DUNGEONS AND DANGER

ST. MARTIN'S PAPERBACKS TITLES BY ELIZABETH PENNEY

THE APRON SHOP SERIES

Hems & Homicide
Thread and Dead
Bodies and Bows

THE CAMBRIDGE BOOKSHOP SERIES

Chapter and Curse
A Treacherous Tale
The Fatal Folio
Madrigals and Mayhem
Vows and Villainy

THE RAVENSEA CASTLE SERIES

Bodies and Battlements
Dungeons and Danger

DUNGEONS AND DANGER

A Ravensea Castle Mystery

ELIZABETH PENNEY

St. Martin's Paperbacks

First published in the United States by St. Martin's Paperbacks, an imprint of St. Martin's Publishing Group.

EU Representative: Macmillan Publishers Ireland Ltd., 1st Floor, The Liffey Trust Centre, 117–126 Sheriff Street Upper, Dublin 1, D01 YC43, Ireland.

DUNGEONS AND DANGER

For information, address St. Martin's Publishing Group, 120 Broadway, New York, NY 10271.

www.stmartins.com

ISBN 978-1-250-37007-5

Printed in the United States of America

St. Martin's Paperbacks edition / June 2026

10 9 8 7 6 5 4 3 2 1

CHAPTER 1

All Hallows' Eve
The Murder

The horned Viking headdress I was wearing slipped as I pushed through the throng on the bluff overlooking the bay. Pausing to nudge the awkward helmet back into place, I took in the scene. *Where is she?* I was looking for one of our guests, and I couldn't find her anywhere in this crowd.

The one-day Viking Fest my brother put on to promote his mead brand was definitely a huge hit. At least five hundred people, most of them dressed in historic costume, milled around the large, grassy area. The aroma of roasting ox drifted from huge grills and glasses were lifted with toasts in the tavern tent. Melodic yet energetic Viking rock provided an atmospheric accompaniment.

A bonfire roared on the bluff and now the evening's climactic spectacle came into view: a burning longship drifting into the cove, fierce flames leaping into the night sky. Exclamations and cheers rose from the crowd as they pushed closer to the bluff's edge, caught by the incredibly cinematic sight.

In the back of my mind, I hoped the filmmaker staying at Ravensea Castle was getting this incredible display on camera for background footage. For the past week, a small team had been producing episodes for *Britain's*

Got Ghosts. Ravensea Castle was one of Yorkshire's most haunted sites, built in 1138 on the site of a former monastery located here due to a sacred spring. We even had a Viking ghost, the Red Maiden, although her life far predated the castle.

I had now reached the edge of the crowd, only a short distance between this area and the formal castle gardens. Besides family and guests, we weren't letting anyone inside the private grounds or the castle tonight.

A slim figure wearing a horned headdress, blond hair streaming and cloak flying, hurried through the trees. As she drew closer, I recognized my sister, Tamsyn.

"Nora?" Tamsyn peered at me in the near-dark. "Is everything okay?"

"I don't—" Something made me glance up at the castle and a chill prickled at the back of my neck. "Look," I said, my voice hoarse.

A woman was standing on the battlements, illuminated by flickering light from the fires. As the two of us stared, she disappeared.

It might have been our guest. Or not. Either way, I needed to investigate. I'd lived at Ravensea long enough—my whole life, actually—that a certain tingling down my spine let me know when the veil was thin and ghosts were near.

"I'm going in." I picked up my long skirts and began to trot along the path.

Footsteps behind me. Tamsyn was following.

We ran through the woods, across the formal physic garden, and up the stone stairs to the terrace. There, we paused to unlock one of the French doors.

We hurried up the grand staircase to the upper floors of the castle.

A woman's scream echoed through the halls, coming

from the direction of the northeast tower. Tamsyn and I veered in that direction, racing through corridors and up the winding stone staircase to the circular room.

We burst through the open door. Tall windows provided a spectacular view of the bay and the burning longboat.

Our attention was captured by a much more startling sight.

One of our guests lay sprawled face down, the handle of a dagger protruding from his back.

CHAPTER 2

THE PREVIOUS WEEK

With Rolf, our English mastiff, and Ruffian, the castle tabby, looking on, I eased my gloved hand between thorny branches to pluck another cluster of sloes. The fat, oval, purple fruits were at their perfect ripe peak after last night's frost.

Most people immediately thought of sloe gin, a common use for the tart berries. They were also rich in antioxidants, vitamins, and minerals. As an herbalist, I used them to make a cough syrup sweetened with honey.

My phone chimed with a text as I placed a handful of sloes in the basket. Deciding I needed a break, I carefully stepped away from the bush and set the basket down to dig my phone out of my apron pocket. Naturally, both dog and cat came over to give inquisitive sniffs and I had to pick up the basket again, cradling it in one elbow while I checked my phone.

The text was from Finlay Cole, the man I had been dating since June. Finlay was a detective inspector in the Yorkshire police force. Although he lived in the nearby village of Monkwell, his territory was large and we sometimes had trouble finding time together.

Hey, love. Free for dinner tonight?

My fingers were poised for an eager yes before I remembered. A new group of guests were due today and while I wasn't required to attend the buffet dinner we'd serve, I often did, as the hostess.

Wish I could, but a group is arriving. Ghost hunters!! Filming for BBC.

We'd been waiting for months for the proposed television feature to come to fruition. Ever since we learned about the show *Britain's Got Ghosts*, we'd gone around saying *Ravensea's Got Ghosts,* because it was true. We probably had more ghosts per square foot than any building on the island.

When we first opened to overnight guests in June, our spectral residents had become more than part of the atmosphere. One ghost, Sir Percival, had actually stepped forward to help us solve a murder.

Another time, then. Miss you.

Finlay had been away this week at a training in York and I missed him, too. Inspiration struck.

Join us? Janet is making cottage pie and her famous fruit crumble. One more won't matter.

Janet Fagan and her husband, Guy, lived at the castle, acting as housekeeper and man-of-all-work. Janet had stepped in when I lost my mother at a young age, and at this point, they were family.

There's an offer I can't refuse. I mean an opportunity to see you.

I sent him laughing emojis in response. Janet's cooking was renowned.

Speaking of Janet, one of the terrace French doors creaked open and she emerged, feather duster in hand. "Miss Nora?" she called after spotting me next to the blackthorn bush. "Your father has a guest he'd like you to meet."

"Be right there," I called back. Glancing between the basket and the sloes still waiting to be picked, I sighed.

Got to go. See you later. x

Later. x

I tucked my phone away and put on my right glove again. Before going inside, I should collect a few more bunches. Too many times I'd made plans to return to a garden task only to be waylaid by something or other. Another few days and these sloes would fall and rot on the ground. What a waste that would be.

After leaving the basket and my gloves in the kitchen, I hurried to Dad's study at the front of the castle. The route took me through the Great Hall, where I paused at the front desk to make sure all was in order for guest check-in. Janet had obviously been busy in here, because the suits of armor, weapons hanging on the wall, and the ancestral portraits were all freshly dusted. The red Persian runner up the wide staircase with its landing had been vacuumed as well.

Ravensea was ancient and rather basic when it came to luxury and elegance, desired attributes of high-end lodging. But we were totally authentic and I leaned on that fact heavily in our marketing. It was very easy for guests to imagine stepping back in time here, I thought with a smile.

The massive front door creaked open to reveal my sister, Tamsyn, bag strap over her shoulder and a cat carrier in one hand. "Hello," she caroled. "I'm home." Then she noticed me standing right there and was taken aback. "Oh, hi, Nora. Didn't see you."

"What are you doing here?" I blurted out. I bit my tongue and tried to reframe. "I mean, nice to see you. I thought you were filming?"

Tamsyn had a leading role on a television drama called *Mist on the Moors.*

"We're on break," Tamsyn said, handing me the cat carrier, which held Primrose, her adorable kitten. "I thought I'd come help with the Viking Fest. I'm sure Will has his hands full."

Our brother, Will, had come up with an ambitious plan to put on an epic, one-day Viking Fest that included games, tons of food and drink, music, bonfires, and more. He hadn't told us what the "more" entailed yet. Top secret.

I set the carrier down and let Primrose out. She began padding around, looking for her friend, Ruffian, I guessed. "He's in the kitchen."

"I'll take her in and let Janet know I'm here." Tamsyn placed her bag at the bottom of the stairs. "What are you up to?"

"Dad has a visitor and he wants me to sit in." Guessing the next question, I added, "I have no idea what it's about."

Tamsyn scooped Primrose up and followed me. I didn't object. She hated to be left out of any action here at the castle, as did I.

The study door was partially open so I knocked on the jamb and went in. Our father, Arthur, was sitting at his desk, curly red hair and beard askew, talking eagerly to his visitor, a slender, floppy-haired man wearing wire-rim glasses. They both rose to their feet upon seeing us.

"Tweedy," Dad said. "I'd like you to meet my lovely daughters, Nora and Tamsyn. Girls, this is Professor Norman Tweedy, from the University of York. He's got some very exciting news for us." Dad rubbed his hands together. "Have a seat and he'll tell you about it."

The professor shook both our hands, saying how nice it was to meet us, and gave Primrose a pat. His hand was cool, almost clammy, and limp. *Ugh.* I surreptitiously wiped my hand on my jeans.

We pulled chairs up and sat to listen. Tweedy looked at Dad, who said, "Take it from the top, why don't you?" Primrose sat on Tamsyn's lap at attention, which I thought was super cute.

"It all started with this book," Tweedy said, picking up a glossy paperback from the desk, titled *Vikings: From Raiders to Traders.* He handed it to Tamsyn, who was closer. "While researching the Viking incursion and eventual settlement in Britain, I came across a very interesting person mentioned in Viking legends. A shield maiden named Rusla. Red—"

"The Red Maiden?" I guessed, referring to one of our ghosts. Sightings of a woman in a cloak and horned helmet were rare but well-documented in the family history.

Tweedy frowned, no doubt annoyed at me upstaging his speech. "We think there might be a connection," he temporized.

Now Dad interrupted. "You said they were one and the same, Tweedy. That's why you think the treasure is here."

"Treasure?" Tamsyn and I said at the same time. Tamsyn handed me the professor's book and I placed it on my lap.

The professor huffed, his thunder completely stolen. "We—I—believe that Rusla made landfall here, to stay at the monastery. When she set sail again, she was caught in a skirmish in the bay and her ship was plundered, burned, and sank. Legend has it that she left a hoard in care of the Dreki, or dragon."

"The Dragon's Lair," I said. Our name for a nearby

cave because of the surf that burst through holes in the rock like nostrils at high tide.

Tweedy nodded. "This piece of land, before the castle was built, didn't have a name back then so I believe the mention of the cove was a marker."

"The Monastery at Monkwell was here," Dad pointed out.

"True, which would have given searchers a direct link to the burial spot." Tweedy swiveled in his seat to face us. "Your father reports that no one has located a hoard at any point in history, which means it's probably still there."

"What is usually in a Viking hoard?" Tamsyn asked. "And what would it be worth? Just an estimate."

Tweedy picked up his phone and scrolled before handing it to Tamsyn. I looked over her shoulder at the webpage, which depicted a fairly recent find in Yorkshire. Mostly coins with some other small metal objects, it was worth millions.

Millions, possibly here somewhere on our property and belonging to us.

CHAPTER 3

We'd been cash-strapped so long, for generations actually, and the idea of a windfall that large made me feel faint with excitement and longing. We could put a new roof on the castle and refurbish more bedrooms for guests. Modernize the loos. Maybe even put in a saltwater pool, spa, and other amenities.

"Now you can understand why the hoard is worth searching for," Tweedy said. "That's why I'm here. Between your father and I, we'll find it if it's still here."

My suspicious mind immediately leaped to the next question. "What do you get out of it?" A pat on the back and a thank-you? I highly doubted that.

Tweedy's smile became tentative. "The usual arrangement, which I've just begun to discuss with Arthur, is a fifty-fifty split. You allow me to search and then we split the money when it's sold. In the UK, we must report any finds as treasure and then they are usually purchased by a museum."

Dad patted printed pages sitting on his desk. "Tweedy brought me a copy of regulations and a contract for me to sign. All very aboveboard."

Before I could comment further or even digest this proposal, Janet rapped on the door and put her head in.

"The film crew is here, milady. Perhaps you'd like to greet them?" The *milady* was a title originating with my late mother. Despite every effort to discourage her, Janet still addressed Tamsyn and me that way. I'd given up. Milady, it was.

Reluctant to leave the conversation with Professor Tweedy, I sighed. "Thanks, Janet. I'll be right there." I rose to my feet. "Please excuse me. Duty calls."

"I'll come with you," Tamsyn said. My sister knew tons of people in the entertainment industry and she had connected us with Brady Benson, the project lead.

"You must come say hello," Dad told Tweedy. "We've got ghost hunters coming to stay. All very exciting. We're one of the most haunted castles in Britain, you know."

"Ghost hunters?" Tweedy's tone was scoffing. "You're pulling my leg, right?"

Tamsyn and I exchanged glances. Tweedy was in for a very rude awakening.

Dad bridled. "Not at all, sir. I don't jest about such matters." His thick brows drew together in a scowl. "I'm warning you, they don't tolerate disrespect."

Tweedy's eyes flared wide and I could guess what he was thinking: that my father was bonkers, barmy, round the twist.

"I'm sorry . . . didn't mean any harm . . ." Tweedy was gabbling now, desperate to maintain access to the possible Viking hoard. "Didn't realize you were serious."

Dad's smile was scary. "We're dead serious about ghosts here, aren't we, Nora?"

"Very much so, yes," I said. "They're our friends." I said the latter just to see the expression of bewildered disbelief on Tweedy's face. Oh my. We weren't getting off to the best start if I was already tempted to tweak him.

Hiding my grin, I started toward the door. The shuffle

and scrape of chairs behind me let me know that Dad and Tweedy were following.

Primrose in her arms, Tamsyn moved ahead to walk beside me. "I'm excited that this finally worked out."

A group of four people stood near the reception desk, three men and one woman. Tamsyn handed me Primrose and began running across the flagstones. "Brady," she cried with a squeal. "This is so exciting."

Brady, on the short side with spiky hair and black-rimmed glasses, returned her embrace, shouting, "Tamsyn, love. Didn't think you'd be here."

"I'm on break," she explained. "Lucky for me."

"For us," Brady said gallantly. "Let me introduce you." With his arm around my sister, he steered her to face the others.

"Hold it," Tamsyn said. "First, meet my sister. She's the innkeeper here." She twinkled at Janet. "And you've met our lovely rock, Janet? We couldn't do it without her."

The other three gave little waves. "Hello, Nora. Hello, Janet," they chorused.

Brady introduced us. The good-looking man with silvery blond hair was Gray Knightly. Ollie Agar was chunky with a thick beard, and Georgia Kane was tall with short platinum-and-pink hair and pretty features. She'd been a production assistant on one of Tamsyn's shows, she said.

Dad and Professor Tweedy had been standing to one side, waiting to be introduced. Tamsyn gestured toward Dad as if announcing him on television. "Meet Arthur Asquith, patriarch and historian here at Ravensea. And his friend, Professor Norman Tweedy."

An odd silence fell. The four friends subtly moved to stand closer together, exchanging looks. "What is *he* doing here?" Gray whispered in Georgia's ear, barely loud enough for me to hear.

Brady finally extended a hand to Dad, who shook it. "It's lovely to meet you, my lord. Thank you for allowing us to film here at Ravensea."

"You're very welcome, young man." Dad gave Brady a hearty slap on the shoulder. "We've never had an official paranormal investigation. With any luck, our dearly departed will cooperate."

"I hope so, sir," Brady said. He turned to Tweedy. "Nice to see you again, Professor." His smile appeared forced.

"What's going on?" Tamsyn asked, puzzled. "How do you know each other?"

Tweedy gave a hearty laugh. "This gang of four are my former students." He adjusted his glasses, his expression mocking. "Such a coincidence that we're all here."

Judging by the expressions on the film crew's faces, it wasn't a happy one.

"That was strange," Tamsyn said as she burst into the kitchen, where Janet and I were preparing lunch. The only standard meal we offered was breakfast, but on occasion, guests requested lunch and dinner. "Brady and his crew were not happy to see Tweedy at all. I had no idea they were connected."

"How could you?" I asked. "We just met Tweedy today."

"True," Tamsyn said, grabbing a cucumber slice off a platter. "And I only know Brady and Georgia through work. Didn't meet Gray and Ollie until today."

"Did anyone elaborate at all while you were getting them settled?" I asked.

Tamsyn had shown the crew to their rooms. Tweedy as well, because Dad insisted on having him stay here instead of in the village—gratis, of course. With the other rooms full, I'd had to put him in the newly renovated northeast tower room. My family had a bad habit of offering free rooms that I was trying to break. In this case, though, finding the hoard would certainly compensate for the lost revenue. If we found it.

"No." Tamsyn took another cucumber slice and this time I pretended to slap her hand. She gave me a cheeky grin and bit into it. "Not that I asked. I could tell questions wouldn't be welcome."

"Hopefully their history, whatever it is, won't matter," I said. "Their projects don't really overlap."

Janet gave the potato soup a last stir and turned off the heat. "Unless they're here for the treasure, too." While we were putting together sandwich platters, I'd shared Tweedy's exciting theory about the hoard.

Tamsyn stared at me in shock. "How can that be . . . ?"

"We only found out about it today," I said. "Dad didn't even know." I pointed at Tamsyn. "You first talked to Brady months ago, right?"

She nodded. "We met up at an industry thing. He told me about his plan to create a ghost-hunting show and I mentioned Ravensea—or he mentioned it. I can't remember."

"And he contacted me." Our communication had gone back and forth over the summer while we hammered out an agreement. Brady was paying a location fee, but my main interest was in the free publicity we would garner once the show aired. We could never afford that level of advertising.

Thinking through the sequence of events reassured me. We were in Yorkshire, after all, and our guests were from York. It wasn't surprising that Brady and his team were interested in history, Tweedy's specialty. Ghosts *were* history, right?

"Arc you ready?" Looking as excited as a little kid, Dad stood poised beside the antique brass gong he'd dragged out of the attic. This was his solution to alert mealtime stragglers. While many guests hovered, eagerly waiting for meal service, others lost track of time.

I placed the final platter of sandwiches next to the soup urn. "We're ready."

BONG. The deep and resonant sound vibrated through the air. It was rather thrilling, really.

Dad chuckled with glee. He made as though to strike again, but I shook my head. "I hear them coming." Footsteps and voices were echoing in the Great Hall. I gestured for him to come closer. "There's obviously some bad blood between Tweedy and the film crew. If things get ugly, try to smooth them over, okay?"

While I was curious as to the source of the conflict, I was more invested in keeping the atmosphere pleasant. Open hostilities would turn what should be an exciting experience into a nightmare. The film crew might even pull out.

"Got it," Dad said. "I'll do my best." On that note, he pivoted to stand near the dining room door. As the guests came in—Brady, followed by Ollie, Georgia, and Gray together, whispering—he gestured toward the buffet. "Help yourselves. Sit anywhere. If you need something, just give a shout."

They swarmed the food, murmuring in appreciation as they stacked sandwiches, crisps, and salad on plates, then ladled bowls of soup.

Tweedy sauntered through the doorway, taking in the scene with what looked like confident ease. If he was bothered by the presence of his former students, he didn't show it.

"How are you finding the tower room?" Dad asked, halting Tweedy's progress to the buffet.

Good job, Dad. Delay him until they've finished serving themselves.

Tweedy rubbed his hands together. "Absolutely perfect. Such a view from there. Plenty of room to spread out and get some work done on my next book." That was the cover story, I gathered. A book. Of course he wouldn't mention the treasure hunt.

Gray shot Tweedy a glare before pointedly turning his back and continuing on to the long table. Brady and Ollie were already seated at the far end and Gray joined them. Silverware clattered and they spoke in low tones as they settled into their meal.

Georgia detoured over to Tweedy on her way from the buffet. "Good to see you, Professor Tweedy. What brings you to Ravensea?" Her expression and voice were friendly, almost flirtatious. I noticed that her three companions had stopped eating to listen.

Tweedy rubbed his chin, studying the young woman with narrowed eyes. "Research, of course. There are fascinating remnants of Viking settlement up and down the coast here."

"Speaking of relics, I'm a Viking," Dad interjected heartily. He struck a pose. "Can't you tell?" Indeed, with his broad height and curly red hair and beard, he did resemble a Viking warrior. "In fact, our family name, Asquith, means 'ash tree' and 'wood' in Old Norse."

"Fascinating, my lord," Georgia said. She glanced

down, seeming to remember that she was carrying her lunch. "I'd better . . ."

"Go eat." Dad made an ushering movement. "Tweedy, help yourself."

Georgia joined her friends and Tweedy wandered over to the buffet, picking and poking along. Once he was finished, Dad and I went up. I grabbed a large bowl of potato soup—one of my favorites—and a roast beef sandwich with horseradish and cheddar.

When I headed to the table, I saw that Tweedy was seated only one empty chair away from the film crew. I could already sense the tension in their ducked heads, the way they shifted their backs toward him. He was slurping soup noisily, not seeming to notice or care about their attitudes.

Dad and I sat at the other end, my father in the head seat.

"Gray," Tweedy said, drawing all eyes. "What have you been up to?" He waved a hand. "Besides taking part in . . . hunting ghosts." He sent a wary glance toward Dad, probably remembering Dad's earlier scolding.

Gray didn't look up from his bowl. "This and that."

Tweedy didn't let up. "You never finished your degree, did you? What a shame. Slinging pints is quite a comedown for a man of your talents."

That meant Tweedy did know what Gray had been doing, and not only that, felt compelled to insult him over it.

"Simple. I ran out of money," Gray said. "I'll go back at some point."

Brady stepped in to encourage his friend. "You'll be all right once the episode is picked up. Especially if they want more."

"Let's hope," Georgia said with a little laugh. "I could use the lolly."

"Still short of spending money, are we?" Tweedy laughed. "But stylish as ever, I'm glad to see."

The young woman dropped her spoon with an exclamation, her eyes wide with outrage and hurt. She turned toward Gray, who put his arm around her.

I sent Dad a frown, signaling that he should rein in his rude and unruly guest.

Before Dad could say anything, Tweedy turned to Brady, regarding him with assessing eyes. "Fancy yourself a showrunner, hmm? I do hope your time management skills and tenacity have taken a step up since university."

Brady reared back in his seat, his face flushing a deep, ugly red. When he appeared about to launch an angry response, Ollie put a hand on his forearm and shook his head slightly.

"That's not relevant now," Brady managed to grit out. "I'd appreciate it if you would drop the topic. We graduated five years ago, for pity's sake."

Dad finally stepped in, his voice booming. "Tweedy, my good chap. Eat up. I've got lots of lovely archival materials to show you." He smiled. "Some are so recently excavated from the repository that I haven't even cracked the covers." He sighed happily. "Or blown off the dust."

Greed flashed in the professor's eyes. "Music to my ears, my lord. Who knows what treasures we'll discover?" His smile was smug. Pleased with the double meaning of his words, no doubt.

As an uneasy silence fell over the table, I abandoned the idea of finishing my own lunch. Tweedy's snide attacks on our other guests had stolen my appetite. Under other circumstances, I would immediately evict him. Unfortunately, with such a huge treasure at stake, we literally couldn't afford to alienate the man.

As host, my role was clear: mediate, mitigate, and manage guest relations. I prayed we would get through the next week without some kind of disaster.

CHAPTER 4

After lunch was cleared away, Tamsyn, Dad, and I met with the film crew in the dining room. Thankfully, Tweedy was occupied in Dad's study, well out of the way. After hearing his mocking opinion about ghost hunting, I didn't want him anywhere near the film shoot. His bad vibes might jinx it.

"When is the show going to air?" Dad asked. He chuckled. "Our ghosts will finally get their fifteen minutes of fame."

Brady appeared uneasy as he shuffled through papers. "About that. Um, how can I put this?" He tipped his chin, gaze on the chandelier, which to my relief was not draped with cobwebs. Janet was such a treasure.

While we waited for his answer, I sent my sister a frown. She was biting her lip, which told me she knew something I didn't.

Brady sighed, then used his thumb to push his black-framed glasses higher. "What we're doing here is an audition of sorts. I'm confident—well, pretty confident—that *Britain's Got Ghosts* will air our episodes. We just have to impress them."

Rather than the slam dunk I thought hosting them here was, it was more of a flyer. For them and us.

A brief silence fell over the table. Tamsyn was gazing at me imploringly and I shook my head. We'd talk about it later.

Dad thumped the palm of his hand on the table. "I'm sure our ghosts won't disappoint. Isn't that what you need? Actual evidence of their existence? That won't be a problem here."

The film crew's expressions eased. "That's all we need," Brady declared. "We've got the right equipment. I've got a lot of production experience and, um, Ollie is very experienced in the field."

He wasn't mentioning Gray or Georgia and I wondered about their interest in paranormal investigation. They were both very attractive and would probably look great on camera. Maybe that was their contribution.

"Ollie is what you might call a ghost whisperer," Brady said. He opened his laptop and tapped away. "In fact, I'll show you his latest episode, which I filmed."

He turned the laptop in our direction and pressed the PLAY button. Ollie was outside a pub from the Tudor period. "This pub on the Yorkshire coast is said to have been a pirate's lair. In fact, it's named after a famous pirate named One-Eyed Jack."

The camera angles, the background music, the use of short, snappy yet leading dialogue were more *Blair Witch* than glossy BBC, I thought. Maybe that wasn't a bad thing. Younger people would like this style and it fit Ravensea as well. We were far from a glossy production ourselves.

We watched a few minutes of Ollie attempting to contact One-Eyed Jack. After wall sconces flickered and the paranormal equipment started to go nuts, Brady stopped the video. "You get the idea. I was hoping that in this meeting, we could plan a schedule for the shoot—who we are going to try to contact, where in the castle we'll film, etcetera."

Everyone looked at Dad. I had an idea who we should try first, since he was among the most active. I wanted to let Dad guide this, though. He was the one who had invested time in researching our family history, including the backstory for each ghost.

"The perfect introductory ghost is Sir Percival, who died in 1461," Dad said. "He has a very colorful and tragic story that I'd like to share with your audience—if that would be all right. It really helped us understand him, didn't it, Nora?"

"It really did." For example, we learned why sometimes we only saw a floating head. Poor Sir Percival, a soldier in the Wars of the Roses, had been beheaded in the castle courtyard after finally returning home.

Brady's face lit up. "That would be fantastic. I would love to get a full interview with you about each ghost and use clips in the episodes."

Dad beamed. "When shall we begin? I don't need much time to prepare."

Brady was slightly taken aback. "Let me get organized, okay? We'll do an interview first and then decide when to approach the spirit."

"Dad, you should do the interviews in the drawing room," Tamsyn said. "In your armchair in front of the fireplace." To Brady, she said, "He gives fireside chats to our guests there, often during our wine socials. Guests go mad for Dad's talks."

She was exaggerating a wee bit, although our guests did enjoy his interesting and colorful stories about Ravensea history.

"Show me," Brady said, pushing back his chair.

Brady, Dad, and Tamsyn went to the drawing room to check it out while the other three crew members took advantage of the break to scatter. I hurried upstairs to the hallway near the King's Chamber, Sir Percival's usual haunt.

Brady—and most people, I had to admit—treated ghosts like a curiosity, like a form of wildlife in a zoo. They certainly weren't consulted for their opinions about being featured on television.

Why hadn't I had these reservations before, I asked myself, feeling guilty. I'd only seen the notoriety and promotional opportunities. Even if they were dead, our ghosts deserved to be treated like . . . people.

As I stood on the carpet near a seriously ugly ancestral portrait, I couldn't help but think of the times I hadn't wanted Sir Percival around when guests were in residence. In fact, I kept a sage smudge stick for that very purpose. Too bad I didn't have something that would summon him.

Only my voice. "Sir Percival?" I called softly. "Are you here?"

A breeze blew along the hall, ruffling pages in an open book on a window seat. Wall sconces flickered, another sign.

"Thanks for showing up," I said. Sparkles of light danced in a corner. "We're going to be doing something . . . different later. We would like you to greet our guests."

A sudden stillness, as if he were saying, *Huh?*

"I know, right?" I laughed. "We have people here who want to meet you."

Again the breeze blew, this time strong enough to close the open book with a small thump.

"Thank you," I called. "I really appreciate it." My heart sang with relief. Sir Percival was going to co-operate.

I hurried down the hall, eager to go downstairs and share the news discreetly with Dad and Tamsyn. On the way, I went past the Knight's Chamber, where Gray was staying. The door was open and as I approached, I heard Georgia speaking.

"What are you going to do?" she asked, her tone urgent.

"I have no idea," Gray said. "But I'm not going to let Tweedy screw me over again. Did you notice how he was mocking me at lunch? He knows my situation is his fault. Well, partly, anyway."

"He's the worst. Did you hear how he insulted me?" Her voice rose in aggravation.

I shouldn't be listening to this. Picking up the pace, I hurried past the doorway, hoping they wouldn't notice me.

No such luck. Georgia was standing right in the line of sight and she jumped when she saw me. "Nora. I didn't know you were there."

"Hello," I said, hoping she didn't realize I had been eavesdropping. I gestured toward the staircase. "Just on my way downstairs."

Gray now appeared beside Georgia. "I have a question for you, if you don't mind."

"Uh, no," I said. "Of course not. Fire away."

He glanced up and down the corridor. "Let's talk in the room, okay?"

Reluctantly, wondering what was coming and why it had to be private, I stepped inside. Gray closed the door firmly behind me. Georgia had retreated to the window, where she hovered, her stance shifting in discomfort.

"What's up?" I asked when neither of them immediately said anything.

Gray was rubbing his chin, as if thinking, and at my question, he darted over to the nightstand to pick up his phone. "Look at this," he said.

On the screen was a document on an academic site. The title was *The Shield Maiden's Journey,* and in a much smaller font, the author was identified as Gray Knightly.

"You wrote this?" A quick scan revealed that the paper discussed Rusla, the same Viking Tweedy had been tracing. The one who had supposedly left her hoard here, at Ravensea. Before there was a castle.

Huh. This was an odd coincidence. Or was it? A suspicion began to form in the back of my mind.

"I did. Part of my degree work." Gray began to pace. "I was the first to put together clues regarding Rusla's journey in ancient documents." He paused. "Tweedy was my professor. He supervised my work."

I guessed where this was headed. "He based his theory—?" I clamped my mouth shut on the question. Probably not a good idea to reveal Tweedy's treasure hunt. The fewer people who knew about the possibility of huge riches, the better.

Gray's laugh was bitter. "He's here about the hoard, isn't he?"

CHAPTER 5

"Urp," was my elegant reply. My suspicion was correct. Gray was here for the treasure as well. Did Brady and Ollie also know about it?

"I told you, Georgia," Gray said. "He's a thief." He took back his phone and waved it around. "He used my research in his first book after telling me it wasn't significant, and now he's tracing Rusla's journey." He sneered. "He is such a hack. Not an original idea in his pea brain."

He could have a point. I'd certainly heard complaints in the past about professors who used their students' research to their own benefit. In this case, Tweedy may have downplayed Gray's discoveries only to run with them himself. Talk about unethical behavior.

In an abrupt change of subject, Gray asked, "What was on this site before the castle?"

"An abbey," I said. It wasn't a secret.

Gray nodded. "I thought as much." He rubbed his chin, looking pensive.

Was he planning on looking for the treasure? Who else knew about it? Was the whole team involved? We had to get control of the situation, which was already going in directions I hadn't anticipated.

"Please don't go poking around the castle without

permission," I said, trying to sound authoritative. "It's . . . not safe." I glanced at Georgia and then Gray again. "I'm serious. Please tell me you understand." Crossing my arms, I stood with feet firmly planted to let them know I meant business.

"Don't worry about me," Georgia said. "I have no intention of exploring." She shuddered. "I might run into a ghost."

That was a strange attitude for a ghost hunter. Still, I was glad for her assurance that she wouldn't nose around. "Gray?" I prodded, wanting him to provide a verbal acknowledgment of my request.

"I won't go anywhere on my own," he said. "Not without your knowledge or permission." He smiled warmly.

Why did I feel like he wasn't being totally honest with me? Maybe he thought he'd get permission from Dad or Tamsyn instead. I'd better fill them in right away.

"Thank you," I said. "Now if you'll excuse me . . ." I gestured toward the door. "I need to get back to work." Namely, go find the other two members of the team and read them the riot act as well.

Downstairs, Dad was back in his office and he didn't know where anyone was. "Tweedy is up in the tower, working on his book," he said.

"That's nice." I wondered whose work he would rip off for that publication. "Oh, by the way, Gray knows about the hoard."

Dad dropped his pen, which naturally rolled under the desk. He bent to look for it. "He does?" he asked, his voice muffled. "Aha. There you are." He sat upright again, triumphant. "Why do things you drop always go *under* the furniture?"

"That's a good question." I'd wondered the same thing. Rather malicious of them, I thought. "Regarding your question, yes, he does know about it. I told him not to go looking without permission."

Dad scowled. "I should say not. I hope he keeps his mouth shut, although that's probably a lost cause. News that juicy travels fast." His frown deepened. "I wonder how he found out? I'll have a word with Tweedy."

"According to Gray, it was his theory first."

My father looked thunderstruck. "That's quite an accusation, Nora. Does it have any merit?"

"Maybe. Gray showed me an article that he wrote about Rusla. Please don't say anything to Tweedy yet—until I learn more. I don't want to make things even more tense around here."

"I get your point. We already had to referee at the first meal."

"Thanks," I said, relieved that Dad understood the volatile dynamics of the situation. Add in a treasure hunt and it was going to be explosive. "Anyway, I'm going to track down the others and warn them not to roam around. The last thing we need is someone getting hurt."

I didn't even want to see the increased liability insurance premiums in that case. And I didn't want to get sued, either.

"I agree," Dad said. "We'll have to monitor where people go, either to film our ghosts or search for treasure."

"I'll let you get back to work," I said, seeing his interest stray toward the documents and books on the desk.

I continued on, looking through the rooms for any sign of Brady or Ollie. I didn't see Tamsyn, either. Maybe she was outside or had gone to the village.

My last stop was the kitchen. Janet was taking a break, feet up and reading a book. "As you were," I said when she started to close the book. "I'm looking for Ollie and Brady."

"I haven't seen them," Janet said. "If I do, I'll tell them you're looking for them."

I wandered over to the stove, noticing that two large casseroles sat waiting to be placed in the oven. Enough for the group of eleven tonight, counting Finlay. Janet's cottage pie was a delicious savory mix of ground beef, vegetables, and gravy topped with fluffy mashed potatoes. "These look fantastic."

"Nice filling meal on a chilly fall night," she said. "I'm also making fresh bread to go with it."

A large bowl covered with a striped towel sat near the AGA range. I took a peek at the mounded dough. "Yum. Fresh bread and butter are perfect with cottage pie."

"Pickled beets and piccalilli from the garden as well," she said.

Piccalilli was a mustardy relish made with cauliflower, onions, beans, and carrots. Thinking about it made my mouth water, so I rummaged in the fridge for a snack. A few cubes of cheddar, Greek olives, and a sliced apple would do the trick.

I sat at the table to eat, pulling out my phone to check messages. Janet went back to reading. Finlay. I needed to let him know the latest plans. And about the treasure. That could wait until I saw him in person. I certainly trusted him to keep it a secret.

After dinner, you can watch us film a ghost encounter. We're starting with Sir Percival. Low-hanging fruit.

That should be interesting. I've never met the gentleman.

You'll enjoy it. He's a sweetie.

Maybe that was an odd thing to say about a headless ghost but I would stand by it.

I'll take your word for it. A pause with blinking dots, then, *I can't believe we're having this discussion.*

Welcome to my life. x

See you soon, love. x

Smiling, I set my phone aside. Finlay Cole had been one of the first guests at Ravensea, when we'd opened last June. He'd stayed here while looking for a place to rent in Monkwell after his job transfer. Solving a murder right here at the castle had launched a friendship that soon became much more. Now, several months in, we spoke daily and got together several times a week, as often as our busy careers allowed.

I'd had no idea that opening a bed-and-breakfast at the castle would lead to romance as well. It was an incidental outcome of my business venture. Speaking of business, I needed to get out to the garden again and keep working. Once we had a killing frost, the herb garden would go dormant for the winter.

The back door opened and Tamsyn came in, holding Primrose. "We went for a little walk," she said. "Primrose likes the fountain. You should have seen her walking around the rim." She put the cat down and pulled out her phone. "I have video evidence."

We watched the video a couple of times. It was really cute.

Then I recalled my mission. "Have you seen Ollie or Brady?" I'd tell Tamsyn and Janet about Gray's startling revelation and its implications after I spoke to the guys. Bringing the topic up now would only delay me further. I really should have been searching the castle instead of eating a snack and texting Finlay.

"They went down into the dungeon," Tamsyn said. She flipped to another screen. "Look at this video, Janet. She's chasing a butterfly."

The dungeon. Were they on the trail of the treasure? I'd better go find out what they were up to. Opening a cupboard,

I grabbed an old green plastic six-volt lantern. The dungeon wasn't fully wired for electricity by any stretch.

"Come look for me if I'm not back in twenty minutes," I said, heading for the back passageway. They were still watching videos and I wasn't sure they heard me.

We didn't use many of the rooms in this part of the castle. I had adapted the distilling room to make herbal products and an old pantry held raw materials and finished inventory.

At the end of the dark corridor, a door led to a flight of stone stairs that went down. And down. And down again. Stone walls on both sides pressed close.

The farther I descended, the quieter it got. The only sound was the faint drip of water. The air was stuffy yet damp, holding the mineral aroma of rock and dirt. I tried not to think about the tons of stone over my head or the fact that I was deep underground.

When I was little, I'd been deathly afraid of the dungeon. Afraid I'd be trapped down there and left to rot. Will, on the other hand, thrived on exploring this part of the castle. He liked investigating the empty cells with their rusted manacles and chains and following the tunnels wherever they led. If my parents knew half of what he'd gotten up to, they would have gone gray overnight.

At the bottom of the stairs, I had a choice of left or right. I went right, because that is where the other entrance, off the Great Hall, tied in. I figured they had gone down that way, not through the kitchen.

I trod past empty rooms, some with doors made of iron bars. At intervals, gates closing off the corridor stood open. Being imprisoned must have been like being buried alive.

A light illuminated the corridor walls in the distance and I heard voices. There they were. As they came into view, I saw they had ghost-hunting equipment with them. They weren't looking for the treasure, I realized with relief.

"Are you getting anything now?" Brady asked. He was holding a strange piece of equipment, a tablet and a box on a handle.

"Not yet," Ollie answered, busy turning dials on a handheld meter. He glanced up. "I sense something here, though."

"Is it me?" I asked.

They both jumped. "Nora," Brady said. "You scared me."

"Doesn't say much for your nerves," I quipped. We all cracked up.

Right then, I heard a creaking sound followed by a slam from down the corridor.

Eyes wide, we all stared at one another. Was that human or haunt? At Ravensea, both were equally likely.

CHAPTER 6

"Let me go find out what that was," I said. Maybe it had been a door to one of the cells. Though why it should close when there was no air movement down here was beyond me.

Moving fast as I could on the brick floor without tripping and falling, I retraced my steps down the corridor. As I feared, the gate between sections was closed. We were stuck in an offshoot reachable only through this gate. Beyond Ollie and Brady was a dead end.

I grabbed the rusty bars and tried to push and pull the door open. It was locked.

"Whoever did this, fix it," I called. "This isn't funny."

Although rust and filth caked my hand, I reached into my pocket for my phone. The idea of being stuck down here was looming like a monster in the shadows. *What if—* I told my brain to shut up and swiped the screen.

No signal. Of course not. This far underground was a dead zone.

What were we going to do? Wait for people to realize we hadn't come back? How long would that take? Tamsyn and Janet hadn't been paying much attention when I said I was coming down here.

"Hey, guys," I said when I rejoined Brady and Ollie. "Bad news. We're locked in."

Brady's eyebrows shot up. "What? Seriously? How did that happen?"

"I'd like to know myself," I said. "One of the gates that seals off the corridor shut and locked. I have no idea how." I put up my rust-covered hand. "I swear I didn't touch it on the way through."

The men exchanged glances. "I bet it was Tweedy," Ollie said.

"Tweedy? Would he really go that far?" He'd proved that he was unpleasant, rude, and infuriating. This was a whole other level, though.

"The man is an absolute sod," Brady said. "I wouldn't put anything past him."

"I have a question," Ollie put in. "Why is he here during term time?"

That was a good question. I underlined my mental note to check out his status at the university. Not that it would affect the treasure hunt. He and Dad had signed an agreement. I was curious, that's all.

"Probably got terminated," Ollie said.

"That would be a blow," Brady put in. "The man doesn't have a life. He's a loner and a loser."

How sad. Not having a life, I meant. Tweedy appeared to be like other academics I'd met, obsessed with their research to the exclusion of anything outside his career. Although, to be fair, tracking down a treasure might make anyone single-minded.

Ollie was still fiddling with the device. "I think Tweedy might be the troll on my channel who calls himself *profskeptic*. I blocked him but he started trashing me all over social media. Like whacking moles to chase down all the posts and comments."

"What makes you think it's him?" I asked. "Although from things he's said, I gather he's not a believer." He hadn't insulted Ollie at lunch, I recalled. He had probably been afraid of Dad's reaction.

Ollie smirked. "That's for sure. As for why I think it's him? It's the phrasing, all pompous and lofty. Remember how he used to tear people apart in class with a smile on his face, Brady?"

Brady shuddered. "Still dream about uni, don't I? It's usually one of his classes and I haven't studied a bloody thing."

I had my own stress dreams along that vein. What a relief to wake up and realize those days were long behind me.

Now I had grown-up problems, like feuding guests and a never-ending repair list.

As if sensing my discomfort, Ollie said, "Don't worry about it, Nora. We'll do our best to stay out of his way."

"Besides, who cares what he thinks?" Brady said. "He's dead wrong about ghosts. They do exist."

The lights flashed on Ollie's meter and he grunted in satisfaction. "Turn on the SLS," he told Brady, then looked at me. "That means Structured Light Sensor." He pointed to a certain spot. "Aim there."

I moved so I could see the screen on the tablet-box device, which displayed a video view of the area.

"Is someone here?" Ollie called. "Say hello."

A crackling sound came over the computer speakers. "I see something," Brady cried. A spot glowed on the screen and then a stick figure appeared, looking as though it was dancing.

"What is that?" I whispered.

"The spirit," Brady whispered back. "That's how they look on this program."

Ollie was staring in that direction. "I see something."

The figure of a woman was forming, vague, a mere outline. Horns on her head. "It's Rusla. The Red Maiden." The men threw me looks but didn't ask questions.

Why was she down here? Previous sightings had been on the battlements. Was her presence a clue to the treasure?

"Is it down here?" I blurted. So much for keeping secrets. I'd have to come up with something and make it quick. However, I had to take advantage of the opportunity to talk to her, insane as that sounded.

Ollie was holding a different device now. "Hush. She's speaking."

The equipment he was using was called an EVP, or electronic voice phenomena, recorder, I'd learned.

I could hear a voice, too, although it was indistinct and interrupted by static. Hopefully they could edit the audio track to make the words clearer.

On the screen, the stick figure faded, then disappeared. Ollie turned the EVP recorder up, then down and off.

"We did it," Brady said, excited. "We made contact." He turned to me. "I want to hear everything you know about Rusla."

Oh, boy. Fortunately, the clang of metal and a shout caught our attention just then.

"Nora?" Tamsyn. "Are you down here?"

I'd never been so glad to hear my sister's voice. We could leave our dungeon prison now.

"Why was that gate locked?" Tamsyn asked as the four of us made our way back to civilization. "We never even close them."

"It was open when I came through," I said. The lock

wasn't a key, it was a bolt that prevented those on the other side from coming back through. Could a ghost throw a bolt? I wasn't convinced they could. "You didn't see anyone else down here? Or coming up the stairs?" We'd been stuck over half an hour so whoever it was left ages ago.

Tamsyn shook her head. "You think it was a prank? Who would do that?"

"No idea," I said. Behind Tamsyn's back, I drew a finger across my lips, signaling to Brady and Ollie to keep quiet about Tweedy for now. I wanted to talk about him with her and Dad later, in private. They both nodded. "We did have a ghost encounter, though."

Tamsyn drew closer to me with a shudder. "I'm not surprised. It's definitely creepy down here. Who was it? A poor prisoner? Or an evil jailer?"

"Neither," I said. "The Red Maiden, we think."

"Really?" Tamsyn sounded amazed. Then she said, "Oh."

Yes, *oh*. Maybe the Red Maiden was telling us that her hoard had been hidden down here, before the castle was built, in the monastery cellars. It made sense to me that a new structure had been built on the remains of the old. Perhaps Dad could unearth some proof that the same site had been used.

"I got her voice on my voice recorder," Ollie said. "I'll try to clean it up and see what she was saying."

Hopefully not: *Dig here*. Which reminded me. I needed to warn them off from exploring on their own without telling them about the treasure. When we got back upstairs, into the daylight. Actually, the mysteriously closed gate had given me the perfect excuse.

In the comforting brightness of the kitchen, which was empty at the moment, I asked if they wanted tea. Or something cold to drink. A look in the fridge revealed we had lemonade. Everyone wanted that and I filled four glasses.

"Listen, guys," I said. "I know you're excited about exploring and encountering our ghosts. But I must ask you not to go off by yourselves. As you can see from today, it might be dangerous."

Tamsyn jumped in. "It's a good thing I knew where you were. Nora, too. You'd still be down there, stuck. It might take us ages to find you."

Ollie put the back of his hand to his forehead in mock dismay. "We could have died down there and become ghosts ourselves." Everyone laughed.

Brady's response was more somber. "I understand what you're saying. Sorry about that. I know you folks are busy so I'll try to minimize disruption."

I set my empty glass in the sink. "We appreciate that. Why don't we work on a shooting schedule? I'm sure you want all kinds of background and filler shots. We just need to know where you are and when." And have the ability to say no, don't go there.

I doubted I'd be able to keep news of the treasure hunt from Brady and Ollie for long. Maybe I'd managed to slow down the inevitable. We'd soon find out.

CHAPTER 7

I had time before dinner so I went to my happy place: the garden. My first stop was the sloes, where I had been interrupted earlier. Ruffian and Primrose stalked creatures through the flowerbeds while Rolf lazed, twitching and snorting in his dreams.

This time of day, the sun was lying long across the land, turning everything golden. If only we could store up this warmth and beauty against the long winter ahead. Although that season had its attractions.

Once I'd picked enough sloes, I moved on to rose hips. These round red berries were a good source of vitamin C and antioxidants. I used them in teas, jelly, and syrups. Plucking berries one by one was slow work, almost meditative, and gradually my racing brain slowed.

I needed respites like this, otherwise I would work and worry myself into exhaustion, trying to solve problems and fix everything. Out in the garden, I could just be, alive to each of my senses, thoughts drifting in and out like the gentle movement of the tide. Recipes and formulations often revealed themselves when I worked like this, as if touching the plants was a kind of connection to their properties.

The crab apple tree nearby was bursting with fruit. A crab apple and rose-hip jelly would look and taste delightful, like rubies in a jar.

Rolf lumbered to his feet with a woof and I turned to see Finlay coming through the garden. He had Lady, his French bulldog, with him.

I put my basket down and went to meet him. While Rolf and Lady exchanged doggie kisses, we indulged in real, grown-up ones.

He finally pulled back, smiling down at me. "I've missed you," he said. He pulled a thorny twig from the sloe bush out of my hair, studied it, then tossed it aside.

"Same," I said, snuggling closer, my arms around his waist. A few inches taller than me, lean and strong, Finlay had chiseled features, dark hair, and a goatee. When we met, I'd immediately found him attractive. Even better, his personality and character lived up to his exterior. He was a keeper.

"How was your day?" he asked. "Mine was filled with meetings and paperwork."

At this point, that sounded appealing. "Come help me pick and I'll tell you all about it." This was going to be fun. Finlay had no idea what was coming.

As we cleared rose hips off the bushes, I told him about Tweedy's arrival, teasingly building up to the big reveal: the treasure.

Finlay's brows twitched as he fumbled for words. Being struck speechless was a rare state of affairs for this brilliant, eloquent man.

I laughed. "Yeah, I probably looked like that when he told us. Let's be real, though. He could be wrong. And if he's not, maybe somebody found it centuries ago." Even this reality check couldn't dent a stubborn optimism, though. I held up both hands, fingers crossed. "I'm praying he is right and that we find it. All our problems solved in one fell swoop." I threw my arms wide. "Yahoo."

"Yahoo, indeed." Finlay grinned. "We'll plan a huge celebration for when you find it."

Another test passed. Other people might have tried to rain on my parade, to minimize my excitement and ease the inevitable disappointment they foresaw. Spoilsports.

I darted forward and gave him a kiss. *I love you.* No, I didn't say it out loud. It was too soon, after only several months of seeing each other. That didn't mean I wasn't feeling it. I adored Finlay.

"But wait, there's more," I said when we finished kissing. I picked up the basket and began pulling more rose hips off the canes.

He goggled at me in disbelief. "You *have* had a busy day."

"I know." I paused for effect. "I was locked in the dungeon with two of the ghost hunters."

"Locked in the dungeon? By accident?" His brows drew together.

"Doubt it. Someone was making mischief, I'm guessing. Tamsyn let us out. Meanwhile, we had a visit from the Red Maiden." Not sure if he'd heard about that particular ghost, I added, "She's the one who left the treasure, we think. Anyway, Ollie picked up a voice recording. And Brady captured her on video. Ghosts look weird on video. Like stick figures dancing."

Finlay gave a head shake, as if clearing his mind. "Really. I can't wait to see that. It's interesting that they can be caught on video and audio. Kind of refutes the naysayers, doesn't it?"

"It does. Of course, we could be accused of faking it. I was right there so I know they weren't. I saw her, too. Sensed her, actually. As I always do."

Finlay didn't scoff at me or try to tell me I had imagined things. Yes, he was perfect. I'd never told any of the other boys and men I'd dated about the castle ghosts. It was as personal and private as sharing family secrets. He seemed to take it all in stride.

"'There are more things in heaven and earth, Horatio, than are dreamt of in your philosophy.'" He was quoting Shakespeare.

"Exactly." Shakespeare had ghosts in his plays, come to think of it. Personal experience or dramatic effect? Both, probably.

"The voice recording." Finlay had gathered a handful of hips and he released them into my basket. "What did it say?"

"Don't know yet. Ollie has to clean up the audio." I marveled at the idea of hearing a ghost actually speak. Communication thus far had been through affecting material things like lights flickering and doors and windows opening and closing. Sounds, too.

"Fascinating," Finlay said. "Thanks for letting me tag along tonight."

"No problem." I was glad he was interested in watching a ghost hunt and not running for the hills. I checked the basket. "I think we have enough. Let's go in."

We often offered wine and cheese socials to guests and Janet and Tamsyn had put together one for this evening. While I went to put away the sloes and rose hips, Finlay joined the others in the drawing room.

After my stillroom duties, I went to the kitchen to help Janet. "What can I do?" I asked while washing my hands.

"Put together the salad?" she suggested. Janet was slicing the loaves of bread. Anything that wasn't devoured tonight we would keep for sandwiches tomorrow.

"I can do that." I ferried heads of lettuce, cucumbers,

and tomatoes to a prep area. We'd do a basic salad with homemade dressing, in case people were fussy. As for me, I liked my salads loaded with dried fruit, nuts and seeds, chunks of cheese. Tonight, I would add arugula and red cabbage, for color and accent flavors. Anyone who didn't like them could put them to one side.

"Exciting doings this week," Janet said as we worked companionably together.

I laughed. "That's for sure. Treasure hunting, ghost hunting, the Viking Fest . . . To think I was getting bored last week." I tore the lettuce into pieces, placing it in a large bowl.

"I've learned to enjoy the boring times," Janet said placidly. "Don't look for trouble. It will find you."

"That's for sure." My heart clenched. I hoped trouble would mosey on down the road and leave us alone.

The back door opened and Janet's husband, Guy, came in. His thatch of hair was windswept, his broad features touched by the strong October sun. Guy was as invaluable as his wife in keeping this place going. He helped take care of the garden and grounds, fixed just about everything, and oversaw any maintenance jobs we hired out for.

"Evening, Nora," he said with a nod as he went to kiss his wife. "I understand you had a little trouble in the dungeon this afternoon."

"You could put it that way." I shivered at the memory. "There's no cell service down there. Someone might be trapped for hours, even overnight." Until they were missed.

"I'm going to go around and make sure those doors can't lock," Guy said as he filled a glass with cold water. "Should have been done ages ago."

"We never spend much time in the dungeon," I reminded him. "No wonder it's never been a priority."

Guy cracked a grin. "I guess it's just become one." He raised his hand beside his mouth and whispered, "What with a treasure being tucked away somewhere around here."

"If you come across it, let me know," I said, laughing. "I'm surprised it hasn't turned up in the garden." Guy had dug every square foot of the kitchen garden by hand. Better for aerating the soil, he claimed.

Unfortunately, the garden represented only a tiny part of the property. We had acres of wood, fields, and formal gardens. If the treasure was hidden on the grounds, finding it would be a daunting task.

After dinner, the ghost hunters convened in the drawing room, where they'd appropriated a big, round table as a workstation. Brady organized equipment while Ollie, Gray, and Finlay chatted. Georgia came over to talk to me and Tamsyn. As for Dad and Tweedy, they were locked in the study, discussing the treasure, I assumed.

Georgia, who was going to be on camera tonight, had curled her hair and put on full makeup. "I've had a few bit parts," she confided in me and Tamsyn. "This is my big break."

"You'll do fine," Tamsyn said warmly. "What shows have you worked on besides the one with me?"

Georgia reeled off a list, and when they started talking shop and gossiping about people I didn't know, I went over to the guys. Standing next to Finlay, I whispered, "Having fun?"

"It's fascinating," Finlay said. "I had no idea you could actually record ghosts."

Brady overheard. "It's a game changer, for sure. Otherwise, all you have is anecdotal experiences, which are almost impossible to verify."

For this session, Brady would be filming while Ollie helped with sound equipment. Gray and Georgia would handle the SLS camera and EVP recorder.

A thought startled a laugh. When they all looked at me, I shared it. "This is Sir Percival's debut on film. We've seen him countless times but never recorded him."

"I hope he doesn't have stage fright," Finlay joked.

"Me too." Brady huffed a sigh. "By the way, Ollie, before we start, play the voice recording from the dungeon for Nora."

"We think we saw the Red Maiden," I added for Gray's benefit. "She's the ghost of a Viking, we believe. She's mostly seen on the battlements, so encountering her in the dungeon was unusual. Not that I spend much time down there."

Gray's eyes sharpened at the mention of the Viking. I was pretty sure he was connecting the dots, the way I had. If it had been just me who saw her, then no one else had to know. Unfortunately, she'd revealed herself to Brady and Ollie as well.

Ollie opened a laptop. "I moved the file over here to adjust the settings." He tapped a couple of keys to launch the player.

"Ekki hér," a distinctly female voice said against a background of static. "Ekki hér."

"What does that mean?" Finlay asked.

Ollie grinned. "Thought you might ask. After putting it through a translate program, I discovered it's Icelandic for *not here*."

"No idea what that means, mate," Brady said. "Was

she talking about her bones? Those would be long gone by now anyway."

"She died at sea, we believe," Tamsyn said as she joined the group with Georgia.

My eyes met Gray's across the circle. Was he thinking the same thing I was, that the Red Maiden had been talking about her hoard?

Did she know we were talking about trying to find it? I have to admit, how much ghosts knew was a mystery to me. Ours seemed to be much more cognizant than the theory that they were merely echoes of the past would suggest.

Um, Red Maiden? How about telling us where it is?

Brady briefed Gray and Georgia about how the episode would be structured while lapel microphones were pinned on and tested.

"Do either of us have to explain who Sir Percival is—was?" Gray asked. "Or will Arthur's interview be sufficient?"

Brady glanced at me, his gaze speculative. I guessed what was coming. "Oh, no," I said. "I don't need to be on camera."

"I think it's a good idea," Tamsyn the traitor said. "You and Sir Percival are practically friends." She was referring to the way he'd helped us solve a murder a few months ago.

I cringed, knowing she was right yet not wanting to appear in a show. Unlike most people, I had zero desire to be on camera. I even disliked having my photograph taken.

Tamsyn eyed me up and down. "The apron is very cool. I like it." She touched my hair, which was pinned up. "I'll fix this and do your makeup." To Brady, she said,

"It won't take long. Ten minutes? We can meet you in the upstairs hall."

Finlay gave me a quick hug. "You'll be fantastic. Put on your Castle Apothecary apron."

"Great idea." I wore bib aprons with my logo while selling at shows or taking merchandise to vendors. The one I had on right now was plain white.

Brady was shuffling through papers and folders on the table. "Aha," he said, opening a binder. "Nora, it would be great to include you. Just chat naturally with Gray and Georgia about Sir Percival. Don't let it stress you out. We can do retakes if necessary." He found a pen. "I'll need you to sign a release first."

Apparently Sir Percival wasn't the only one who would be debuting on film today.

CHAPTER 8

We convened in the upstairs hall, Sir Percival's usual haunt. I went to stand next to the ghost-hunting team, my heart pounding with stage fright, while Finlay and Tamsyn watched from the window seat.

"All right," Brady said. "Nora, you and Gray and Georgia come along the corridor. Nora, mention that you're hoping to contact Sir Percival and give us a couple of anecdotes about him."

I said a silent prayer that Sir Percival would cooperate tonight. "Okay. I'll give it a try."

"Just act natural," Brady said before lifting the camera. "Ollie?"

"All set," Ollie said.

"Quiet on the set," Brady called. "Camera is rolling. Action."

My legs were moving but my brain and mouth were frozen. How did Tamsyn do this all the time? Even when she didn't have a script, she was warm and natural in front of the camera.

Gray fortunately broke the ice. "Nora, tell us who we're going to contact tonight."

I inhaled. "His name is Sir Percival. And far from

being a knight-errant, he was a Yorkshire hero in the Wars of the Roses."

My reward was a whirling set of sparkles in one corner. He was here—and he was listening.

"Sir Percival is a family favorite," I said, unable to hold back a smile.

Heavy velvet curtains swung gently despite the lack of a breeze.

"Really?" Georgia's eyes widened in shock. "Why is that? Aren't you afraid?"

"No. Absolutely not. He's one of our ancestors."

Behind his camera, Brady gave me a thumbs-up even though I had the sense we were veering off course. Instead of spooky encounters, this ghost-hunting session would have the atmosphere of a family get-together.

We stopped on the "mark," an area of the landing where a portrait hung and Sir Percival was often encountered. Gray fiddled with his SLS camera. "Georgia, turn on the EVP." Gray looked up, right into the camera. "We're going to try to contact Sir Percival, Ravensea Castle's favorite ghost. Will Sir Percival respond well to visitors? We'll find out."

He did and he didn't, that was the truth of it. Depending on whether he liked you.

The sparkles intensified and I nudged Gray to point the camera in that direction. "I think I have something." Brady moved to film over Gray's shoulder.

The screen showed a dancing stick figure, as it had in the dungeon.

"You're looking well tonight," I said to Sir Percival. "Welcome."

"Is that really a ghost?" Georgia's voice rose to a squeak. She wasn't acting. She was scared.

"It is," Gray said. "You can see no one is in that corner." He squinted. "Why doesn't he have a head? Oh, there it is."

On the screen, Sir Percival's head was floating above his body.

"He was beheaded, poor thing," I said. "Right here at the castle. That's totally normal for him." Maybe my brief snippet of biography would increase viewer interest. Dad could give the full story of Sir Percival's life—and death. He'd been betrayed by a relative who sought to take the castle and Sir Percival's wife, Sibilla. My middle name is Sibilla.

The EVP device Georgia was holding began to crackle. She stared at it, seeming to be frozen.

"Turn it up," Gray said.

Seeing that she was still confused, I took the device and found the volume knob. I gave it back to her.

More crackling, then a very clear voice said, "BOO."

Georgia screamed and dropped the device onto the carpet. Over on the window seat, Tamsyn and Finlay were starting to crack up. I hid a giggle behind my hand. Georgia was flapping her hands around. Gray opened and closed his mouth, as if not sure what to say.

Brady said, "Cut." He lowered the camera. "What was that, Georgia?"

She put both hands over her face. "I don't know. He frightened me. I . . . I guess I didn't think there would be real ghosts."

I plucked the EVP off the carpet. "They're real, all right." I gave the EVP to Ollie. "This is amazing. He's never said anything. Just made sounds happen."

Tamsyn stood, gesturing with both arms. "Drinks in the drawing room."

The group began to troop in that direction. Finlay

waited for me. I put up one finger, indicating he should wait. Once everyone else was on the stairs, I said, "Thank you, Sir Percival. I appreciate you showing up tonight."

A strain of ghostly laughter drifted through the hall. Finlay startled. "Did you hear that?"

"I did." I smiled at the ceiling. "Hilarious, Sir Percival. Truly."

I joined Finlay and we started toward the staircase. "He was amazing, Nora. It's going to make a great episode."

"Totally. Georgia freaking out like that will go viral, I'm pretty sure." Not exactly the elegant debut she was striving for, I guessed. I couldn't hold back a question. "Did I do okay? Please, be honest."

He stopped walking to look at me. "I thought you were excellent. Very relaxed. And no, I'm not just saying that."

My shoulders came down. "Phew. Dad and Tamsyn have no problem appearing on camera. I think the performing gene skipped me."

"I'm not one for public appearances, either," Finlay said. "Unfortunately with my job, I'm often the spokesperson for the press. And I lead a lot of meetings, of course."

He didn't talk much about his position as detective inspector handling serious crimes, and I never asked questions. I'd dealt with murder as a bystander, and I couldn't imagine what it was like to have homicide as your job. Although I did like investigating. The nosy gene was strong in me.

In the drawing room, Brady and Ollie were checking the recordings while Gray and Georgia sat on a sofa together. Georgia still looked upset. She'd run her hands through her curls until they were standing on end.

"They're harmless," Tamsyn said, handing Georgia a

glass of my brother's mead. "No one has ever been hurt by a ghost here, have they, Nora?"

"Um, no." I veered toward the drinks table. "What do you want, Finlay?" He chose beer and I poured myself a glass of mead. "I find our apparitions reassuring, actually."

"How's that?" Brady asked, his attention caught.

"Because they're proof that life does go on after death." I picked up my glass. "I find that comforting." Especially after losing my mother at age ten. The thought that she might be gone forever was unbearable. Ghosts—and our church—gave me hope that I'd see her again.

Ollie played the voice recording again. "BOO." Georgia shuddered.

"He obviously has a sense of humor," Ollie said. "That's amazing."

"Are you going to edit out my reaction?" Georgia asked. "I must have looked like a fool."

A silence fell as we all looked at Brady for his response. "Uh, no," he finally said. "That was cinematic gold, Georgia. A totally natural and unstaged reaction. People are going to love you for it."

"They'll adore you," Tamsyn chimed in. "Ask me how I know." She laughed merrily. "A vlogger released a reel of my bloopers and I could have died. But my fans loved them and I soon had a ton more followers."

Hope shone on Georgia's face. "Really? Okay, Brady. Run with it. I'll try not to play the fool next time."

"No, don't hold back," Brady said, which made us all laugh, even Georgia.

She lifted her glass toward him. "Fine. I'll be myself."

"Nora," Brady called. "I'd like to ask you a question."

"Sure." I wandered over to the table where he and Ollie were working. "What's up?"

"The next ghost." Brady was searching through the loose papers and folders on the table as he spoke. "I was wondering what—who—you would suggest."

I gave that some thought. We wanted one who was reliable when it came to human interaction. The perfect encounter came to me. "You want the friendly ghost."

Ollie laughed. "That's what you call it?"

"Her. And yes. You'll see." I held back the details. "She lurks in one of the unoccupied towers. It's a big empty room."

"We'll try her next, then." Brady was still shuffling, his movements almost frantic. "Tomorrow night. In the morning, I'm filming Arthur talking about Sir Percival's story." He gave a huge, huffing sigh. "Did you move my folder, Ollie?"

"What folder?" Ollie was still playing with sound levels on his laptop.

"My . . . an important one." He stabbed a finger toward the table. "It was right here." He pivoted to call to Gray and Georgia. "Did either of you move a folder off the table?" They both shook their heads.

Brady scrubbed his face with both hands. "I'm losing it. That was a very important document. A treatment for a show, for the BBC. If you see it . . ."

"You have a digital copy, don't you?" Ollie asked, not sounding too concerned.

"Of course I do," Brady said. "It's just . . . I don't want people getting their hands on it, that's all. That project is very important to me. To my future."

"It will turn up, mate," Ollie said. "Unless one of the ghosts nipped it."

Everyone laughed. Even Brady gave a reluctant chuckle.

"We'll keep an eye out for it," I told him. "It must be

here somewhere." Maybe he'd left it in his room or another place he'd been sitting. Or Janet might have tidied it away, although she was good about leaving guest things wherever they'd been dropped.

I still smiled about the bra that had been dropped on the upstairs carpet between rooms late one night, we surmised. Janet had placed it neatly on a side table.

Finlay gently touched my arm. "Before I go, want to take a turn around the garden with me and Lady?"

"Love to." I placed my empty glass on the used glasses tray, then took off my apron. "Let's go through the kitchen and I'll grab a fleece." The October evening would be chilly.

Lady, Finlay's bulldog, was in the kitchen with Rolf and both of them wanted to come for the walk. We left them unleashed. Lady was familiar enough with the property that she didn't take off and get lost.

With the two dogs running ahead, stopping to sniff now and then, Finlay and I strolled along the path to the bluff. The wide, grassy area had been sectioned off with stakes and fluttering pink ribbon, I noticed.

"For the Viking Fest." I pointed. "The stage is going there. Vendors in that spot. Cooking and eating tents here."

"I've seen the posters around town," Finlay said. "How are ticket sales going?"

"Pretty much sold out, my brother said. Five hundred people. Mostly dressed in costume, I'm assuming."

"I've already ordered my horned helmet, cape, and breastplate," Finlay said.

I looked my boyfriend up and down, imagining him clad as a Viking warrior, liking the image. I slid my arm through his. "I'm going to be a Viking shield maiden. What fun."

Finlay pulled back, then grabbed me and picked me up. "I'll sling you over my shoulder and carry you away." Holding me exactly like that, he began to trot toward the cliff. Calling out and waving my arms, I pretended to object. The dogs capered and barked, not sure what was going on.

He set me down at the bench that overlooked the bay, panting. "Phew. That was a workout."

I cuffed his arm. "Hey. I'm not that heavy."

Slinging an arm around me, Finlay led me to the bench and we sat. "You aren't. You're perfect. I need practice."

I snuggled close. "You can pick me up and carry me away anytime." For an independent woman, I sure found the idea strangely appealing. Maybe because I trusted Finlay implicitly.

The dogs flopped at our feet, panting, and we sat back and looked at the view. Inky sky and bay, a star-studded sky with a sliver of moon. The night was almost perfectly silent, except for the gentle hush of waves against the shore and the chirp of late crickets.

"I still can't get over that you can record ghosts talking," Finlay said. "I had no idea that was possible."

"It is amazing. I've seen it in videos, of course, but we've never tried it here." I thought of the Red Maiden's message to us. *Not here.* "I wonder if the Red Maiden was talking about her treasure, which would be helpful. Searching in the dungeon is less than pleasant."

"Do Ollie and Brady know about the treasure?" Finlay asked.

"I have no idea and I certainly don't want to ask. I'm trying to keep a lid on the news." A sinking feeling told me that effort was probably hopeless. Information that exciting traveled fast—and leaked like water from a holey bucket.

"She must have been talking to you, then," Finlay said.

An interesting possibility. "I wish she would tell me where it is. If it is still here." The prospect of finding a multimillion-pound treasure was mind-boggling, especially in light of how we'd struggled over the years.

Although the Asquith fortune was once quite sizable, death duties and poor decisions had decimated it over the years. There was never quite enough money coming in to keep up with repairs to the castle as well as the cottages and commercial buildings the estate owned. The rental properties were a priority, of course.

Not that I minded hard work. It was more the constant grinding of trying to make ends meet, let alone get ahead.

"If you found it, would you still stay open to guests?" Finlay asked.

I thought about that. No need to ever work again? That sounded tempting. For about five minutes. "I would, yes," I finally said. "I would definitely upgrade accommodations. The extra money would allow us to do more here. Maybe we could set up a small museum. Put on plays and other cultural events related to our history. Reenactment weekends, that kind of thing."

"I see many costume rentals in my future," Finlay said.

We were sitting very close, my head resting on his shoulder. The night air was chilly, plus I loved being close to him. Glued together, practically.

"If we had the money, we could even film original shows or movies." I was really dreaming now. "Tamsyn could be in charge of the production. She'd probably enjoy that."

"The castle is certainly the perfect place to do that,"

Finlay said. "Plenty of space and lots of atmosphere baked in."

"A Ravensea Castle Production." I could see the logo: the castle standing proudly on the bluff.

Rolf scrambled to his feet, followed a few seconds later by Lady, who gave a woof. I sat up and looked around, expecting to see someone coming across the bluff.

No one was approaching us, but I did see a light bobbing in the woods to the right of the castle. Our chapel was in those woods, as was the sacred spring.

"Another ghostly visitor?" Finlay asked lightly. "I've heard of floating orbs."

"Why don't we find out?" I pushed myself off the bench. If people were prowling around the property at night, I wanted to find out who.

The four of us set off across the bluff toward the edge of the woods. The light continued to bob along toward us. Whoever it was, they weren't trying to avoid anyone, it seemed. Although they might not be able to see us, they could certainly hear the dogs barking.

"Enough," I called, wanting them to quiet their racket.

They thankfully subsided and the light stopped moving. When we drew closer, I heard a man say, "Good boy. Good girl." He was patting Rolf and Lady.

Professor Tweedy. A distinct feeling of suspicion started to rise. Had he been searching for the treasure without telling us?

CHAPTER 9

With a huge effort, I refrained from hurling accusations at the professor. Instead, making an effort to sound casual, I said, "Lovely evening, isn't it?"

I didn't trust him, especially after Gray revealed that Tweedy had stolen his work. At the same time, I didn't exactly believe Gray one hundred percent. Sometimes people had an axe to grind. They also used whatever they could to discredit a rival.

Gray could have been lying. Perhaps he had used Tweedy's research to formulate a theory about the treasure, not the other way around.

All these thoughts went through my mind like lightning, between the time I greeted Tweedy and he answered me.

Tweedy shone his light around. "It is lovely. I don't get much opportunity to spend time by the sea and I savor every moment."

In unspoken accord, we fell into step, taking the path through the garden to the castle. This area was thickly wooded and Tweedy's light provided welcome illumination. The dogs romped ahead, pausing now and then to make sure we were still coming.

"I love being on the water," Finlay said. "That's why

I transferred here from London. Even bought a small sailboat. I go out as much as my job allows."

"What do you do?" Tweedy asked. When they'd met earlier, at the social, Finlay's job must not have come up.

"Detective inspector, Yorkshire force."

Tweedy's flashlight beam veered wildly for a second and I guessed he was startled by Finlay's revelation. "Interesting. Yes, that must be a fascinating line of work." He chuckled. "Kind of like mine. Searching out the truth using the few clues you have."

"You could put it that way," Finlay said. "I'm sure yours is much more fun."

"True, that." Tweedy said. "Piecing together the past is endlessly fascinating to me. It's all about the stories I discover."

"Dad feels the same way," I said. "He's working on a family history." And a booklet with our ghost stories, which I didn't mention because I'd seen Tweedy's skepticism. As an innkeeper, I tried to be tactful to keep everyone happy and minimize conflict. The ghost hunters and Tweedy were a much more challenging mix than most.

"I heard there's a Viking Fest here this weekend?" Tweedy asked.

"That's right," I said. "My brother, who owns a meadery, is hosting it. Everyone is dressing up in period costume. You should as well."

"Like time traveling," Finlay commented. "Only with indoor plumbing and antibiotics."

We were renting loos, but close enough. "Do you know your way from here?" I asked Tweedy. Finlay and I were going to enter the castle through the kitchen door.

"I do, yes." The professor continued along the path toward the terrace.

"Cuppa or nightcap?" I asked Finlay, suppressing a yawn. It had been a long and jam-packed day.

"I'll take a cuppa," Finlay said. "Then head out. I've got an early meeting."

The kitchen was empty, with only one light burning above the stove. Everyone else was in bed or watching telly. I put the kettle on and began rummaging through the tea bags. "Regular tea or herbal? My Calming Chamomile and Strawberry Dreams are both relaxing." Herbal tea blends were among the products I offered at Castle Apothecary.

"Strawberry Dreams, please." Finlay added fresh water to the dog dishes and both dogs began to lap noisily.

I put two tea bags in mugs and opened a tin of biscuits and set it on the table.

"Do you trust Tweedy?" Finlay asked casually as he selected a chocolate-covered biscuit. He took a bite and chewed.

"Not really." I came over to the table and perched on a chair, ready to leap up and make the tea when the kettle boiled. "Gray was his student and he said some things . . . and I don't like him prowling around at night."

"That struck me as strange," Finlay said. "Why not go exploring in daylight?"

Because then we would all know about it, was my thought. "Did you know that he gets half if he finds the treasure?"

Finlay coughed and patted his chest. "Half? How is that fair?"

I shrugged. "It's the standard arrangement. The finder and landowner split any proceeds. We didn't know about the treasure, you see, which means he's entitled to a share." Half of something was better than all of nothing.

The kettle squealed and I jumped up to make the tea.

"I'll make a point of hanging around while he's here," Finlay said, taking another biscuit. "That might discourage any bad intentions, if he has any."

"Is that the only reason?" I teased as I delivered the mugs to the table.

He waited until I set them safely down before grabbing me around the waist. "You know it isn't, my fair lady."

I laughed as I allowed him to pull me onto his lap. "Pray tell, kind sir. I take it we're practicing for the festival?"

He kissed me. "Something like that."

The tea was soon cold but we didn't care as we cuddled in the warm kitchen.

As a result of a late night with Finlay, I was both groggy and dreamy-eyed the next morning. At one point, I found myself adding pancakes to the scrambled eggs pan in the dining room.

"Oops," I said to no one, using the tongs to move the stray pancakes.

"Nora." Tweedy appeared at my elbow. "I have a question for you."

"Yes, Professor?" I forced myself to stop working and give him my full attention. This group of guests was like a ravenous horde when it came to meals.

Tweedy gave me a tight, tense smile. "I'm in need of clerical assistance, I find. Correspondence, typing up notes for my next book. Do you know someone who might be interested? Only a few hours a day and it pays very well."

I honestly couldn't think of anyone. I didn't have time and Tamsyn despised clerical work.

Georgia, already seated at the dining room table,

turned around in her chair. "I'll do it. As long as it doesn't interfere with our filming."

Tweedy's smile was wry. "Oh, yes. The filming. We can work around that, I'm sure. Do you have experience?"

"Tons." Georgia picked up her phone. "I'll send my CV. What's the best email?"

Tweedy went to tell her and I returned to the pancakes. Georgia's eagerness to work for him told me that she needed the money. I guessed the crew wouldn't be paid unless the episodes were picked up.

I sighed. I wished we could find the treasure. It would be nice not to worry about the budget. I was constantly weighing income and outgo, hoping we wouldn't fall too deeply into the hole. Even with a location fee from Brady, I had to be careful not to overspend.

One step at a time, I reminded myself. We were all doing our best.

After breakfast, Brady interviewed Dad, who was seated in his throne-like chair next to the drawing room fireplace. Dad had done a great deal of research into Sir Percival's life and he told the story with great energy and élan. I was sure he would come across very well on television, with his booming yet eloquent voice and curly red hair and beard. He was a character.

Meanwhile, I went upstairs to tidy the bedrooms. Tamsyn usually helped me but today she was watching the shoot as Dad's coach. After some reluctance when we'd first opened, Tamsyn now pitched in whenever she was here, which I appreciated.

I unlocked the door to the linen closet, where we kept the housekeeping cart and spare sheets and towels. I added fresh towels to the cart. We didn't change sheets every day, to save energy—mine and the electric bill. Then I checked the cart's bathroom stock. I made the personal grooming products our guests used, figuring it was a way to promote Castle Apothecary.

For the men, I chose a citrus vetiver scent that was both bold and refreshing. For Georgia, a rosemary lemon soap and a jar of salts for the soaking tub, in case she'd used the one already provided.

Once my cart was fully loaded, I backed out of the closet and set off down the hall, my key ring jingling. I couldn't help but think of the many housekeepers who had trodden these halls in previous centuries. At one point, Ravensea had dozens of staff. If—if—we found the treasure, I could hire people to help.

There was a daydream. As I traveled to the farthest room, the Queen's Chamber, I noticed that the door to the southwest tower stairs was open.

Ravensea has four towers. The family rooms were on the third floor, off the southwest tower, which was closest to the kitchen wing and Janet and Guy's quarters. Tweedy was staying in the northeast tower and the friendly ghost haunted the northwest tower.

No one had a reason to be in the southwest tower. Another case of unauthorized exploring? Perhaps. The battlements the Red Maiden frequented were reached via those stairs. Is that why someone was up there, to try to reach her?

Brady was in the drawing room right now, with Dad. That left Georgia, Gray, Ollie, and Tweedy. I thought Georgia and Tweedy were working together right now, but I wasn't positive.

I abandoned the cart in the middle of the hall and went to find out.

We hadn't been up here for ages, and the winding

stairs were dusty and cobweb-draped. And dark, with only a few slit windows to provide light, so I had to watch my step as I ascended. We'd added lighting to Tweedy's tower or we wouldn't have let anyone stay there. It wasn't safe. If anyone took a tumble down these stone steps, they'd be severely injured or killed.

The last window near the top had been shuttered, making the landing pitch-dark. I dug around in my apron for my phone and turned on the flashlight app. I'd need it going down, that was for sure.

I pressed the latch and the thick oak door swung open. The tower room was empty but the door to the battlements stood open. If they were still in the tower, they were either outside or had continued up to the next floor or the tower's flat roof.

My stomach sank and my head swam at the idea of going up to the roof. It was dizzyingly high.

The battlements first. As I crossed the room, I spotted footprints in the dust. There was a clue. They looked like trainer tread and were quite large. One of the men, then.

It was Ollie, standing on the battlement walk and staring out to sea. In centuries past, sentries and soldiers would have defended Ravensea Castle from these heights.

With the wind howling around the tower, he didn't seem to hear or notice me. While I watched, he rested his hands on the wall and closed his eyes.

He tilted his head back and called out, "Rusla? Rusla? Are you here?"

CHAPTER 10

Instead of summoning the Red Maiden, he had called up a very angry Asquith. Making sure the door stayed open behind me, I advanced along the walkway. Because he was standing with his eyes closed, I cautioned myself to be careful not to startle him. The last thing I wanted was to send him over the low wall if he jolted in surprise. It wasn't more than waist-high and frankly, being up here made my stomach quiver. With my fear of heights, I would have been on the boiling oil detail rather than battlement patrol in the old days.

"Rusla," he called again.

My footsteps crunched on the gritty walkway and his eyes flew open. "Easy," I said when he flinched. "As you can see, I'm a live human."

"Nora. What are you doing up here?" Ollie picked up a water bottle, which sported a logo from his video series, and drank. He seemed perfectly at ease.

"I think the better question is, what are you? Does Brady know you're up here?" That was the only reason I could maybe approve, that Brady was having him do some ghost scouting.

The flush on his cheeks and refusal to meet my eyes gave me the answer.

I folded my arms against the wind, which was chilly. "Either you're trying to get a jump on the other team or you're here for another reason." I wasn't going to tell him about the treasure if he didn't know.

He capped his water bottle. "Uh. Uh, my own research."

I didn't budge. Instead I shifted my stance to block the path back to the door. I kept my gaze fixed on him, afraid that even turning my head toward the view would set off my phobia. When it was really bad, I couldn't move. Could. Not. Move. I could enjoy this glorious view anytime, from safely behind a window.

After a minute of my silence, he caved. "Gray told me about the hoard, okay? I'm hoping that Rusla will communicate with us again and tell where it is." His lips curved in a rueful smile. "After letting us know where it was not."

I'd thought the same thing. But we couldn't have people running around searching for the treasure willy-nilly. Tweedy had given us an agreement. Did he have the exclusive right to search? I couldn't remember.

"I can't fault your logic," I said. "However, the situation is complicated." A gust of wind buffeted me, almost knocking me over. "Why don't we take this inside?"

He hesitated, seeming as if mustering an argument. Then his shoulders slumped and he started walking toward me.

Once we were both inside the dusty tower room, I closed the door and bolted it.

"Are you going to banish me from the castle?" he asked, dejected. "I'm sorry, Nora. I shouldn't have gone poking around on my own."

I gave him as stern a look as I could muster. "No, you shouldn't have. You probably don't know this, but

Tweedy has an agreement with my father giving him the right to search for the hoard."

Ollie made an enraged sound and stomped his foot. "Tweedy got to you first? I was afraid of that. He's such a conniving little crook."

Was he? Another question was, were the ghost hunters also in that category?

"I can't give an opinion about Tweedy's motivations," I said. "I can only deal in facts. He arrived first, brought the knowledge of the possible treasure to us, and we agreed to let him look. Besides breaking that agreement, we can't have people poking around here without permission. If something were to happen to one of you, we would be liable."

"I didn't think about that," he mumbled.

Even though I had warned him and even after we'd been stuck in the dungeon.

"Of course not. The idea of treasure blinded you." I was getting heated now. "What were you thinking? Please, stop. Otherwise we're going to have to cancel the show."

Ollie's face blanched. "Don't do that. It's not Brady's fault. He'll kill me if we're booted because of me. He's been working on this project for ages."

Although tempted to come down even more heavy-handedly, I managed to hold back my wrath. "It needs to be discussed. I want to make sure we're all on the same page." With that, I made a sweeping gesture for him to precede me out of the room. "I need to get back to work."

He clumped down the tower steps. I waited to give him a head start. Safe inside now, I took in the spectacular view of the coastline. The sky was that deep, endless blue that we get in October, studded with puffy cumulus clouds. Golden sunlight gilded rippling waves on the bay, and in the distance, I spotted several white triangles of sail. A perfect sailing day indeed, and I wondered if Finlay would be going out.

"Rusla," I said aloud. "If you can do me a favor, I'd appreciate it. Let us, the rightful owners, know where the hoard is, please?" Silence met my plea. "Okay, be that way." Feeling rather foolish, I crossed the room to the doorway. I'd gone from encountering our ghosts whenever they decided to grace us with their presence to trying to communicate with them. They were probably annoyed. I would be, if I were them. *Rest in peace, not.*

Lunch was a hearty Scotch broth served with egg mayonnaise or ham and mustard sandwiches. The gang ate heartily, as did I, hungry after my chambermaid duties.

Tweedy wasn't at the table. He was taking his lunch in his room, with Georgia in attendance.

"I'm not sure I like Georgia working for Tweedy," Gray complained. "I wanted her to practice using the equipment this afternoon."

Brady, who was always thinking of an angle, said, "Why don't we film you teaching her? The viewers will love it. They'll probably all run out and buy their own SLS cameras and EVP recorders."

"I have an order coming," Dad said. "I never realized we could enhance the communication with our ghostly residents."

Picking up an egg sandwich half, I took a big bite to stop myself from making an objection to this news in front of our guests. Dad was falling into the same trap as I had: wanting more from our ghosts instead of mutual benign tolerance. If we kept it up, the ghosts would probably leave of their own accord.

Ravensea, the formerly haunted castle. How empty it would feel.

Ollie and Gray knew about the treasure. Did Brady? Probably. I needed to talk to Dad and Tamsyn and get their thoughts about this situation. I wanted to take a close look at the agreement with Tweedy.

"What's on the agenda this afternoon?" Ollie asked, sending me a covertly guilty look. He cleared his throat. "I was thinking of working on my video channel. I need to do maintenance and updates."

Brady set his soup spoon down and picked up a ham sandwich. "We don't have anything official until this evening, when we're filming in the tower. You're on for that, Ollie. I thought I'd take a walk through the property to shoot background footage." He took a bite and chewed. "If that's all right with you, Arthur."

"Of course, of course," Dad said. "I'd be happy to show you around. Nora, are you free to join us?"

I would make it a point to be. I wasn't letting anyone on the crew roam around unescorted. Not after this morning. "I'd love to come along. It's a beautiful afternoon for a ramble."

After changing into walking boots and putting on a fleece and a windbreaker, I went to the kitchen for provisions to stow in my small pack. Janet gave me several water bottles, a packet of cookies, and dog biscuits for Rolf, who wanted to come along.

Dad and Brady met us in the garden, Brady with his camera at the ready. Dad was sporting a walking stick and cloak that made him look like a sage guiding us on a journey. When Brady turned the lens on him, I understood. My father was going to act as host today.

"Good day," Dad said. "I'm Arthur Asquith and we're

on the grounds of Ravensea Castle, my family's abode for almost one thousand years."

I made sure to stay out of camera range as we set off through the garden. I also tried to keep Rolf under control, which was hopeless. We finally gave up and I was sure that many shots would show Rolf galloping through like a repeating motif.

While not filming, Brady enthused over the garden, asking me a ton of questions regarding the plants, bushes, and trees. I told him that there had been a medicinal garden here since the Middle Ages and probably before that. Asquith women had always treated resident people and animals with herbal medicines, teas, fortified wines, and skin care products.

"Fascinating," he mused. "We might want to do a feature interview with you."

I put a hand to my windswept hair. "When I'm better prepared, please." Despite my reluctance to appear on camera, I enjoyed opportunities to educate and inform the public about herbal medicine.

Our next stop was the bluff, where Will was adjusting some of the grade stakes with their fluttering pink ribbon. "Hello," he said as we approached. "What's up?"

"Will, this is our head ghost hunter," I said. "The ghost hunter-in-chief? Brady Benson, meet my brother, Will Asquith. Will makes mead and is in charge of the Viking Fest here this weekend."

Will pulled off his work glove to shake Brady's hand. "Having any luck? I know our ghosts can be shy."

"We are," Brady said. "It's going quite well, actually. So far, we've encountered Sir Percival and the Red Maiden. The friendly ghost is on the docket for tonight."

Will threw me a mischievous smile. "You are in for a treat. She's, ah, very affectionate."

Brady laughed. "I can't get over you Asquiths. You talk about these ghosts like they're members of the family."

"They are," we all said at the same time, which made us laugh. "We also think alike," I added.

"Great minds, you know," Will put in.

"I can see that," Brady said tactfully. "A Viking Fest, huh? What's on the agenda for that?"

Will explained the setup, how there would be feasting and music and sales of artisan products. Bonfires, too, once night fell. "I have a spectacular finale planned. And no, I'm not telling you, Nora. Don't even ask."

I pretended to be offended. "Be that way."

"Would you mind if I filmed the event?" Brady asked. "I can use the footage for the show, probably. I'll share the raw takes and you can use them however."

Will's eyes lit up. "That would be awesome. With everyone in costume, it's going to look like we took a time machine back a thousand years."

"It's going to be a blast," I said. With all that was going on this week, the Viking Fest hadn't really been on my radar. Now I was getting excited. And the best part was, Will was in charge and had a team of his employees to work the event. I didn't have to do anything except show up in my horned helmet and garb. Finlay and I could drink tankards of mead and dine on beef roasted over a fire.

Brady and Will chatted a few moments more and then the filmmaker said, "I'll let you get back to work. Arthur and Nora are giving me the grand tour." He patted Rolf's shaggy head. "And this chap as well."

"Rolf's a good boy," Will said. He found a stray treat in his pocket and fed it to him. We all indulged Rolf.

As Brady and Dad started striding across the bluff, Rolf in the lead, I lingered. "I've got big news, Will." I quickly told him about Tweedy and the treasure hunt that had led him here, to Ravensea.

"A treasure, ay?" Will eyed the castle walls. "That would solve a lot of our problems, wouldn't it?"

"It sure would." Seeing that Dad and Brady were looking back at me, wondering what I was doing, I hurried on. "There's a lot more to tell you. I don't have time now. Keep an eye out, will you, for people skulking about? Our ghost hunters have gotten wind of the treasure. I found one up on the battlements this morning."

"Yikes." Will bared his teeth. "I'll do that." His brows drew together. "I sure hope word doesn't get out before the festival. We might have five hundred people roaming around looking."

I hadn't thought of that. "Oh no. What should we do? I could warn them to keep quiet, which is in their own best interests . . ."

"You know how that goes. News like that travels fast." Will rubbed his chin, thinking. "I am hiring security guards. Maybe I should beef up the detail. We aren't going to let anyone into the castle garden or any of the buildings."

"Good idea," I said, thinking how tempting it would be for people to go inside the castle even without the lure of possible treasure. "We can talk about that more later, too. I'd better run."

I meant that literally. I had to trot along the bluff path to catch up to the others. "There you are, Nora," Dad said, as if I had appeared out of nowhere. "I was just telling Brady about the monk."

"Ah. Yes. I forgot about him."

Dad made a sweeping gesture. "Before Ravensea was here, there was an abbey in this location. Holy men and women lived here, and the abbess, Tilda of Monkwell, was especially respected."

"Monkwell. Monks. The sacred spring." Brady connected the dots. "Did they build the chapel?"

"No, that's newer," Dad said. "Fifteenth century."

After a short walk through the woods, we reached a clearing where the simple yet picturesque stone chapel stood. An arched oak door on one end provided entry. There were a couple of small lattice-paned windows on each side and one large stained glass window over the altar.

"Tell me about the ghost," Brady said.

Dad looked at me so I took the baton. Tamsyn and I had seen him most recently, about ten years ago. "The monk hangs around the chapel and the sacred spring. He appears mostly on foggy days or nights, when his figure, all in black, drifts out of the mist." I shuddered at the eerie memory. "When my sister and I saw him, he looked like a shadow at first. Then he sort of solidified, if you know what I mean, until we could see a man in a hooded cloak."

"Ooo, he sounds great," Brady said. "On foggy nights? Are we getting any of those soon?"

"It's possible at this time of year," I said. This time someone else could enjoy the creepy encounter. The ghost hadn't done much, just stood there looking at us. Or so we assumed. We couldn't see his eyes under the hood.

"Can we go inside?" Brady asked, his face glowing with interest. "What a great little church. You can tell how old it is just by looking."

"Rolf, stay." Dad pulled a ring of keys out of his pocket and unlocked the door. As they entered the chapel, a patch of red mushrooms with white stems under a tree caught my eye. Poisonous mushrooms. Concerned, I went over to take a closer look.

Rolf came trotting over and I warned him to stay back. Thankfully, he listened.

Russula emitica weren't the deadliest of fungi, but the effects of ingesting them could be very unpleasant. The problem was how pretty they were, how harmless they looked. Like some people, I reflected.

As I studied the clump, I noticed that several of the mushrooms had been cut, it looked like, leaving the bottom of the stems. Animals wouldn't touch them. Had someone picked them on purpose?

CHAPTER 11

I was taking a picture of the mushroom clump when the sound of huffing breath reached my ears. I looked up to see Georgia striding along, earbuds in and arms swinging. She was out for a power walk.

Her gaze fell on me and she jumped, then laughed. Pulling her earbuds out, she said, "Nora. I didn't see you there."

"Sorry to startle you." I pointed to the clump. "You didn't pick any of those, did you?"

She looked down and noticed the mushrooms. "No," she said, sounding offended. "Why do you ask?"

"They're poisonous," I said bluntly. "And it looks to me as if a few are missing."

She took a comically big step back. "Oh no. Will you die if you eat one?"

"No, probably not. But I don't recommend it." If someone made that mistake, they'd be pretty sick for a day or two.

"What's that building?" Georgia asked, pointing to the little stone church.

"Our private chapel. Want to look inside? Brady and Dad are already in there."

Georgia studied the building. "I'd love to. It's adorable."

Leaving Rolf guarding the entrance, we stepped through the open doorway into the small, sacred space. It held a few rows of chairs facing a rudimentary altar. The window above cast colored light over the shadowed interior. Brady was filming while Dad stood out of the way.

"Do you ever use this place?" Georgia asked, her voice hushed.

"Once in a while. Family functions." We'd held a private funeral here for my mother, after the one we had at the church in town. I still spent quiet moments here thinking about her.

"It's a perfect place to get married," she said. "Although it doesn't hold many people."

"Tamsyn and I have always talked about that," I said. "We'd want a private ceremony and then a big bash at the castle." Until recently, neither of us had been close to getting married. Now we were happily involved with very nice men, and who knew what the future might hold?

Tamsyn was dating a coastguard officer, Brian Taylor, who was also a property heir. He was out of town right now or he'd be at the castle with her.

Brady lowered his camera, and he and Dad made their way down the aisle toward us. "The sacred spring next?" Brady asked.

"You have a sacred spring, too?" Georgia exclaimed. "This place has everything."

"Good afternoon, Georgia," Dad said, inclining his head. "Nice to have you join us. The sacred spring is why the abbey was founded here. A source of fresh water and one of those special places, they thought. The veil is thin, you see."

In Celtic mythology, a thin place was where heaven and earth seemed to touch, where the boundary line wavered. That could explain why the castle and grounds were teeming with ghosts.

"I can feel it," Brady said, staring up at the big stained-glass window. "It's peaceful here, as if the rest of the world is far away."

We trooped outside and Dad locked the door. Then he and Rolf led us down a path through wind-twisted trees to the spring. We were close to the shore, and although the water wasn't visible, we could hear waves crashing on the rocks.

The spring was another of my favorite places, a cave carved out of solid rock and set in a hillside. After ducking through a low opening, carved steps led down to a small cavern. The crystal-clear water gurgled out of a channel and into a basin. A tin dipper sat on the ledge for those who were thirsty.

"Is it safe to drink?" Brady asked.

"Better than safe," Dad said. "It's full of minerals and life-giving properties." He paused. "And we've had it tested." That was a requirement before we could allow people to drink from the spring.

"I want to try it." Brady picked up the dipper and scooped some water.

After he drank, Georgia wanted a taste. While we waited, my gaze fell on the back of the cavern. On the left side, there was a narrow cleft in the rock. Our parents had warned us not to explore back there in case we got lost or stuck. For once, we had obeyed them, although we'd loved exploring other, larger caves along the shore.

The monks and nuns knew about this spring, obviously. Had they hidden the treasure in the cleft?

It might be worth investigating. When our visitors weren't with us.

We returned to the castle in time for social hour, which Tamsyn and Janet had handled. They'd even whipped up several hot appetizers: cheese puffs, bacon-wrapped prawns, and mini quiches. A fire was crackling in the large hearth and our other three guests were drinking wine and chatting. Will was here, I noted with pleasure. I wanted him to talk to Tweedy, too. We needed him on our team.

Tweedy immediately buttonholed Dad and Will while Ollie and Gray called Brady over for an update. Georgia and I went over to the food.

"I'm starving," Georgia said. "So much for the calories I burned during my walk."

"It all evens out in the end," Tamsyn said. "Would you like red, white, or mead? The mead is made right here in Monkwell by our brother, Will, who is right over there."

"Mead, please." Georgia's eyes danced with interest. "Oh, he's dishy." Still watching him, she accepted a glass of mead from Tamsyn.

Should I warn her off? Or was that presumptuous of me? Will was a big boy. He could handle Georgia if she did make any moves.

Tamsyn lowered her voice. "I thought you and Gray were an item."

I'd thought that too, and was curious to hear Georgia's response.

Georgia shrugged. "No, not really. We've gone out a couple of times. Brady thought we'd look good together on camera." She took another big swallow of mead and put her glass down to load a plate with appetizers.

"Great spread," I told Tamsyn as I did the same. "Thanks."

"I'm quite enjoying cooking," she said. "I'm practicing recipes for when I see Brian."

"Going all domestic on us, huh?" I grinned, liking the idea of Tamsyn becoming more involved with the bed-and-breakfast. When her career allowed.

"Maybe," Tamsyn said cheekily. She poured a glass of mead for herself. "Let's sit down."

The three of us moved to a nook holding a love seat and a couple of armchairs. Ruffian and Primrose, who were lurking, hoping for crumbs, joined us. Ruffian was teaching the kitten all his tricks.

Georgia pulled out her phone. "I'm going to be getting a few packages delivered. Please let me know when they come, will you?"

"We can do that," I said, curious about what she was having mailed here. None of my business, though. I nibbled on a mini quiche, which had ham, cheese, and red peppers in a delicate, flaky crust.

Putting her phone aside with a sigh, Georgia sat back, her gaze on the ghost-hunting team. "I hope and pray our episodes get picked up. I had to beg, borrow, and steal to be able to take time off from work."

"I know the feeling," Tamsyn said. "I used to wait tables and bartend until I got a regular role on a show. I was literally living hand to mouth."

Georgia shifted to face my sister. "It must have felt amazing when you made it. All that hard work and sacrifice paid off."

Tamsyn nodded. "I'm very grateful. It's not just talent. It's timing and luck, too. And there are still ups and downs. My previous show, *Highland Lass*, got cancelled earlier this year. It was sheer good fortune that I was offered another role right away."

Although one might accuse Tamsyn of modesty—she was considered an up-and-comer, one to watch—I knew she was being honest. As her sister, I got a peek behind the scenes at the instability and angst she experienced.

Georgia leaned forward, sending little glances toward Tweedy, who was still talking to Dad and Will. "That's why I jumped at the chance to work for the professor. He's paying me really well and it's easy stuff—transcribing notes, sending emails, that kind of thing."

I refrained from comment. I didn't like the man, but it wouldn't do Georgia any good for me to maybe sour their relationship with criticism.

"There is something strange, though," Georgia said, her voice barely above a whisper. "He's got this notebook that he forbids me to touch. I moved it once and he practically jumped down my throat." She pressed her lips together. "I told him that if he shouted at me one more time, I would quit." Her smile was satisfied. "He backed right off. I tell you what, though. I'm dying to get a look in that notebook now."

My first thought was that the notebook contained Tweedy's theories about the hoard. Of course he wouldn't want anyone seeing it. I wondered if he had any idea that the ghost hunters were also interested in the treasure. I didn't want to be the one to break it to him, that was for sure. He'd probably explode.

After dinner, we gathered to film the next episode. This time Ollie would be the ghost hunter. Will had volunteered to give the spiel about that part of the castle and what we knew about the ghost. In return, Brady was going to caption Will as the owner of Monkwell Mead, which would be a boost to Will's business.

This tower was similar to the others, reached by a winding staircase and capped at the top by a large room. In the future, when we had the funds for renovation, the towers would make lovely suites. Right now the room was a bare, cold space with high ceilings and tall, drafty windows.

At Brady's direction, Ollie and Will moved to the center. Battery-operated lanterns and candles had been set up; otherwise we would have been in the dark. An early October dusk was falling, the good weather giving way to ominous dark clouds. Bad weather was on the way.

"Camera is rolling," Brady said. "Action."

Ollie made a sweeping gesture. "Tonight we're in a tower at Ravensea Castle in Yorkshire, near the village of Monkwell. With me is Will Asquith, whose family has owned this castle . . . how long, Will?"

Will chuckled. "Since it was built in 1138."

Ollie's brows rose. "That's a very long time, for sure. How old do you think tonight's ghost is?"

Footsteps scuffed on the stairs and Tweedy came into view. Dad put a finger to his lips. "We're filming," he whispered.

"Cut," Brady called. He turned to see what the disturbance was. "Ah, Professor. Coming to watch the pros at work?"

Tweedy made a scoffing sound. "Something like that."

"Sorry," Dad said. "I was trying to warn him."

Brady shook his head. "No problem. Quiet on the set. And that includes you, Tweedy," he added under his breath.

Tweedy opened his mouth to retort, then thought better of it when we glared. He clamped his mouth shut and leaned against the wall, arms folded and a mocking expression on his face.

I was very tempted to tell him to leave. He was obviously there to make people uncomfortable. I wished Gray had come to us first. I would rather share the treasure with him than this odious man.

An idea pinged in the back of my mind. But there was no time to think about it now.

Ollie took up the dialogue where they had left off. "How old do you suppose tonight's ghost is?"

"Well, you never ask a lady how old she is," Will said, joking. "The thing is, we have no idea. We don't know her name or the circumstances of her life. How she died, either. Why she haunts us here."

Ollie looked thoughtful. "Hmm. A real puzzler. I usually like to call spirits by their names. However, in this case, I'll have to play it by ear."

"Don't worry," Will said. "She'll come. She always does."

Tweedy made a choked, scoffing sound behind his fist, earning more dirty looks from us. Surprisingly, Brady didn't turn around with a reprimand. Maybe the camera hadn't picked it up.

"What do you call her, if she doesn't have a name?" Ollie asked.

"The friendly ghost," Will said with a grin. He put up a hand. "Before you ask, you'll soon understand why."

Ollie pursed his lips. "Ooh. I can hardly wait." He looked down at his EMF—electromagnetic field—device, the only equipment he was using tonight. No SLS camera or EVP.

Will moved back, letting Ollie take center stage to work his magic. From what I'd read about him, he was known for his ability to communicate with the departed. An unusual talent, for sure.

He fiddled with the device, noting aloud that he was watching for changes in temperature and electromagnetic fields.

A gust of wind blew through the room, making the candles flicker. I smiled at this classic sign of haunting.

"Is someone here?" Ollie asked. Lights began to glow on his device. "I see the temperature has dropped."

It had indeed, at least ten degrees. Even Tweedy looked surprised. One candle went out as if snuffed, then another.

"Hello, there," Ollie said warmly. "Good of you to join me."

A battery lantern went out with a pop of the bulb.

Ollie stood still, waiting. "They call you the friendly ghost. I think that's great. I'd like to be your friend."

I was holding my breath, waiting for the ghost's trademark touch. How would he react? Even if you were expecting it, it was quite unsettling.

Tweedy let out a squawk. "Stop," he cried. "Stop it, I say." He brushed at his head, flapping his hand around. Then his chest arched, shoulder blades together as if he was shrugging something off. "What is it? Get it off me."

Brady turned the camera toward him.

"Don't you dare film me. I don't give you permission." Tweedy basically shoved his way past me and Tamsyn and thundered down the stairs.

The remaining candles flickered and went out.

CHAPTER 12

We were silent for a moment and then chatter broke out. "That was incredible," Ollie said. "Even if she ignored me." He went to join Brady, to review footage of the scene.

"The friendly ghost is just like a cat," Tamsyn said. "She went for the one person who doesn't want her around."

I wondered if the professional skeptic was now a believer.

"Serves him right," Dad said. "If it wasn't for—" He broke off, realizing Gray and Georgia were listening. He didn't know yet that they knew about the Viking treasure. Dad cleared his throat. "The ghosts are part of the family. Anyone who can't accept that is out of luck."

"Tweedy always thinks he knows best," Gray commented. "It's maddening."

Georgia gave a shiver, her mouth dropping open. "She's back. Brady, she's back." Georgia began to giggle nervously. "She's patting my hair."

"That's what she does," Will said. "I remember the first time it happened to me. I thought one of my sisters was teasing me. Then I turned around and neither of them were there."

Brady focused his camera on Georgia. "Step into the room, G."

She took a few tentative steps. "I wonder if she'll come with me."

"Only one way to find out," Brady said.

Ollie moved to stand along the wall, leaving Georgia alone in the middle of the room, which was lit only by a couple of battery lanterns on the floor. The effect was eerie.

Georgia closed her eyes. "Are you here?" she whispered. "Let me know." A smile broke across her face. "Hello, there. She's back."

Ollie was checking his meter and he grunted in satisfaction. Brady swung the camera toward him. "The readings are off the charts," he said, which would make a useful snippet.

Back to Georgia. "I wish we knew your name," she was saying. "My name is Georgia." She smiled. "We'd love to know your story."

A high-pitched giggle drifted through the room.

After a moment, Georgia shook herself and opened her eyes. "I think she's gone." Her expression was sad. "I wish we knew who she was."

"I'm working on that," Dad said. "The closest I've gotten is a woman in the seventeenth century that may be a possibility. Anne Asquith."

"Can't wait to hear about her, Dad," I said. When we redid this tower for guests, we could call the room Anne's Abode. If she let us put people here. How many other innkeepers had to take ghosts into consideration, I wondered. We were unique in that regard.

Brady started putting equipment away. "I guess that's a wrap for tonight, folks. We'll try again at another time, with the SLS."

Ollie stayed behind to help but the rest of us trooped downstairs. "Want Ovaltine?" Tamsyn asked me. "I'll bring up a tray."

"Love a cup, thanks." When Tamsyn was staying here, we often chatted over hot drinks before bed. It was well past time for a debrief with my sister.

"Tamsyn, we have a problem." Mugs in hand, we were curled up on the window seat in my bedroom with both cats snuggling close. Outside, rain had started to lash down and trees were bowing and bending in the wind. A fall storm was upon us.

"I'm all ears," Tamsyn said. Primrose crawled into her lap and she patted her silky fur, murmuring endearments.

"The Viking hoard," I said bluntly. "The ghost hunters know about it."

Tamsyn put a hand to her mouth. "Oh no. How did that happen?"

"I think Gray already knew. He was one of Tweedy's students and, according to him, he was the one to figure out the Red Maiden's route."

"Tweedy stole the idea from him?" Tamsyn shook her head. "I really don't like that man."

"Me neither. Anyway, I think Gray was hoping to propose the hunt to us. Tweedy got here first. Georgia definitely knows about it because I overheard them talking. And today, I caught Ollie up on the battlements trying to summon Rusla."

I stopped talking to let my sister absorb all this. "I warned them not to prowl around without permission. For all the good that will do, right? Millions of pounds are at stake."

"What about Brady? Does he know?"

"I'm not sure. It's hard to imagine that he doesn't." I picked up an oatmeal cookie and nibbled at it. Cookies often help me think better. "We could kick them all out, I suppose. I was pretty tempted to when I found them in the dungeon and on the battlements. Someone could have gotten hurt. Or worse."

"True." Tamsyn took a cookie. "Hmm. The thing is, they know about it. That cat can't be put back in the bag." She smiled at Primrose. "No, I'm not talking about you, sweetie. Sure, we could bar them from the castle, but they could easily sneak onto the property and look around."

These were the thoughts that had been circling my brain as well. "I do have an idea: If you can't beat 'em, join 'em. We tell them they have permission to search and they get a finder's fee. Say, ten percent."

My sister thought about that as she sipped her malty drink. "Less for us—and Tweedy—versus more help searching. This place is huge. Not to mention that the treasure must be well-hidden or else it would have been discovered by now."

I'd assume it had, except a record would have been made in the family papers. Dad had been studying them for decades, literally. "We could be talking a lot of money. I found stories about a couple other Yorkshire hoards." Picking up my phone, I brought up the news articles. "They were buried in farmer's fields, for pity's sake. It's incredible no one found them until recently."

Tamsyn groaned. "The grounds. I haven't even thought about searching there. We have acres of land, most of it forested."

The task really was daunting. "I wish we had a treasure map. Wouldn't it be nice if the spot was marked with a big *X*?"

Tamsyn rolled her eyes. "I wish."

I daydreamed about that for a moment before remembering the spring. "Today when Dad and I took Brady to the sacred spring, I had a thought: What if the monks and nuns hid the treasure in the cave? They might have fled there to hide when Rusla was fighting with the other ships."

"I can see that," Tamsyn said. "We'll have to check it out." She grimaced. "Not that I'm looking forward to crawling into that crevice. It's pretty narrow, as I recall."

"It is. At least at the beginning. There could be a whole cavern in there for all we know."

We lapsed into silence, listening to the rain patter down and the purring of cats. I thought about ways we could divide the castle and grounds for a search. What would be fair when it came to assigning sections? Drawing lots, maybe. We'd also have to wait until after the Viking Fest for a full-scale effort. With Will appropriating the bluff for the next few days and five hundred people descending on Saturday, there was too much going on.

One thing was for sure. Whether putting the cat back in the bag or unringing the bell, our only hope was to try to control the number of people who knew about the treasure and had access to the property. Otherwise we'd be inundated with treasure hunters.

After breakfast the next morning, I retreated to my still-room to make sloe cough syrup, realizing that if I waited any longer, I would lose the whole crop. Tamsyn had taken over room duties today, which was helpful. Tweedy left to go somewhere and the rest of the guests had scattered. We'd have to set up a meeting with them later.

I still hadn't broached the topic with Dad. He wasn't

going to be pleased at all that people were prowling around without permission. He might even banish them with a thunderous barrage of the colorful medieval epithets he favored.

While I washed the sloes and set them to simmer on the gas ring, I thought of several favorites. Raggabrash, meaning disorganized. Moonsick. Turd. Yes, turd. First used in reference to pig manure, it had been very popular in the year 1000. What's old is new again, right?

Keeping an eye on the bubbling fruit, I puttered around the workshop, checking bars of soap curing on the racks and doing a quick inventory of salts, lotions, and creams. At this time of year, I had to keep an eye on the stock levels. The shops and other businesses I sold to around Yorkshire were entering the busy holiday season. Between stirs of the pot, I brainstormed gift-box ideas I could offer my customers.

I strained the sloes, added raw local honey to the juice, and returned the mixture to the ring. Someone rapped on the door and I went to answer.

Dad was standing behind a handcart holding several boxes. "Special delivery," he said.

I held the door open. "Thanks for bringing those down."

"Thought I'd save you the bother," Dad said. "You should have seen the load of boxes this morning. Most of it was stuff for our guests."

"That's right. Georgia said she was having orders sent here." I nipped over to the stove and turned off the gas, worried the jam might burn if I didn't watch it closely.

He pushed the dolly into the storeroom and stood it upright. Between the two of us, we got the boxes unloaded. The boxes contained oils, natural fragrances and colors, and other supplies for the business. I made a quick check, comparing them against the orders on my phone. "One more, coming later."

"I'll bring it down when it shows up," Dad said. He started toward the door. "I'd better get back to work."

"Wait a sec." Although I could tell he was pining to return to his study, where he spent most of his time, I said, "I have a question for you. Did you sign the agreement with Tweedy?"

He nodded. "Yes, I did. After running it by our barrister, of course. It's pretty straightforward, really."

"Is there a time limit?" I asked. If not, Tweedy might be moving in here indefinitely. I shuddered at the thought.

Dad cocked a brow. "What do you take me for, lass? He gets one shot at the hunt and that's it. If the treasure isn't found by the end of next month, the deal ends."

We were almost at the end of October so that made sense. "Got it. When you have a chance, I need to discuss the treasure hunt with you." I gestured toward the stove. "I can't right now, though. My syrup . . ."

"Grab me anytime. Only thing on the docket is meeting with Tweedy when he gets back from York. We'll be laying out the final plan of attack regarding the hunt." Dad shook his head. "To think there's been a treasure here all along. After all the struggles we've endured."

"That's for sure. I'll be up after I bottle the syrup. See you then." I wanted to get Dad on board with my plan before Tweedy returned. We needed to present a united front.

Dad left with the handcart and I checked the syrup. The glossy, delicious-smelling concoction was ready to be bottled.

Leaving it to cool, I went out to the kitchen to grab a

cup of tea. I was waiting for the kettle when the front bell rang. Thinking it was my package, I turned off the gas and went to answer the door.

Instead of a uniformed delivery person, a middle-aged man dressed in a black leather jacket, pressed jeans, and polished ankle boots stood there. Judging by his attire and the Audi parked in the courtyard, he wasn't from around here.

"Can I help you?" I asked.

He was staring up at the towers and battlements. Didn't blame him. Ravensea was a truly impressive sight. He dragged his gaze downward. "Good day. I'm Simon Audley. I'm here to see Brady Benson."

"Please come in," I said. "I'll locate him for you." I hoped. I had no idea where he was.

I showed him into the drawing room. "Would you like tea or coffee? Biscuits?"

"That would be lovely." He was looking around taking in every detail. "I'd love to be introduced to the Asquiths, if that's possible."

A glance at my purple-spotted apron helped me understand his confusion. "I'm Nora Asquith, actually."

His brows rose. "Oh, I'm sorry. I assumed . . ."

"We're working proprietors," I said. "Besides the bed-and-breakfast, I'm an herbalist." I had an idea. "Actually, I'll introduce you to my father. You two can chat while I find Brady. And make the tea?"

"Coffee, please. And biscuits would be lovely." He smiled. "It was a long drive from London, especially with the fog."

London, huh? I bet he was here about the ghost-hunting show. Which meant we'd give him the first-class treatment. Which, to be fair, all our guests received.

"Make yourself at home," I said. "I'll be right back."

Dad was behind his desk, poring over documents and books while classical music played on the sound system and a cozy fire crackled in the small iron grate. The fog Simon had mentioned curled against the windows like smoke, the aftermath of last night's storm. Hopefully it would dissipate before tomorrow's festival.

"What's up, Nora?" he asked absently. "Here to talk?"

"We have a visitor. A Simon Audley, from London. He's here to see Brady, which might mean he's interested in the ghost hunting show."

Dad's head came up. "He's from the BBC?"

"Not sure. I wanted you to meet him, keep him entertained while I look for Brady. Do you have any idea where he is?"

Dad rose in his chair, stretching. "Haven't seen him since breakfast. Maybe Tamsyn knows."

Which meant finding her first. I left Dad in the drawing room with Simon and then hurried to the kitchen to make coffee. While waiting for the water to heat, I texted Tamsyn. Much faster than making the rounds of the rooms looking for her.

An answer came back quickly. *He went down to the beach.*

Where are you?

In town with Janet, picking up our costumes. Darby ordered them for us.

Darby Walsh was Will's girlfriend. She owned Tatiana's Bower, a delightful boutique that carried my products. Tamsyn had ordered Viking Fest costumes through her.

We have a producer here. I think. Simon Audley. He's from London, anyway.

Simon IS a producer!! We'll be right back.

I put together a tray and delivered it to the drawing room. Dad and Simon were already deep in discussion and barely noticed me. Glad to see our visitor at ease and comfortable, I didn't mind. I hurried away, grabbed a jacket, and went out into the garden. No Rolf today. He must be with Guy somewhere.

The fog bank was dense now, smothering the landscape in a gray blanket. I could only see a few feet ahead of me on the path. Drifts of white wound around topiary bushes and bare trees, making them eerie and mysterious.

Perfect for a ghost hunting show. Maybe that's why Brady had come out.

The bluff was deserted still, although Will had said some vendors would be rolling in tonight, along with the crew putting up the stage. Generators had already been delivered, hulking like crouching beasts in the murk.

Authenticity had its limits. These reenactors needed electric power for music, lights, and refrigeration.

The beach, Tamsyn had said. I took my time going down the wet path to the shore. Our beach was a rocky stretch of coarse sand pocked with clumps of seaweed. Not exactly a spot for bathing beauties on towels under umbrellas.

The fog was even thicker down here. Instead of seeing at a glance if Brady was on the beach, I'd have to walk most of it to find out.

Halfway along, I could barely make out a figure in the mist walking toward me, arms swinging side to side. How strange. What were they doing?

I continued on, my boots squelching in the wet sand. As we drew closer together, I saw that it was Brady, wearing a rain slicker with the hood pulled up. He was holding a metal detector and sweeping it back and forth across the sand.

Betrayal stung. Et tu, Brady?

He wasn't filming. He was searching for the treasure.

CHAPTER 13

"Hoy!" I cried, like an angry fisherman. "What are you doing?" My boots slapped as I covered the remaining distance.

He stopped moving and waited for me, still holding the metal detector. "Nora. You caught me." He gave me a sickly smile.

His cavalier response almost made the top of my head come off. "Catch you? This is our property." I stomped a boot with each word, splashing sea water. "You don't have any right to search without permission."

Brady's posture sagged. "Yeah. I know. I was going to tell you about it if I found anything."

I folded my arms. "Give me one reason why I shouldn't boot you all out. I don't give a fig about the television show." As I said that, I felt a sense of liberation. I'd put a lot of eggs in that particular basket. The free publicity and promotion had blinded me to any of the downsides that came with allowing people in to film. I'd been banking on Brady's talent and skill not to make a dog's dinner out of it.

Alarm flashed across his face. "Yeah, you're right. I was totally out of bounds. I've always wanted to try metal detecting and this seemed like a good place."

Metal detecting. Did he not know about the hoard? Maybe not. “Um, what exactly were you looking for?”

“Oh, I don’t know. A stray coin. Maybe brass from a ship’s rigging. Jewelry. A mate found a gold ring on a beach down near—”

“So you don’t know.” The words slipped out and I groaned at the faux pas.

“Know what? Is there treasure on this beach?” Brady looked eager. “I’m hooked on looking for artifacts. In London, I go mud larking all the time. Do you believe that the Thames still spits stuff up, centuries later?”

Time to get this conversation back on track. “I didn’t come down here about that.” I pointed to the device. “A man named Simon Audley is here to see you.”

“Simon? Really?” A huge grin broke across Brady’s face. “He’s a producer. I’ve been trying to get a meeting with him for ages.”

Without discussion, we started trudging across the sand toward the path.

“For the ghost-hunting episodes?”

“Not exactly. Yes, maybe those. But I’ve got another concept I pitched. A whole series that goes beyond ghosts. Other mysterious legends and myths. Historical sites wrapped in mystery. Actually, I’m calling it *Our Mysterious Isle*.”

“Ooh, I like that title.” Even with his brief description, I could picture the series. “I’d love to watch something like that.”

“Me too,” Brady joked. He started running across the sand toward the cliff. “I can’t believe he came down. He didn’t say anything about it in his last email.”

“He’s in the drawing room with Dad,” I called to his back. I wasn’t going to run back up the cliff. Not when I had Tamsyn as eyes and ears in the castle.

While Brady huffed and puffed up the path, I stopped to send her a text.

Brady on the way. Be there soon. Let me know if I miss anything.

She sent a thumbs-up.

After reaching the top of the path, I stopped to catch my breath. I really didn't want to go back inside yet. Tamsyn and Dad could handle Simon and Brady.

I needed to get my thoughts and emotions under control before addressing the issue that was becoming critical. Brady had seemed unaware of the Viking hoard, although he could have been playing me for a fool. Maybe he knew about it but didn't think I did. The others were certainly aware. Why wouldn't Brady be?

The grinding of engines caught my attention. Will's ancient Land Rover was making its way down the old service road to the bluff, followed by a flatbed truck carrying a number of portable loos. Despite the fog and cold, the event setup was progressing.

To stay out of their way, I decided to go in the other direction, toward the chapel and sacred spring. It was beautiful out here, peaceful, the roar of the surf faint and seemingly far away. I enjoyed roaming the grounds in all seasons, in all weather.

In the woods, I could barely see the path due to the thick fog. Only my familiarity with the landscape kept me on track. As I often thought while wandering, except for my modern clothing, I could be existing in any period of time.

Over a thousand years ago, monks and nuns had trod these paths on their way to the spring. In later centuries, they'd been replaced by ladies in silk dresses with petticoats and dandies in breeches and hose. More recently, during World War II, we'd had residents patrolling while keeping an eye on sky and sea for German planes and boats.

Now it was just me, in my Wellies and neon anorak. Paws pounded behind me, followed by a loud panting sound. And Rolf.

I turned to see the dog barreling along, followed by Guy, dressed in rain gear as well. "Trying to get the wee devil to settle down," Guy said when he reached me. "He's excited about the action on the bluff."

I patted Rolf, who licked my hand with his huge tongue. "The loo delivery? That's only the beginning."

Guy groaned. "I know. I'm thinking we should send him away for the night. Maybe out to Liv's farm."

My friend Liv Becket owned a dairy farm that provided milk and cream for her ice cream shop, the Lazy Mermaid. Finlay rented the flat about the shop from her, which gave me another opportunity to eat far too many of her delectable desserts. Rolf liked visiting the farm, as would any dog.

"That might be a good idea." Otherwise he'd be barking his head off at all the action. "Or he could stay at Finlay's, with Lady."

Guy grinned. "They're quite the pair, aren't they? A real Lady and the Tramp."

"Where are you heading?" I asked. "I was going to stop by the spring."

"Sounds like a plan." Guy fell into step beside me and Rolf went galumphing ahead, stopping now and then to put his nose to the ground.

We were content to stroll in silence, taking in the vistas revealing themselves around each curve of the path.

A groaning noise reached our ears. Guy and I stopped short, staring at each other. Even Rolf halted, muzzle up. "What was that?" I asked.

"An animal in trouble?" Guy guessed. "Or a person?"

The noise came again, accompanied by coughing. That sounded more human, although I wasn't totally sure.

"We'd better find out." Bracing myself, I began trotting down the path. "Rolf, stay." I didn't want him bolting ahead and getting into something he shouldn't. Like a tangle with an injured wild animal.

We came around the corner to find Ollie sitting on a rock, a hand clutched to his stomach. His sticker-adorned travel mug was lying on the ground, next to a pool of vomit. He'd put those same stickers on his water bottle, too.

"Ollie!" I cried. "Are you all right?"

He shook his head. "No," he rasped. "I'm ill. It just hit me suddenly."

A sudden bout of flu? Or food poisoning? But we'd all eaten the same food at breakfast. Maybe he was allergic to something.

"How do we get him back?" I asked Guy. I didn't think Ollie should try to walk.

"I'll bring the Landy down the back road," Guy said. He leaned over, hands on knees, to address Ollie. "Can you make it to the chapel? I'll pick you up there."

"I'll try." He grimaced in pain. "That's where I was, actually, when this started."

We were only a five-minute walk from there so with my help, he probably could make it. If not, we'd have to gather additional people to help carry him. Or call an ambulance.

"Do you want to see the doctor?" I asked. He was the best judge of how ill he felt.

"No, no. I'll be all right. Once I can lie down and rest."

"Okay. If you feel worse, even one little bit, you tell me," I said sternly. "We'll take you to the hospital."

He nodded. "I will."

"I'll be off, then," Guy said. "Be right back." He and Rolf vanished into the woods.

"Let me know when you're ready," I told Ollie. "It will be at least ten or fifteen minutes before Guy can get back here." I pictured the duo returning to the castle, hopping in the Land Rover, and driving to the meeting place. I'd forgotten the chapel had an access lane. We usually walked over, through the gardens.

"In a minute," he said, still clutching his stomach.

I leaned against a tree to wait, watching him for any additional signs of distress. Although pale and sweaty, he looked alert.

"I saw him," he said, so softly I had to strain to hear.

"Saw who?" My pulse gave a leap, which spoke to how on edge I was. He could be talking about running into another guest or a local resident.

"The monk."

Well, there went that theory. There hadn't been a monk at Ravensea for a thousand years. "You did?"

Ollie nodded. "Yeah. He was outside the chapel. At first, he looked like a shadow, especially in this dense fog. Then he came . . . gliding toward me."

I was riveted. There hadn't been a sighting of the monk for years. "What did he do?"

"Nothing, really. He was holding a small oil lamp, like the kind genies use."

I could picture what he meant. Resembling a teapot, this ancient design had a spout for the flame and a handle for the holder's forefinger.

An interesting object, especially in the daytime. Did it have symbolic meaning? Was the monk trying to communicate with Ollie?

"Did you sense him, um, saying anything?" I asked.

Ollie bent over, retching. Nothing came out this time. "Sorry," he said, wiping his mouth. He picked up his to-go mug and took a swallow. "I didn't have a chance. Right after I saw him, nausea struck. I had to leave. Made it this far."

I doubted the two events were connected. It was a shame he hadn't received a clear message from the monk. The ghost's appearance might be a sign that the treasure was in the sacred spring. Or, more likely, Ollie had summoned him with his ghost hunting skill.

A motor rumbled in the distance. Guy was on his way.

"Can you stand up?" I asked. "I'll help you get to where Guy can pick us up."

Ollie pushed himself upright, legs planted wide and wavering. He reached out with one arm and I slung it around my shoulders.

"Steady now," I said. "We'll get there."

Guy parked, leaving the Land Rover running, and came to help. Between us, we got Ollie into the back seat. I hopped in front and we took off for the castle.

Guy drove us to the front entrance, where we both got out to help Ollie inside. Fortunately, he hadn't been sick again. Maybe whatever it was had worked its way through.

"We'll get you upstairs," I said. "Don't eat anything for a few hours, okay? I'll bring you ginger tea to settle your stomach."

Seeing that Guy had him, I darted ahead to open the door. As the three of us edged inside, Brady came down the stairs, scowling and thumping his feet heavily. After taking us in, his expression shifted to concern. "What's up? You okay, mate?"

"I've got a bug," Ollie croaked. "Came on me sudden like. I'm going to take a nap. Maybe I'll feel better."

"Let me," Brady said, indicating I could step aside. "We'll help him up to his room."

Relieved of duty, I left them to it and went to make Ollie tea. Thinking I had a few minutes, I detoured to the drawing room. Simon's car was still parked outside. Why wasn't Brady meeting with him?

Tamsyn was sitting with Dad in front of the fire. "Hello," I said. "Where's Simon?"

My sister made a disgusted face. "With Tweedy. He managed to scoop poor Brady's meeting. By the time Brady got here, they were already talking in Tweedy's room."

That was quick work. Tweedy hadn't even been here when Simon arrived.

Checking to make sure no one else was in earshot, I said, "You'll never guess what Brady was doing on the beach." After a pause, I said, "Using a metal detector."

"What?" Dad roared, his face flushing with anger. "That knave. How dare he take advantage of our hospitality this way?"

I put up my hands. "Hold on. That's what I thought. He said he was looking for random finds. Not sure if I believe him, but . . ."

"They're all in on it." Tamsyn's bottom lip quivered. "I'm so sorry, Dad. I had no idea when I asked you if they could film."

Dad, who had been ready to let loose another barrage, clamped his mouth shut. "Hmm," he said, scowling. "What do you mean, all of them?"

I guess we were talking about this now, and it was all my fault. I should have made the Brady reveal later.

"As I told you before, Gray said that he'd originally developed the theory about Rusla," I said. "While one of

Tweedy's students. He claims that he was going to talk to you about the hoard but Tweedy got to you first."

My father's brows furrowed. "Go on."

"Naturally, Georgia found out, because she's quite close to Gray. I warned them not to go off and search without permission. Then I found Ollie up on the battlements trying to summon Rusla. I told him off as well. Now we have Brady using a metal detector."

"Why didn't you tell me any of this?" Dad asked, an undercurrent of warning in his tone. "You should have come directy to me, lass. With all of it."

"I know, Dad. I was trying to think how best to handle the situation." I sent my sister a pleading look. "Tamsyn and I had an idea."

She got the message and stepped in, taking the heat off me. "We thought that since they know—which is unfortunate but now can't be fixed—that they could help search for the treasure. Maybe get a finder's fee. A small one. Say, ten percent."

"This place is huge," I said. "You've given Tweedy a month. That really isn't much time. Not that I want you to give him longer," I added hastily.

"I'm listening," Dad said. "What do you have in mind?"

"I thought we could divide the property into sections. Maybe draw lots, to be fair. Once they're done searching their area, that's it."

"Or we could boot the lot of them and forbid them entrance ever again," Dad suggested.

Right now, that sounded like a plan. I was tired of the whole thing.

"You decide," I said, meaning it. "Right now, I need to go make Ollie a cup of ginger tea. He's ill. Guy and I found him out by the chapel, throwing up. Oh, he saw the monk, he said. Carrying a lamp."

Dad looked thoughtful. "Interesting. The monk is usually empty-handed. He stands and glowers at people from under his hood."

"It could be a clue," Tamsyn said. "Right, Nora?"

"That's what I was thinking." I wanted to suggest that we reserve the spring for the family, but my conscience interfered. We hadn't known about the hoard until Tweedy told us. If he hadn't, then Gray would have. Maybe. He already had access to the property while filming, so who knows?

I heaved a sigh. "I'd better get going and check on poor Ollie. He's pretty sick. I hope none of the rest of us catch whatever it is."

Unless . . . the idea that struck me was truly horrible. What if someone had tried to poison Ollie?

CHAPTER 14

Once acknowledged, my terrible idea wouldn't leave me alone. Was ginger tea the right treatment? Perhaps not, if he'd ingested a poison.

I hurried upstairs, intent upon checking on Ollie and questioning him. While we might need to act fast, I didn't want to jump to conclusions either.

His door was closed and I knocked before opening it. "Ollie? Can I come in?"

"Yes," he said with a groan.

All the curtains were closed and Ollie was a lump on the bed, shoes off but still clothed and covered with the spread.

"Are you feeling any better?" I asked.

"A little. My stomach still hurts."

"I've reconsidered," I said. "I think we should take you to the hospital. But first, I need to ask you a couple of questions."

"Okay." He sounded weak.

"What did you eat today? And drink?"

"I had the scrambled eggs and toast for breakfast. A couple of sausages. Coffee. That's it."

We'd all had the scrambled eggs and sausage. Unless he'd gotten a bad sausage, which was possible although unlikely. Janet was very careful to make sure pork was fresh and well cooked.

"Are you ever allergic to any of that?"

He shook his head.

"You're positive you didn't eat anything else?"

"One hundred percent."

I remembered the cup he'd had with him. "What was in your to-go cup?"

"Coffee. I brought it with me on my walk."

I glanced around the room. "Where's the cup—oh. I think we left it." If my theory had any merit at all, the contents of that cup would need to be examined. Although how someone could doctor it was beyond me. The coffee had been in an urn that we'd all served ourselves from.

"If you're amenable, I'd like to have you checked by a doctor," I said.

He sat up. "Please don't bother. I'm feeling better." He threw back the coverlet. "In fact, I'm going to get up."

I couldn't force him to seek medical treatment. "If you throw up again or feel any more worrisome symptoms, tell me immediately. Promise?"

"Okay. Do you have any seltzer water? I think that would do the trick."

We kept fizzy and still bottled water on hand. "I'll bring you a bottle." Or actually, I'd have Tamsyn run it up. I needed to go find his cup.

The Landy was still out front so after asking Tamsyn to bring Ollie his water, I jumped in. Driving would be much faster than walking.

I didn't use this vehicle often and it took a moment to get the hang of the sticky old gears. I lurched out of the courtyard and down the side lane leading to the chapel.

I parked and left the motor running, figuring it would only take me five minutes to reach the spot where we'd found Ollie. A big rock beside the path, near an oak, I recalled.

The fog was burning off now, trailing like tatters through the trees. Running, I made it to the spot in good time. There was the rock and the tree shedding its big, rust-colored leaves.

No cup, though. It was gone.

Uncomfortably aware that the engine was still running, I traveled farther along the path, checking to make sure I had the right spot. The cup wasn't sitting near any of the other rocks I checked. No, I was pretty sure I had the right place.

As I ran back to the Landy empty-handed, a question burned in my mind: Who had taken the cup? Had someone come along and grabbed it, thinking Ollie had left it? That was possible.

Or had it been the person who tainted his coffee? Brady knew Ollie had gotten sick. I wasn't sure where Gray or Georgia were right now. Tweedy had still been with Simon, I assumed, because Simon's car was still in the courtyard.

When I returned, I took the Landy around behind the castle, to the old stables where Guy usually parked. Where we all parked.

"Thanks," Guy called as I got out, leaving the keys. "I meant to bring that around." He was working in an open bay, tinkering with the lawn tractor before putting it away for the winter.

"Not a problem." I crossed the gravel to talk to him. "I had to run back to the spot where you picked Ollie up. I was looking for his to-go coffee cup."

He wiped the oil stick before dipping it. "Special cup,

was it? Guess we left it in the rush." He pulled the stick out and examined the level. "How's the young fellow doing?"

"Much better. Guy, his cup was gone. It wasn't where he left it."

He inserted the dipstick and twisted the lid. "I guess it was special if someone grabbed it."

"No, no. I don't think that's it. I'm worried his coffee was poisoned and it made him sick. I wanted to get the cup before someone dumped out the liquid and washed it."

Guy's brows flared. "Poisoned? My, my, Nora. That is a very serious accusation."

"I know. But he said he wasn't allergic to anything he'd had for breakfast. If it wasn't an allergy, maybe a sudden flu? Although he's feeling much better, he says. Flu doesn't clear up that fast."

"Very strange indeed. Why would anyone target Ollie? He seems like a regular chap."

I couldn't think of a reason, either. The treasure, maybe.

In that case, everyone looking for it was at risk.

Another delivery arrived in late afternoon. This time it was costumes for the ghost-hunting crew. Tamsyn had them brought to the solar, which had now become costume central. Ours were there, along with a makeup table and station for hair.

"What is this?" I asked my sister, who was arranging the costumes on a rack. "You've taken over my office."

"Just for a day, Nora," she said, sliding the hangers along. "We can all get ready here before going out to the event."

Brady popped into the room. "The others are on board, Tamsyn. They'll be here in a moment."

On board with what? The simple idea of dressing up like a Viking had turned into a production. But what did I expect? My sister was a professional actor. Of course she was maximizing this opportunity.

Speaking of opportunities, I took one and asked, "How'd it go with Simon? If you don't mind me asking."

Brady folded his arms. "Not that great, actually. Tweedy ended up taking most of his time. I barely got a 'we'll see' out of him before he left."

"Ugh," Tamsyn said. "That's the absolute pits. I thought he came to see you."

"Me too." Brady sniffed. "From what little I gathered, Tweedy proposed a show a lot like mine. And he's got the cred I don't—namely, being a professor of history."

Tamsyn came over, holding a helmet. She gently placed it on my head. "There you are, Rusla."

I put a hand up to steady the horned hat. "Me? I get to play the lead role?" In what, I still was not sure.

"Your hair is redder than mine. Plus you're fierce. If I didn't know better, I'd think you were her direct descendant."

"Really?" I was flattered by the idea that a Viking shield maiden might have been an ancestor. Not possible, though. Rusla had died off the coast of Yorkshire, without issue, as they say.

That we knew of. Had she left a baby behind, in care of the monks and nuns? Intriguing though it was, I was too busy right now to pursue this train of thought. That was Dad's department, chasing down theories and legends and whims through history.

Speaking of Dad, I heard his deep voice in the drawing room and a moment later, he and the rest of the team plowed into the room. Including Ollie, who looked much better.

"Line up, everyone," Tamsyn said. "I'm wardrobe mistress today. The costumes will be staying here, but I'm going to explain your role."

"Our role?" Georgia said. "I don't understand."

"Brady and I cooked up a plan," Tamsyn explained. "Yes, we all could put on helmets and cloaks and act the fool. Or we can be characters from Rusla's story. This will give the ghost-hunting show verisimilitude."

"Oh, like a reenactment," Gray said. "Great idea."

"Can I be Rusla?" tall, blond Georgia asked.

"Afraid not," Tamsyn said. "That's Nora. She resembles our Red Maiden much more closely. You, Georgia, are an abbess. You'll look gorgeous."

That was my sister, able to make the role of a religious sister seem highly desirable.

"I'm glad you're okay," I said to Ollie as the others obediently queued up. "But I couldn't find your coffee cup. It was gone."

"Hmm. Strange. Maybe someone found it and brought it back here."

Or disposed of it, with the evidence. Although, now that he'd recovered, my theory about poisoning seemed less likely. The missing mug was still troubling, though. Things people left usually sat there until one of us swept the grounds.

"I was rather fond of that cup," Ollie was saying. "Hopefully it will turn up."

Me too, otherwise I had nothing. Which was probably for the best. I really didn't need a murder or attempted murder to solve right now.

Tamsyn had marked each hanger with a name. Dad

was a Viking king, Rusla's father. Tamsyn, my warrior blood sister. Gray and Brady were Anglo-Saxon sailors, who Rusla had fought, and Ollie was a monk. Although not at this meeting, Janet and Guy would play Anglo-Saxon residents of Yorkshire.

"What's Tweedy going to be?" I asked. "Or is he not included?"

"Shouldn't be," Brady grumbled. "Not after the tricks he's been pulling."

Hums of agreement went around the circle. No one liked the man, which made it a shame that we had to deal with him.

"He's a merchant," Tamsyn said. "It's his ship that Rusla raided."

The ghost-hunting team exchanged complicit glances. I could guess what they were thinking. They wanted to best Tweedy and, in their eyes, he would deserve it. I couldn't disagree, especially after his trick this afternoon with Simon. He was blatantly out for himself.

Brady's missing file. Had Tweedy taken it, to get inside information on Brady's presentation? It wasn't hard to imagine him stooping that low.

Unfortunately, he had the upper hand when it came to the treasure. He'd gotten here first. Now who would be the first to actually find the hoard? Finders keepers indeed.

"I'd like to meet this afternoon after we're done here," Dad said, his helmet still perched on his head. I could see it becoming a permanent part of his wardrobe. "We need to discuss the treasure hunt and how it will proceed."

Startled exclamations and gasps flew around the room. Had they really thought we hadn't caught on? Brady and Ollie sneaked glances at me, probably wondering if I'd ratted them out. Oh yes, I had.

After a tense moment, Brady, as leader of the team, stepped up. “We’re very happy to do that, sir.” If he had any wits, he probably sensed how close he had come to being banished.

Judging by the grim expressions on the others’ faces, they realized the same was true for them as well.

CHAPTER 15

We planned to convene in the dining room, with food and beverage service. Janet thought, and I agreed, that a difficult conversation went down better with refreshments.

On my way through the Great Hall, I spotted Ollie's travel mug sitting on the desk. How did that get here? Maybe someone had found it and brought it back to the castle. Thinking of fingerprint evidence, I used a tissue to pick it up at the bottom and gently shook it. Liquid sloshed inside, which meant it probably still held coffee. I didn't want to open it and check in case I smudged any prints.

We now had a way to find out if Ollie had been poisoned. I just needed to convince Finlay to have the coffee tested.

I sent him a quick text. *Are you around later? Need to talk. x*

Want to have dinner at the White Rose? A local inn and pub.

Sounds good. Meet here first? With the guests on their own tonight, I didn't have dinner duty. Finlay agreed to come over right after work. We could decide what to do with this possible evidence before going out to eat.

Hearing voices in the upper hall, I glanced around for

somewhere to hide the distinctive mug. After deciding a big bottom desk drawer was perfect, I used the tissue to convey the cup to the drawer and closed it. Opened the drawer again and added a sticky note: *Don't Touch! Nora.*

All I needed was Janet or Tamsyn thinking they were helping by washing the cup.

Footsteps tromped down the stairs. The ghost-hunting crew, all wearing expressions of mingled excitement and trepidation. I felt exactly the same way. While the subject needed to be addressed and hashed over, I wasn't looking forward to it.

Conflict was not my forte. I just wanted guests to enjoy staying here while I holed up in my workroom and made my herbal products for them to enjoy.

Janet and Tamsyn had put together a great spread: local cheeses, crackers, pickles and olives, cured meats, fruit, and veggies. Ollie was the only one not eating, I noticed. Probably a good idea to take it easy until he was fully recovered. I was grateful he hadn't had to be hospitalized.

I put a few things on a plate and went to sit beside Dad, at the head of the table. Tamsyn took the seat on his other side.

Tweedy sat at the other end, of course. As if he were equal in stature to Dad. My father waited until everyone else was seated then said, "Are we ready to begin?"

The ghost hunters nodded. Tweedy said, "What's this all about, Arthur? I can't quite wrap my mind around it." With a casual shrug, he stacked cheese and meat between two crackers and took a bite.

Gray was glaring at him, but Tweedy didn't notice. He opened his mouth, getting ready to blast the professor, I guessed, so I jumped in. "You'll get a turn, Gray."

Huffing, he shifted around in his seat, making his displeasure obvious.

"All right," Dad said. "Why don't we cut to the chase? I'm not a fan of long-winded meetings, are you?" He cleared his throat. "A couple of days ago, Professor Tweedy approached me with a proposal. He claims that Rusla, the Red Maiden of Viking lore, left a hoard hidden on Ravensea Castle property."

Gray sighed loudly but didn't say anything. Slinging an arm over the back of his chair, he picked up his wine, swirled the glass, and drank.

"Tweedy and I signed an agreement that if he should find the treasure within the next thirty days, we would split its value."

Everyone remained quiet, which was amazing to me. Finally, Brady's hand rose. "Why are you involving us in this discussion?"

"Very good point, Brady," Dad said. "Nora will explain."

What? No fair, Dad. I'm not prepared.

"Nora alerted me to a . . . um, situation that's been occurring, and she actually has a solution to propose."

"A solution?" Tweedy burst out. "To what?" He stabbed a finger toward my father. "Our agreement is binding. I made sure—"

"Hold on, hold on," Dad said, his voice edging louder. Everyone braced for an outburst. "Nora?" he said in a softer tone. They all relaxed.

"Um, okay," I started. Not the most assertive introduction. "Over the past couple of days, I've become aware that you all know about the treasure." Noticing Gray's expression, I put up a hand. "We won't go into how or when or any of that. With the signed agreement in force, we're, um, stuck right now.

"So . . ." I drew out the word. "As you can see, this is a huge place. We'd like to propose that if you wish, you can join the treasure hunting team—"

Tweedy bolted to his feet. "Hold on. That is unacceptable. How much will they get? I'm not sharing any of my proceeds."

"I'm thinking that the finder, or finders," I went on, ignoring Tweedy, "will get ten percent. A finder's fee." I paused. "You have to admit that ten percent of millions is still a lot of money."

"Many hands make light work," Dad said. "It's a daunting prospect to search such a vast property. Remember, this treasure, if it is still here, was hidden more than a thousand years ago. The castle wasn't even here then."

Tweedy shrugged as he sank back into his chair. "It will have to come out of your half," he said. "You wouldn't even be looking if it wasn't for me."

Fists clenched, Gray jumped up, his chair rocking back. Ollie had to grab it to prevent it falling over. "You stole my work," he said, his tone low and venomous. "I'm the one who first traced Rusla to this part of England. I find it a bit rich that you're taking credit for discovering the hoard. You are unethical and a thief, Tweedy. Plain and simple."

Lizard-like, Tweedy didn't even blink. "All's fair in academia, my good chap. He who publishes first wins."

Now Brady stood. "And he who steals ideas for television? You're despicable." He leaned both hands on the table, practically spitting out his words. "You stole my folder, didn't you? You don't have ideas. You plagiarize."

Tweedy actually smiled. "I have no idea what you're talking about, old chap. Simon asked me to put forward a proposal on Rusla, the Red Maiden. A multipart series about her life and travels." He turned to Tamsyn. "I believe he's going to contact your agent about you in the lead. It will be *Vikings* with a feminist twist."

Conflicted feelings shone clearly on my sister's face. Rusla would be a plum role, especially with top billing. But accepting it meant making enemies out of Brady and the others. And working closely with Tweedy, no doubt, as the show's creator.

Gray made a choking sound, drawing everyone's eyes. "You are despicable," he said, his voice low and ominous. "I was the one who brought Rusla to your attention in the first place. In fact, I'd like to see your proposal, see how much you—"

Tweedy interrupted. "No one has a copyright on ideas. Or historical figures. You should know that."

Georgia looked like she wanted to say something but subsided when Tweedy glared at her. Was she afraid to lose her position with him? That didn't quite add up. It was only part-time and temporary.

Dad picked up a knife and tapped his glass. Once he had everyone's attention, he said, "I understand the need to air grievances, and you may do that elsewhere. Right now I need to know who wants to participate in the treasure hunt. I will be having an agreement drawn up by my attorney for you to sign."

To Tweedy, he said, "We'll take the hit. Remember, you have until November thirtieth. After that, our agreement is null and void. Oh, and by the way, there will be no treasure hunting until Sunday. The Viking Fest is tomorrow and a lot of people will be on the property. We don't want to give them the wrong idea, do we?" His bared-teeth grin scared even me. "You will behave or you're out." His eyes fastened on Tweedy. "And that goes for all of you."

The ghost hunters all said they wanted to participate,

of course, and Dad took down their legal names and addresses. Then everyone scattered, stopping by the food table to grab snacks on the way out.

"That went well," I said with a touch of sarcasm as I picked up my glass of wine. I hadn't even had a sip yet.

"I'd say it's more trouble than it's worth," Dad mused, "except for the size of the hoard. If it's anywhere as valuable as the others they've found . . ."

"We'll get through it," Tamsyn said. "One way or another. I'm glad you put a time limit on the Tweedy agreement, Dad. I can't wait to see the back of him."

"Me either." I took another sip of wine, ordering myself to relax. "What do you think about playing Rusla?" I had to ask.

Tamsyn made a face. "It would be difficult to say no, that's for sure. She's a fantastic character." She shrugged. "It might not be green-lit, anyway. Most shows aren't."

I set my empty glass on the tray with other dirty dishes. "By the way, I'm having dinner with Finlay at the White Rose."

Tamsyn checked her phone. "And I'll be on a date with Brian." Her coastguard love.

"Oh good," I commented. "I've been hoping we'd see him." Brian was wonderful.

"I'll be glad when the Viking Fest is over," Dad put in. "We've got five hundred people coming. It's an invasion."

"You'll be the star of the show," Tamsyn said, patting his shoulder. "Best of all, we don't have to do anything. Will's got security hired and plenty of helpers. It should be fine."

"Long as they stay out of here, I'm fine with it," Dad said. "I am looking forward to the roast ox. I haven't had that in ages."

"Bit large for the AGA," I joked. "It will be a sight, that's for sure." Will was going all out for authenticity.

I helped Tamsyn load the trolley with the food and used dishes and rolled it back to the kitchen. Then, after updating Janet and Guy, I went upstairs to change for dinner. After a shower, I donned nice jeans, a soft green cashmere sweater, low-heeled ankle boots, and a suede jacket.

As I curled the ends of my hair and put on makeup, I thought about my role tomorrow as Rusla. We Asquiths weren't redheads, exactly. More like strawberry blonds. We had hazel or green eyes. The Vikings had settled Yorkshire so it was possible that we had Nordic blood in our line. Would I have been a shield maiden if I'd lived back then? Doubtful. I wasn't exactly aggressive, though I could see myself defending home and family.

Rusla had been a warrior, an explorer, and a raider. She hadn't sat at home waiting for the men to bring back the loot, she'd gone after it herself. She must have had a very strong personality in order to control a ship full of men and to convince them to do her bidding. I winced at the thought of the brutality she must have endured—and dished out—but I had to admit to admiring her sheer determination to go after what she wanted. She didn't wait for permission, or for a man to do it for her.

My phone pinged. *I'm here*. Finlay. We were close enough now that he let himself in. A good thing because it took me several minutes to travel down two flights of stairs to the front door.

He was standing at the bottom of the grand staircase waiting for me, and his smile was just what I needed. "Hey," he said softly. "You look great."

"You do too." I practically flew down the rest of the stairs and threw myself into his arms. We kissed and then I snuggled into his arms with a sigh.

“Rough day?” he asked.

“Uh-huh. I can’t wait to tell you about it.” Before I said more, I listened for voices or movements in the rooms around his. This wasn’t a conversation I wanted anyone to overhear. Not hearing anyone, I gestured for him to follow.

I opened the bottom drawer of the desk and pointed to the cup. “That is evidence. Maybe.” Using a fresh tissue, I picked it up and set it on the desk. “This is Ollie’s cup. While Guy and I were walking earlier today, we found Ollie in the woods, sick to his stomach. We had to give him a ride back to the castle.”

“You think he drank something noxious.” Finlay had put together the pieces in his usual lightning-fast way.

“We’d all eaten the same food at breakfast, so I thought it was a possibility.”

Finlay glanced toward the staircase. “How is he now?”

“Fine, I think. I had him rest for a while and drink ginger tea to settle his stomach. We had a group meeting this afternoon and he seemed back to normal.”

Cupping one elbow, Finlay rubbed his chin, thinking. “Could it be a bug? Or maybe he snacked on something he didn’t tell you about.”

“Those are possibilities, yes.” I picked up my phone and scrolled. “Look at this mushroom I found near the chapel. It’s called *russula emitica.* As you can see, part of the clump is missing. It’s not likely that an animal would eat them.”

He took the phone and studied the photo. “How would they be given in liquid? I mean, that’s the assumption, right?”

I had a theory. “The mushrooms can be simmered to extract the poison. Someone could have used the electric kettle in their room without anyone noticing. He was drinking coffee out of this mug, which would hide the bitterness. Especially if he added sugar."

"The trash," Finlay said. "We need to see it."

He believed me. Even if I was wrong, at least he wanted to determine that instead of dismissing my concerns. We still didn't know who or why, of course. Ollie seemed fairly harmless. A quiet ghost hunter from York. Now if Tweedy had been poisoned . . .

"Tamsyn did the rooms today," I said. "I'll text her."

Wanting to mess with her, I asked: *Did you empty the room trash today?*

The dots flashed as she considered an answer.

An emoji with rolling eyes came first. *Checking up on me? Yes, I emptied it. The bag is in the big bin.*

Thanks. It might contain evidence, that's all. I followed that with a cheeky grin emoji.

What?

I'll fill you in later.

We are at the White Rose if you want to join.

Perfect. Save us seats.

We kept the trash in a big, locked bin out back near the old stables. One requirement of running a bed-and-breakfast was properly handling the rubbish. Before we opened to guests, we had only household trash and Guy took care of it for us.

I retrieved the key and a flashlight from the kitchen and we went out the back way. I aimed the light while Finlay unlocked the padlock. He flung back the lid and we peered inside. A large, clear plastic bag lay on top.

"That's the room trash," I said. We used clear bags in the rooms and for disposal.

He lifted the bag out, holding it away from his body. "Where can we examine this?"

"How about the stables?" This building had multiple bays now used for parking vehicles, repairs, or storage. I led him to one that was empty except for gardening tools. I flicked on the light switch and overhead bulbs came on.

"I'll need to get gloves from the car," he said. "I should have thought of that."

"Well, this isn't exactly what I had planned, either." I went over to the workbench and scouted around. "How about a pair of gardening gloves?" I held up a pair large enough for him. "If you find any clues, then I suppose we'll need an evidence bag, right?"

"True. I have a kit in the car." Finlay took the gloves and put them on. "Do you have newspaper or anything to spread things out on?"

I found a piece of cardboard and placed it on the floor. Finlay untied the knot and gently eased the contents out onto the cardboard. Nothing too disgusting—mostly tissues, an empty bottle of shampoo, scraps of note paper, snack wrappers, used tea bags, and the like. Typical bedroom trash.

Finlay gently pawed through, searching. A flash of red caught my eye. "There," I said, pointing.

He unwrapped a section of paper towel to reveal a *russula emitica* cap and a piece of stem. We had evidence. The question was, which room had it come from?

I took a picture of the mushroom. "I'm going to ask Tamsyn if she noticed the mushroom when she emptied the cans. Is that okay?"

"Absolutely. I'm going to go get an evidence bag. We'll also analyze the liquid in that cup. If it was poisoned, we'll open a case." He stripped off the gloves and fished in his pocket for his car keys.

"I'll wait here." I attached the photo to a text and sent it to Tamsyn.

Did you notice this when you emptied the trash?

No. What is it?

A nasty mushroom that makes you throw up.

Oh. I get it. Ollie.

Maybe. Finlay's going to find out.

Too bad Tamsyn hadn't noticed which trash can the mushroom was in. It had probably been wrapped in a paper towel or tissue, though, to hide it. At least we'd found it before it had been taken away. The same with the cup. I sent a silent thank-you to whoever had brought it back.

Footsteps crunched outside and I looked up from my phone, ready to greet Finlay. But then they stopped. Hackles rose on the back of my neck.

With the light on in the bay and the doors open, I was completely visible to anyone out there. A perfect target.

CHAPTER 16

Instinctively, I took a step back, trying to retreat into the shadows. Then I listened hard, waiting for the next step. Toward me? Or away?

I heard nothing. They weren't moving. My heart was pounding, breath caught in my throat. Trapped, waiting for someone to pounce.

Forget this. Tired of cowering, I ran across the bay to the door. "Who's there?" I called. No one answered. I ran out into the stable yard, moving beyond the circle of light for a better view.

There. A dark figure was standing by the gate to the vegetable garden.

I strode in that direction, hoping to get close enough to see who it was. Maybe one of the guests had been wandering around and ended up back here, in the private area. If I went at them shouting, they'd think I was out of my mind.

"Hello," I called. "Are you lost?"

The figure opened the gate and darted through. I broke into a run, hoping to catch up.

Too late. They had disappeared through the far gate into the gardens proper. I'd never catch them now.

Another set of footsteps crunched on the gravel, this

time from the direction of the drive. "Nora?" Finlay called, a note of concern in his voice. "Where'd you go?"

"I'm right here." I trotted over to the bay. "Someone was out in the dark, watching me."

He frowned. "Watching you? Did they say anything?"

"No, which was strange. If it had been someone innocently wandering around, they would answer me, right? Instead they stood there until I went after them."

He was crouched by the strewn garbage, a plastic glove on, gently picking up the mushroom. "Nora. You went after them?"

"Yeah. I know I shouldn't have. I was tired of being afraid, you know?"

He sealed the bag and began writing on it with a marker. "Yeah, I do know." I half expected him to deliver a warning but instead he clamped his mouth shut.

Good man. I appreciated his not going all patronizingly protective on me. Besides, he probably realized that warning me was useless, sad to say. Maybe it was my Viking blood that made me reckless at times. If I had any in my DNA, that is.

Once Finlay was done with the mushroom, I put on the gardening gloves and scooped up the trash and returned it to the bag. Then I had a thought. "Maybe we should keep this out and go through it more thoroughly in the daylight, for clues."

Finlay eyed the bag. "There's nothing stinky in there, right?"

"Only tea bags. And an apple core. Those will keep for a bit."

"Okay, let's take the bag inside. Is there somewhere safe you can put it?"

"In the stillroom closet. I keep my work area locked."

Still wearing the gloves, I carried the bag into the

castle through the back door. Finlay had his kit and his next stop was the front desk. I gave him the key to the desk, which was on my ring. "I'll meet you there in a few."

By the time I got to the Great Hall, Finlay was sealing the mug in a bag. He filled in the label. "Ready to go to dinner?"

"Ready to get out of here for a while, that's for sure." I tucked my phone and keys in my handbag.

Gray came bounding down the main staircase. Good thing he hadn't showed up a couple of minutes ago. I wanted to keep the mushroom and the cup a secret.

"Nora," he called. "Have you seen Georgia?" He gave Finlay a nod of acknowledgment.

"I haven't. Actually, I thought you all went out to eat."

"Not yet." Gray reached the bottom of the staircase, his expression troubled. "When I saw her earlier, she seemed upset. Wanted to be alone, she said. Now I can't find her."

Had that been Georgia I'd heard walking around outside the stables? No wonder she hadn't responded to me. She'd wanted privacy.

"What was she upset about?" I asked, although it wasn't any of my business. I needed to gauge the seriousness of the situation.

He shook his head. "She wouldn't tell me." His brow furrowed. "Probably something to do with Tweedy. She was working with him this afternoon."

"Maybe she's taking a walk," I said. "Have you tried her phone?"

He gave me an are-you-kidding look. "She's not answering."

I slung my handbag strap over my shoulder. "I don't know what to tell you. If she doesn't show up by bedtime, text me. We'll send out a search party."

My heart sank. It really wasn't safe for people to wander around the property alone at night. "Scratch that. Let me know when she shows up. Or else I'll be worrying all evening."

"I will," Gray promised. "You're going out?"

"Just to the White Rose for dinner. Send me a text so I have your number."

"Maybe we'll see you there." He began climbing the staircase again, taking the steps two at a time.

Spirits dampened by this latest situation, I turned to Finlay. "Let's get out of here before something else happens."

Tamsyn and Brian had commandeered a large round table in the back of the pub. To my delight, I saw that one of my best friends, Liv Becket, and her husband, Tom, had joined them. They owned a dairy farm and an ice cream shop, the Lazy Mermaid. Finlay, their tenant, lived upstairs from the shop.

Liv got up to hug me, quite an effort due to being seven months pregnant. This would be their fourth child. "Nora. I haven't seen you in forever, it feels like."

"How are you feeling? You look great." She was tall and naturally beautiful, with streaked blond hair and a sturdy build.

She rubbed her belly absently, shrugging. "Not bad. Ready for it to be over. Glad we're in the slow season at the shop now." Although they made ice cream for restaurants and local stores year-round, running the retail shop was time-consuming.

"Is it okay to bring Rolf over to the farm tomorrow?" I asked as I took a chair beside Finlay. "We're worried he's going to go ballistic with all the people around." He wouldn't actually see them but he'd hear and smell them. Not to mention the roasting meat.

"Absolutely," Liv said. "My parents will be with the kids while we run our booth at the Fest." She made a comical face. "Ice cream isn't exactly authentic but Will thought we should be a vendor anyway."

"I doubt much there will be period correct," I said. "Except maybe the roasted ox and the mead."

"No electric guitars in ancient Norseland," Tom said, pretending to strum. "We'll have to put up with it, I suppose." He was referring to the Viking rock band Will had booked for the festival.

"I've been listening to Drakkarflame in the car," Finlay commented. "Really cool stuff." He and the guys began talking about music.

Conscious that there were listening ears around us, I didn't bring up the treasure hunt or Ollie's possible poisoning by mushroom. I did tell Tamsyn the latest. "Georgia is missing."

"What do you mean?" Tamsyn asked.

"Gray intercepted us on the way out. He said she was pretty upset about something and took off. If you see or hear from her, let me and him know."

"I will." Concern creased Tamsyn's forehead. "I hope she doesn't get lost or hurt."

"Me too," I said with a heavy sigh. "It's like renting rooms to toddlers. They need constant watching."

A server came to the table just then to take our drink and meal orders. We had fish and chips all around, with brown local ale to drink. Except for Liv, who had water with lemon. The drinks came immediately, with a promise that the food wouldn't be long.

"How's the ghost-hunting show going?" Liv asked.

"I remember some spooky times with you two when we were kids."

"The sleepover with the friendly ghost," Tamsyn said. "We all went running to Janet, remember?"

"I do remember that." It was after my mother's death, which was why we ran to Janet. Plus Dad would have been livid. We hadn't told anyone we were going to sleep up in the tower room. We had grabbed blankets and pillows and sneaked up there after the adults were in bed: me, Tamsyn, Liv, and a friend of Tamsyn's.

I discreetly checked my phone. Still no word from Gray about Georgia. I sent him a text. *Did you find her?*

Liv gave a shout of laughter. "I almost peed my pants when she ran her hands over my head."

"I bet Tweedy did, too." I told Liv about the incident, how the ghost singled the skeptical professor out for her affection.

"That's a riot." Liv sat back in her chair. "Here comes dinner."

Two servers appeared, both carrying several plates. The fish and chips were golden and steaming hot, the aroma mouthwatering.

We ate in companionable silence for a while, the only remarks exclamations of enjoyment or requests to pass the vinegar and salt and pepper.

"I meant to tell you, Nora," Finlay said. "I'm on duty tomorrow night."

I frowned in dismay. "You're not coming to the Fest?" That was disappointing.

"Sorry. I should have been clearer. I'm working the festival. They assigned several officers for the detail and then one called in sick." His smile was rueful. "I decided to take one for the team and volunteered to replace her.

It helps morale if superior officers work in the field now and then."

"I suppose," I said, still disgruntled.

"I'm still going to be in costume, though," Finlay said. "I told them it was a condition of me taking the shift. Why don't we try to connect for the main meal?"

That sounded like a compromise. "I'll get tickets for the first seating. I know the festival organizer." I'd use my inside track, I thought with a smile.

Finlay's mention of a costume sparked comments about each person's planned attire. Tom and Liv were appearing as a yeoman and goodwife, which was typecasting, actually.

To our disappointment, Brian wasn't able to attend due to his work schedule. He promised that he'd be off next week, and Tamsyn told him she expected him to come stay at the castle. I was glad he agreed, because we didn't see much of him. He and Finlay were good friends as well.

"Dessert, anyone?" the server asked after we collapsed back against our chairs, replete, our plates clean. We all shook our heads, thanking her. Brian lifted his hand, indicating he would take the check. We all squabbled before accepting his generous gesture. The server took his card and the bill folder away.

"My turn next time, mate," Finlay said.

"I'm going to call it a night," Liv said, rubbing her bump. "Big day tomorrow."

Tamsyn yawned. "Sorry. I'm right behind you." She leaned close to Brian. "See you next week?"

He gave her a quick kiss. "Definitely." The server brought back his card and he tucked it into his wallet.

"You aren't hanging out with Brian tonight?" I whispered in my sister's ear. Between her filming schedule and his career, they only saw each other a couple times a month.

"I would, except for the Fest," she said. "Will wants all hands on deck for setup."

"That's right." A groan escaped my lips. Will had assigned me to help direct traffic when vendors arrived with their tents and trailers—starting at seven AM. Which meant getting up at six.

On the way out of the restaurant, I spotted Brady, Ollie, and Gray sitting at the bar, pints in hand. Georgia wasn't with them.

"Excuse me," I said to the others before marching over there.

"Did you find Georgia?" I asked without preamble. "Or is she still wandering the property alone in the dark?"

Gray swiveled on his stool to half face me. "Oh. Nora. Hi. She came back a few minutes after you left. Didn't want to come out with us to eat."

I gave him a curt nod before marching away, whispering under my breath, "Thanks for letting me know."

Finlay gave me and Tamsyn a ride to the castle, which loomed mysteriously out of the dark, only a few windows lit. In the cobbled courtyard, he parked next to the front door.

"I'll go make hot chocolate, Nora," Tamsyn said, reaching for the door handle. This offer was her way of saying she wanted a gossip.

"Be right in." I wasn't quite ready to say good night to Finlay. And I had a question for him.

First things first, though. After a thorough kiss, I snuggled close against his warm bulk. He kissed the top of my head.

"I hate to say good night," he whispered.

"Me too." Still leaning against him, I sighed. "Hopefully we'll both get a break soon and can spend some real time together." I imagined us going away for a weekend or even longer. Staycations didn't work when you were an innkeeper, I was learning.

Finlay stroked my hair. "I'd like that. We'll plan a trip." He paused. "Maybe to Cornwall."

Cornwall? Finlay had grown up in Cornwall and his mother, Paula, still lived near St. Ives. Did he want to introduce me to his mother?

"What are you thinking?" I asked cautiously. Maybe I had it all wrong. Maybe he just had a special location or place to stay in mind.

"Well," he said slowly, continuing to stroke my hair gently. "I thought we could stop by and say hello to my mum—"

"I'd like that. I've never been to Cornwall," I added hastily to divert the conversation to safer ground. The tingling warmth I felt in my midsection told me that we were taking an important step. Still, I wanted to let things develop rather than try to pin them down at this stage.

"It's a magical place," he said. "I can't wait to show it to you."

As soon as I went inside, I was going to google our trip and check it out. Which reminded me: Tamsyn and the hot chocolate. It was going to be cold chocolate if I didn't get moving.

"I should go," I said, reluctantly peeling myself away. "See you tomorrow." Which reminded me: "Why are you really working the Fest?" I asked.

"It's precautionary," he finally said. "After the evidence we found tonight, I'll be hanging around more." We'd swung by the local police station to drop off the mushroom and the cup before joining Tamsyn and Brian at the White Rose.

"Surely they didn't analyze the coffee already?"

"No, no. That will take a day or two. The fact that someone picked a poisonous mushroom and brought it to their room concerns me. That's very strange behavior."

"It is." During our dinner and this snuggle session, I'd been able to push Ollie's illness and almost everything else to the back of my mind. I had been concerned about Georgia roaming around at night. But Gray had said she was all right.

I heaved a sigh. "I really should go." After a final, lengthy kiss, I forced myself to slide over and open the car door.

"I'll check in when I arrive." His gaze lingered on my face. "Text me to say good night, okay?"

"I will." I heard the subtext: let him know everything was okay. I almost invited him to come in and stay, as my personal bodyguard. Instead I reluctantly got out and shut the door.

Before going inside, I watched the twin red circles of his taillights move through the entrance arch and across the causeway.

Finlay wanted me to meet his mother.

That was amazing.

A chilling thought brought me down to earth.

He was also worried about a possible murder attempt.

My insides twisted.

Despite the promise of treasure waiting to be found, I wished this trouble hadn't come to the castle. The murder we had solved last summer had been more than enough.

CHAPTER 17

"Sorry," I said, pushing through Tamsyn's half-open bedroom door. "I got held—" I stopped short. Georgia was sitting next to Tamsyn on the window seat, mug in hand and Ruffian on her lap. I didn't know what surprised me most: that she was here or that our standoffish cat had given his sign of approval. Tamsyn's kitten, Primrose, was curled up on her bed pillows.

Tamsyn pointed to a tray on the dresser. "Your hot cocoa is over there." She shifted over, as did Georgia, to make room on the long, wide cushion.

I retrieved my mug and sat beside Tamsyn, next to the wall. I was dying to know why Georgia had disappeared earlier but didn't want to bluntly ask. Asking her if she was the mysterious prowler near the stables would also be awkward. Who would want to admit that they'd run off rather than answer someone calling out? Totally embarrassing.

"Did you eat dinner?" I asked instead. "I saw the guys at the White Rose when we were leaving."

Georgia nodded. "Your lovely Janet made me a sandwich after she found me huddled in the drawing room. I felt quite coddled." The hand not holding the mug gently scratched the top of Ruffian's head. He purred loudly and we all laughed.

"He likes you," Tamsyn said. "And believe me, that's rare. He's very choosy."

"I'll take it," Georgia said. "Sometimes a cat is your only true friend." She ducked her head then and I thought I saw the shine of tears.

A little dramatic but I could sympathize with the sentiment. Cats and dogs were reliable and loving. They didn't ask difficult questions or make demands. Not too many, anyway. Ruffian had the habit of bopping people on the nose at dawn, when he was hungry.

"What's going on?" Tamsyn asked gently. She threw me a look over her shoulder, communicating that she'd waited for me to show up before asking. I gave her a tiny nod in return.

Georgia swiped at her eyes. Yes, she had been crying. I hopped up and grabbed a box of tissues from Tamsyn's bedside and brought it over.

She took one and wiped her eyes, then her nose. "Sorry. I'm just—such a loser. "

We made polite little noises of disagreement, waiting for her to reveal more. What was it? A love story gone wrong? A professional setback? That her clothing order had been the wrong size or poor quality?

Georgia crumpled the tissue in her fist. "Tweedy fired me."

"What?" Tamsyn and I said in unison. "Why?" I added, hoping she would give us details.

Instead of meeting our curious gazes, she put the mug down on the windowsill and began gently patting Ruffian again. "I don't know why, exactly. I did everything he said. In fact, I went above and beyond." She gave a dry little laugh. "You know how hard it was to translate his atrocious handwriting? And put up with his lectures? I should have been paid double."

"Maybe it's not a bad thing, then?" I ventured. I wouldn't want to work for Tweedy, no matter how hard up I was.

"He promised me a job," she said, her voice almost a whisper. "On his new show. But then he dumped me . . . after everything."

Tamsyn glanced at me again, her eyes wide and horrified. My expression was probably equally aghast. Tamsyn narrowed her eyes, chewing at her lip. If she had ideas how to proceed, I welcomed them.

My sister inhaled. "He didn't, um, take advantage of you, did he?" she asked delicately.

Georgia's head came up, color flaring in her cheeks. "What? No. Nothing like that." She grimaced. "Yuck. I'm not that hard up."

What did "everything" refer to, then? What had Tweedy asked her to do? Obviously she thought his request had created an obligation on his part.

Tamsyn was quickly backtracking. "Of course not. It's just, well, I've been around the block and know all about the good old casting couch. Jobs in television are hard to come by. As you know."

Georgia rolled her eyes. "Tell me about it. Anyway, he said he'd hire me as an assistant, maybe even co-producer, on his new show." Her mouth turned down. "Brady would have flipped. Glad I didn't mention it to anyone yet."

I was reminded that Brady had been hoping to produce his own show. Instead, it appeared that Tweedy had scooped the attention of the visiting studio executive and possibly knocked Brady out of the running. Someone had taken Brady's folder, he thought. Had it been Georgia?

What a cutthroat business, and Georgia was right. Brady and possibly Ollie and Gray would regard a defection to Tweedy as a huge betrayal. Especially because they despised him so much.

I took the opportunity to dig into the backstory. "You were all Tweedy's students, right?" That much I had gathered.

Georgia nodded. "We all took a seminar on settlement in Britain, from the Celts to the Norman Conquest. Tweedy's specialty area, as you know, is the Vikings, first as invaders and then settlers, especially here in York." She leaned back, relaxing as she got into her story. "The four of us formed a study group. It was fun. We'd go to the library together, help each other develop our topics and papers. Hit the pub for darts and beer. Hold all-night study sessions."

"Did you ever date anyone in the group?" Tamsyn asked.

"No. Well, Gray a few times. We were mostly platonic, which was nice." Georgia smiled. "They respected my brains."

"As they should," Tamsyn commented. "When was the class?"

"Five years ago," Georgia said. "I finished my degree, as did Ollie. Brady and Gray dropped out for various reasons. Gray hopes to go back, but Brady thinks it's a waste of time. He doesn't need a degree to work in television. Not once he has credits." She took a sip of cocoa. "He's been obsessed. We did a couple of trial run episodes in York, based on Ollie's channel."

"Is Ollie ambitious, too?" I asked. "He's certainly got natural talent when it comes to ghosts."

She frowned. "Not really. He just wants to do his thing. If he earns money from his channel, he's happy. His day job is in IT. He consults, helps people set up security systems."

Cameras and recording systems. Skills that translate to making a show. Or vice versa.

Back to Tweedy. I thought of a question I'd had. "Why is Tweedy here during term time?" I asked. "Shouldn't he be teaching right now?"

Ruffian, still in Georgia's lap, woke up. After a prolonged stretch, he jumped down and landed with a surprisingly loud thump, which made us laugh. Primrose, sensing action, leaped off the bed and ran to join him. In response to some mysterious cat decision, the pair ran out the open bedroom door, Primrose at Ruffian's heels.

"And they're off," Tamsyn said. "A midnight prowl around the castle."

"My lap feels cold now," Georgia joked. "Come back." She shifted on the window seat. "Back to your question, Nora. Tweedy is on sabbatical. From what I gather, his research about the hoard came together late this summer and he requested a leave."

"That makes sense." I'd thought maybe he'd gotten canned, which would be strangely satisfying. What was it about the man that aroused such immediate dislike? I didn't usually react that way.

We were silent for a moment, the lull that often naturally falls during conversations. A spatter of rain hit the windows and I hoped it was only a passing shower. Tomorrow was supposed to be sunny and clear, a perfect late October day.

"There's something I need to tell you," Georgia said, the words slow and hesitant.

Tamsyn's mouth opened but then she shut it, apparently deciding to let Georgia proceed at her own pace. Taking her cue, I didn't immediately start firing questions either.

Georgia shifted on the cushion again, as if she wasn't

quite comfortable. "I'm not saying this just because Tweedy fired me."

Which made me think that the firing was her motivation.

"I was going to come to you, promise."

This I also doubted. Until tonight, she and Tweedy had been in cahoots regarding the new show. Her loyalty had lain with him, not us.

She squared her shoulders, chin lifted, as if steeling herself to tell us the big reveal. "Tweedy is planning to cheat you out of the treasure."

CHAPTER 18

Silence again, only this time it felt like the aftermath of a bomb blast. A dense emptiness followed by a rushing in of sound and fury. And sheer rage.

"What the actual—" Tamsyn said, almost cursing, which was so not like my usually refined and restrained sister.

Leaping off the cushion, I took a page from Dad's book. "That scurrilous, churlish, venomous cur. We must exile his treasonous arse without delay." I struck a pose, my finger pointed to the door as if ordering Tweedy from the premises.

Tamsyn nodded with approval. "Exactly."

Georgia sat with shoulders hunched. "I should have told you sooner—"

She should have, yes, but in the interest of extracting information, I said, "Did he actually tell you that?" I advanced toward her, stopping only inches away to glare down at her. "What were his exact words?"

Georgia put up her hands as if to ward me off. "He kept hinting. 'Finders keepers, losers weepers; cat's away, mice will play.' That kind of thing. Often enough that I put two and two together." She was actually shivering.

Was I that intimidating? "He has a notebook he told me not to touch . . . I took a peek."

I rested my hands on my hips. "He actually wrote down that he planned to steal the treasure for himself?" I was ready to storm the tower where he was staying and demand he hand it over.

Her eyes shifted back and forth, not meeting mine. "No . . . he drew a map. And there were a lot of notes about the sacred spring."

The sacred spring. I'd also thought that the treasure might be there, hidden by the religious community when under attack. Not only did the cave have hidden recesses, even barbarians might have hesitated to violate a sacred site.

Tweedy hadn't mentioned the spring as far as I knew. He and Dad had been focused on castle maps, especially the dungeons. Come to think of it, Finlay and I had seen the professor alone at night, coming from the direction of the spring. Had he been exploring the cave?

Although, Georgia might be lying. Maybe she was trying to knock Tweedy out of the running for the treasure. If Dad cancelled the agreement with the professor, then the ghost hunters would be in a much better position. If we allowed them to be, that is.

Could Dad get out of the agreement? That was a question for an attorney. Unfortunately in this case we weren't back in the days when the nobleman held his own court and set the punishment. I had no doubt that Asquiths of yore would execute rough justice for a traitor like Tweedy. If Georgia was telling the truth, I reminded myself.

Realizing I was still looming over our guest, I took a step back.

"We'll talk about this in the morning," Tamsyn said crisply. "Thanks for letting us know." Her tone and demeanor clearly conveyed that Georgia was dismissed.

"Yes, yes, that will be fine." Georgia slid off the cushion. Then, noticing her mug on the windowsill, she picked it up and carried it to the tray before slinking out of the bedroom. Bombshell delivered. Now it was our job to deal with the fallout.

We waited until she was gone. In fact, I peeked down the staircase to make sure before shutting the thick oak bedroom door.

"I can't believe it, but I'm not surprised," I said, summing up my conflicting feelings. "Tweedy already cheated Gray, according to him, anyway. Why not pretend to look, then covertly steal the treasure? Finlay and I saw Tweedy coming from the direction of the sacred spring one night." Absently, I began arranging bottles and brushes on Tamsyn's dresser.

"Hold on," Tamsyn said. She was on her feet and pacing around. "Tweedy went to the spring at night?"

"It appears that way. We were on the bench when we saw a light in the woods coming from that direction. We went to check it out and it was Tweedy."

Tamsyn took a few steps, pivoted, and returned. "The only thing holding me back is that she might be lying to pay him back for firing her. I'm sure he'll deny it when we confront him."

"I agree. Her proof is pretty nebulous. A couple of idioms and notes." I stopped fiddling with the perfume bottles. "I would love to get a look at that notebook."

"Nora. What are you thinking?"

I threw her a smile. "You really want to know? I was thinking about sneaking into his room and reading the notebook. I know that's not cool but neither is trying to cut us out of the deal." I returned to fiddling and she continued to pace. "We need to talk to Dad, see how he wants to proceed." Then I remembered and groaned. "The Fest. We can't bring up such a hot topic with that going on. This place will be a madhouse tomorrow."

"Which means five hundred witnesses if he tries to go snooping around," Tamsyn reminded me. "He'll wait until after the festival and by then, we'll have told Dad. Tweedy is not going to get his mitts on a single artifact."

Rapping on my bedroom door woke me up. *What time is it?* I sat bolt upright to stare at the clock. Uh-oh. I was supposed to be dressed and downstairs already, to help with the Fest. Why hadn't my alarm gone off?

"Come in," I called to whoever was knocking. Then I reconsidered. "Who is it?"

"Janet," a muffled voice said. "I'm delivering breakfast."

A glance at my outfit revealed that the T-shirt and boxers were fit for company. Now fully awake, I hopped out of bed and went to the door.

"Janet," I cried, opening the door to reveal her standing there with a tray. "You didn't have to bring me breakfast." She already did too much.

"Trying to help, that's all." She entered the room, Ruffian and Primrose on her heels, no doubt lured by the smell of scrambled eggs and bacon. She set the tray on a small table near the window. "You've got a long day ahead of you."

I gave her a hug. "Thank you." I grabbed a piece of bacon and sat. "Tell Will I'll be right down." She'd included a huge mug of hot coffee and I took a first heavenly sip.

Instead of leaving, Janet hovered near the window, peering out into the dawn. The grinding of engines told me that people were already arriving to set up.

"There's something I need to tell you," Janet said.

Uh-oh. The toast I was chewing turned to cardboard. "Go ahead." Naturally my first thought was her health and Guy's health, followed by a problem with the castle. Though she wouldn't preface a castle problem. She'd blurt it out, no problem.

She perched on the chair opposite. "I was paying a visit to the loo in the middle of the night when I heard someone come in through the back." Janet and Guy had an en suite bathroom off their bedroom above the kitchen.

Not a health problem, then. Relieved, my appetite came roaring back. I nodded to show I was listening and began shoveling eggs and bacon into my mouth. I wouldn't bother showering right now. I would do that later, before I donned my costume.

"You know we lock that door so whoever it was must have gone out that way. I couldn't imagine what you might be doing outside at three AM, milady, or your sister either. I thought I'd better go down and find out."

I put my fork down and took a long swallow of coffee. "Who was it?"

Her lip curled, an expression I rarely saw on our sweet Janet. "Tweedy."

Last night's conversation with Georgia came back to me in a flash. My immediate thought was that he had been treasure hunting. "Was he carrying anything?"

She gasped, getting my meaning. "If he had been, I would have demanded to see whatever it was. But he was empty-handed." A pause. "And wearing disposable gloves. That was the really odd part. Besides taking a stroll in the middle of the night, I mean."

I let out a bark of laughter. "I bet I know what he was doing. Finlay and I got there first." Tweedy must have tried to poison Ollie. Was Janet's eyewitness account enough to arrest him? That would be perfect. We would have a valid reason to break the agreement.

Janet frowned in confusion. "What am I missing?"

"Sorry." I crunched a piece of bacon. "The other day in the chapel woods, I came across a type of mushroom that can make you sick. Ollie's symptoms fit, so on a hunch, Finlay and I checked the room trash, which Tamsyn had taken out to the bin. We found pieces of the mushrooms and Finlay took them into evidence and sent his leftover coffee to the lab."

Janet sucked in a sharp breath. "Ollie was poisoned?"

"It's possible," I said. "He recovered within hours, which wouldn't happen with the flu. It might with food poisoning. We need the lab results to be sure."

"Who would do such a thing?" Janet asked. "Ollie is such a nice, unassuming young man."

"I agree. After what you just told me, I think it probably was Tweedy." Anger tightened my midsection. "Tamsyn and I had a very interesting talk with Georgia last night." Conscious of the ticking clock, I gave a short overview of our chat. "Georgia might be lying, but I'm going to proceed as if she's telling the truth. We just need to figure out how to tell Dad. He's going to go ballistic."

Grim satisfaction lit Janet's eyes. "I wouldn't blame him. That man is nothing but trouble."

Hearing shouts and vehicle noise out on the bluff, I groaned. "If only we didn't have the Fest today. I think we should wait until tomorrow to talk to Dad." Not that it would be easy to sit on such explosive information. "Because of the treasure hunting agreement, Dad is going to need to speak to an attorney and figure out how to proceed." I glanced around the room.

"What are you looking for?" Janet asked.

"My phone. It's on the bedside table." Before I could get up, she brought it to me. "I'm going to tell Finlay about Tweedy's midnight ramble. Maybe he will have time to question him. If he poisoned Ollie and we can prove that, then problem solved."

Good morning. Big news. Tweedy was poking around in the garbage, we think. Janet saw him coming into the kitchen at three a.m., wearing plastic gloves.

"No answer yet," I said after thirty seconds. He was either still sleeping, lucky duck, or busy. Only a few crumbs were left on my plate so I stood, picking up my coffee. "Thanks again for bringing breakfast. I'd better get dressed and hop to it before Will comes looking for me."

Janet rose as well, smoothing her apron. "I'll head him off. See you downstairs."

As she left with the tray, I checked my alarm to find out what had gone wrong. I'd set it for tomorrow by accident. Thank goodness for Janet or I'd still be snoozing.

I eyed my rumpled bed with longing. Instead of sweet dreams while sleeping in, I was dealing with attempted murder and a cheating treasure hunter. Not to mention the horde of five hundred would-be Vikings soon to arrive.

CHAPTER 19

Tamsyn and I were assigned to stand in the festival area and direct vendors to their booths. The double row of jaunty canopy tents with their tiny roof flags looked fairly authentic even with the power lines snaking through the grass. Each vendor pulled up in a vehicle, unloaded, and then drove away to park. Staying true to the festival theme, the products included Viking-inspired leather, jewelry, handcrafts, art, candles, and clothing.

Meanwhile, preparations for the main banquet were already underway and the mouth-watering aroma of roasting ox drifted from the huge oven they'd brought in. A spit over a pit had been ruled out as too complicated, since that method took a full day or even longer. Maybe next year.

A streak of tan fur bolting from the woods fringing the castle caught my eye. Rolf, his tongue flapping and no doubt dripping with saliva, was headed straight to the food tent.

"I totally forgot," I cried to no one as I ran to intercept him. He was supposed to go to Liv's farm for the day.

It took several burly Vikings to halt the two-hundred-pound dog, who feinted this way and that, determined to reach the roasting meat. A spare bone from the butcher chef finally clinched the deal. Rolf collapsed on the grass, bone between his paws, and I quickly tied a donated woven leash to his collar.

Tamsyn came across the grass, phone extended. "You and Rolf already went viral."

I didn't dare to let go of the leash. "How did you find out?"

"I set up an alert for the event tag, #vikingfestravensea." She played the video for me, a less than flattering display of me darting around, screaming for the dog to stop. Then the men in their horned helmets descended, using their combined weight and muscular arms to bring Rolf to a halt.

"Ugh. Let's pray it gets buried by other posts."

"Why?" she asked, replaying the video. "You look cute."

As I rolled my eyes in response, Tom's blue pickup truck, stenciled LAZY MERMAID ICE CREAM on the doors, came bouncing across the bluff. Another attendant waved Tom to an end booth. Tom and one of his farmhands got out and went around back to unload a portable freezer. Liv must be coming on a later trip, which gave me an idea. Maybe Tom could take Rolf back to the farm.

"Come on, Rolf," I said, tugging the leash so he would get up. With the bone clenched between his teeth, he was docile enough now. When Tom returned to the truck for another load, I asked, "Can he ride with you to the farm? If not, I'll take him over."

Tom threw a glance at Rolf. "Sure thing. He'll have to ride in back."

Carrying his bone, he happily trotted up the ramp. I followed and secured his leash to a tie-off. "You be good at the farm," I told him. "I'll come get you tomorrow." He treated my bare hand to a nice, thorough slobber from his big tongue. "Thank you for that," I said with a laugh, wiping my hand on my jeans.

"Ready for a cuppa?" Tamsyn asked as I clambered down the ramp. "Will said we can go. His other helpers have arrived."

"Phew. I'm definitely ready for a break." Now that I'd helped for a couple of hours, I had a better grasp on just how much work went into an event this size. And the gates weren't even open yet.

As we made our way toward the castle gardens, I saw Finlay standing with another officer I knew, Constable Advick Kumar. Both were wearing helmets and cloaks over leggings so they'd blend into the crowd.

Be still my heart. Finlay looked gorgeous. He could carry me off to his lair anytime.

"Good morning, Nora, Tamsyn," Advick cried as we approached. "This is amazing. So much fun." He glanced at his boss. "Not that I will forget my duties. No, not for a moment."

I grinned at the charming constable, who was enthusiastic and intelligent in equal measure. "I'm sure Finlay will give you a few breaks. It's going to be a long day." The gates were opening at noon, with the under-wraps grand finale scheduled for ten this evening.

"We're on our way to the castle for a cup of tea, if you'd like to join us," I went on. I raised my brows at Finlay, signaling that I wanted to speak to him.

"I'll go," he said. "Advick, check the bakery booth for me, will you? I heard the honey buns are especially good." The bakery booth was already open for business, serving tea, coffee, scones, cakes, and pastries.

"Thank you, DI. I will do that." Advick strode away, his cape flying behind him.

"Now there's an assignment anyone would enjoy," I

quipped. I started to slip my hand into Finlay's but then pulled back with a grimace.

"What's wrong?" he asked.

"Dog spit. I had to intercept Rolf before he reached the food tent." As I said that, we heard thunderous woofs from the direction of Tom's truck, which was traveling slowly across the bluff toward the lane leading out. "And there he is, barking farewell, on his way to the farm." I cringed. "I hope he doesn't bark all the way. Poor Tom."

Tamsyn whipped out her phone. "Want to see the video? It was really funny." I scowled at her behind his back and she smiled sweetly in return.

Finlay laughed aloud at the antics. After handing the phone back, he said, "Off duty," before gathering me in his arms for a kiss. "Never a dull moment with my girl," he murmured.

"That's for sure." I rolled my eyes. "And the day is young."

In the kitchen, Janet was pulling a pan of scones out of the oven. "Perfect timing," she said. "I've just put the kettle on."

I gave her a kiss on the cheek. "You must have radar for hungry people. I'm ready for my second breakfast." Conscious of my dirty hands, I went to the sink and washed them.

We found seats around the table and sat, filling Janet in on events so far, including Rolf's forlorn journey. I hopped up to distribute cups of tea as she poured.

"He'll be all right once he gets there," Janet said, bringing over the plate of cinnamon scones. "He does enjoy an outing."

"Especially with a friend," Finlay put in. "I took Lady over there earlier." Finlay usually kept the white bulldog in doggy day care while he worked. I'd thought of offering to take her in but the timing wasn't quite right. I wanted to be sure he and I were on firm footing—so far, so good—and also to wait until after the filming. It was too hectic around here right now.

"Aw, so cute," Tamsyn said. "They're the best of buddies."

I let people enjoy their scones before I brought up the topic weighing on my mind. "Finlay, Janet saw something interesting last night. Janet, can you tell him about it?"

Janet set her mug down. "Last night, in the wee hours, I heard someone come in through the back door. Which is locked, so they went out that way."

Finlay nodded, indicating that she should go ahead.

"It was Professor Tweedy, wearing those disposable gloves on his hands."

"He must have been going through the garbage," I said. "And you know what that means."

Finlay pursed his lips. "It's certainly indicative yet far from conclusive."

Annoyed, I sucked in a breath. Why did he have to go all official on me right now? "It's obvious. He was looking for the mushrooms we found in the trash. Can't you question him about it? Or just ask what he was doing out there?"

"Not yet," was the maddening reply. "We aren't getting the lab results back until Monday. Until then, we're only guessing that the mushroom was the cause of Ollie's illness."

Guessing? I was absolutely convinced that the dots connected. Ollie's symptoms were a match to *russula emitica* symptoms. Out of an abundance of caution, Tweedy had used gloves to handle the mushroom. Or to poke through the trash. Who would want to do that barehanded?

I sank into gloomy silence, pretty sure I was pouting. In my mind, we had a real gotcha moment. Then I remembered what Georgia had told me and my sister last night. "But wait, there's more. Right, Tamsyn? Janet already knows," I added.

Tamsyn's eyes flared in alarm. "You didn't tell Dad yet, I hope."

"No, I did not. We agreed to wait until after the Fest. Janet won't spill."

Janet drew a finger across her lips, indicating her mouth was zipped.

"According to Georgia, who Tweedy fired, he is planning on cheating us out of the treasure," I said. With each word, my anger grew. "He's a thief." I amended that.

"Well, a would-be thief." Then again. "Actually yes, he is. He stole Gray's research about the Red Maiden. That's how he was able to get ahead of Gray when it came to hunting for the treasure."

"He's a nasty piece of work," Janet said. "I can't wait to see the back of him."

Even Finlay, who didn't know Janet that well, looked surprised. She never said a harsh word about anyone so Tweedy really had gotten up her nose, as the saying went.

A tempting idea trickled into my mind. Finlay couldn't question Tweedy, but I could. Although I wouldn't want to mess up his case, if the results came back as poison. What if I just said that Janet had seen him and got his reaction? I wouldn't have to accuse him or mention the gloves. Maybe I could couch it in helpful terms. *Did you lose something?*

I glanced up to see Finlay watching me, his lips curved

in a slight smile. Had he guessed what I was thinking? Hoping not, I returned the smile, then lifted my mug. "Who's ready for another cup?"

After another cup of tea and our fill of scones, Finlay returned to his duties and Tamsyn and I went upstairs to shower and change into our costumes. I'd braid my hair, I decided, a common hairstyle among Viking women.

Before getting dressed, I perched on the window seat to take in the activity on the bluff. The vendors were bustling around their booths, getting ready to open, and over on the stage, a band was setting up equipment. In addition to the Viking rockers, we'd have minstrels and folk musicians playing throughout the day.

On the edge of the bluff, men were building a large bonfire. This would be lit with great ceremony at sunset. It was Halloween, also known as All Hallows' Eve. While the Vikings hadn't celebrated Halloween or the Celtic Samhain, they'd had a similar holiday called Vetrnætr, or Winter Nights. Like the more modern holidays, the harvest was celebrated and the dead honored. All marked the dying of the year and the gathering of provisions to make it through a long, cold winter.

Long, cold winters were not my favorite, although I enjoyed hunkering down and spending time in my workshop. Using the summer bounty from my garden, I experimented with new formulations, making notes about the previous season and plans for spring. This after a hectic lead-up to the holidays, of course. For the next month, I would be a virtual machine churning out orders for the shops I supplied.

"Nora?" Tamsyn put her hand around the doorway. "You're not even dressed."

I glanced down at my towel. "I won't be long. Will you braid my hair?"

She held up a comb. "I was hoping you'd braid mine."

"I will. Let me put my clothes on."

The shift and overdress were loose and comfortable, I was glad to discover. The costume came with a belt and an attached pouch, perfect for my cell phone. I put on warm wool socks and low-heeled ankle boots, which were authentic enough to pass muster. Not that anyone would be looking at my feet. Not with a horned helmet on my head.

We braided each other's hair and then donned our cloaks, ready to join the growing crowd on the bluff. Music was playing now and the gates were open for the ticket holders to come in.

While I'd been getting ready, the idea of speaking to Tweedy had been nagging at me. I had to confront him. He'd already caused enough havoc by coming here, potential treasure or not.

The big issue was his plan to cheat us, if Georgia had been telling the truth. I wasn't going to bring that up, not without Dad in the loop and a plan of action prepared. I wasn't that impulsive.

I wanted to know why he was sneaking into the house in the middle of the night, wearing a pair of disposable gloves. That was seriously suspicious behavior knowing what we did about the mushrooms. Ollie could have become seriously ill or even died, although that was rare with those particular fungi.

Watching my sister as she made final adjustments to her costume in a full-length mirror, I wondered what excuse I could give her. She probably wouldn't like me talking to Tweedy. I wrestled with my conscience about lying to her. Our relationship was better than ever and I didn't want to damage it.

Tamsyn leaned close to the mirror, studying her makeup. Our eyes met in the glass and she frowned. "What? Is something wrong?"

"Not at all. You look gorgeous, as always." I shifted on the bed, where I was sitting. "I'm going to go talk to Tweedy about his after-midnight excursion."

Her expression turned somber. "Is that really a good idea? If he's guilty, he might—"

"Attack me?" In the mirror, I watched a smile break across my face. I couldn't quite imagine the prissy little man doing something that would dishevel his outfit. "Come with me, then. He won't attack both of us."

"He wouldn't dare." Fist raised, she struck a fierce pose. In her helmet and cloak, she truly was formidable.

A few minutes later, we were creeping up the stairs to the tower where Tweedy was staying. He might not even be up there, but if he was, I wanted the element of surprise. I hadn't been in the room since he'd checked in. He'd refused housekeeping service, except emptying the trash can, which he left on the step outside the room. This meant less work for us right now, anyway, though we might have an unholy mess on our hands when he left. It was basically the same amount of effort either way.

The door to the tower room was closed. I knocked three times, calling, "Professor, are you in? It's Nora Asquith."

We waited. Only silence. I tried again, this time knocking hard enough to hurt my knuckles. We really should install a bell or even an intercom. The doors on the tower rooms were much heavier than the ones on our regular rooms. Fortresslike, in fact.

This time the door opened a crack to reveal the professor. The slice of his body I could see revealed that he was in costume, as planned. He was dressed as an Anglo-Saxon merchant. Perhaps we should have ordered him a thief's costume. Or one that jailbirds wore.

"Yes?" His voice was testy, as though we'd interrupted him. "What is it?"

"We need to talk to you," Tamsyn said in her most honeyed tone. She even brought out the batting eyelashes and sweet smile. The big guns. "It will only take a minute."

He grunted but opened the door wider and stepped back to let us enter.

The room was in decent order, I noticed. The bed was unmade, as to be expected, and the table was heaped with books and papers, a laptop computer sitting in front of a chair. Otherwise, it was fine. No dirty dishes or used tissues scattered everywhere.

He didn't allow us all the way in, which squashed my plan to look around for his famous notebook. The one he wouldn't let Georgia see. Not that I would be able to leaf through it, not while he was there. Or when he was out, either. I would never stoop to that level, even if it might contain proof that he planned to rob us blind.

"We have a question for you," I said bluntly. Something about the man, the way his beady eyes kept darting between us, made me uneasy. He wasn't a nice person.

"Go ahead." He was equally terse. He gestured toward the table. "As you can see, I'm extremely busy."

Tamsyn set her lips and I could guess what she was thinking. She didn't say anything so I kept the ball rolling. "Janet saw you coming in through the back door at three in the morning. What were you doing outside at that time of night?" I decided to hold back the gloves for future use if necessary. "We're liable if guests get hurt and wandering around in the dark, it's very risky." The liability excuse was great and I was proud I'd thought of it.

Judging by his hasty movement backward, Tweedy was surprised. "I, um, er, I was . . ." He cleared his throat. "I accidentally threw a piece of paper away that I needed. A . . . a phone number . . . on a scrap of paper, which is why it ended up in the—"

"And you wore gloves, why?" Oops. Forget holding that detail back.

He blinked at me several times, making me think he was formulating an answer. He held up his hands. "Because I don't like touching dirty tissues. What other reason could I have?"

I had no answer to that. Well, I did, but Finlay had said we needed to wait until the lab results came back.

"Thought it was strange, that's all." I couldn't resist delivering a verbal slap spurred by his illicit plans to search our property and steal from us. "You should be careful, you know, especially when creeping around at night. Poking around in places you shouldn't. The castle can be a dangerous place."

His features dissolved into a snarling grimace. "Are you threatening me?" He pointed to the door. "Get out. Right now."

I should be delivering that order to him. Soon enough, I told myself. I wanted to hurry but Tamsyn walked out the door slowly, head up, like the queen she was, and I copied her.

We were barely through when the door slammed behind us and I heard the snick of a bolt sliding home.

CHAPTER 20

"That went well," I whispered to Tamsyn as we descended the stairs, adding an eye roll to show I was being sarcastic.

"I don't know, Nora. It might have made things worse." Tamsyn looked worried.

I halted. "Worse than poisoning someone? At least he knows we're on to him."

"That's true," she admitted. "I hope the violence doesn't escalate. People lose their minds when it comes to treasure."

Yes, they do, as history shows us. I'd like to think I would resist throwing aside all my morals and scruples for riches. I mean, you can't take it with you and murder is forever.

A roar went up from outside. The Viking games were about to begin. I'd done all I could and it was time to have fun. For the entire glorious afternoon, I would allow myself to become immersed in my role as a Viking maiden and forget all the worries weighing on my mind.

Just about everybody I knew in Monkwell was at the Fest, it seemed, along with a plenty of strangers. Most of us were dressed in costume, and if I ignored the few details of modern-day life—a phone pressed to a blacksmith's ear, bright pink clogs worn under a fishwife's flowing skirts—we could have stepped back in time a thousand years.

I was eating a lingonberry tart and watching axe throwers when Will joined me, handsome in his red-and-purple attire as a Viking nobleman. "Great event," I told him. I took another bite. "Fantastic food, too."

Thunk. The thrower who was up hit the bull's-eye and we all cheered.

"I'm pleased with how it's going," Will said, gazing around the area. Next to us, men grunted as they lifted huge rocks, and a distance away, Knattleikr players ran back and forth in a game similar to field hockey. "Everything okay at the castle?"

We both looked toward our home, the battlements drowsing in the afternoon sun. Will had put up signs warning that the castle was off limits and instructed security to keep people out of the gardens.

"Define okay," I said. "Matters are coming to a head. But we aren't going to deal with them until tomorrow."

"We found a few holes here and there on the bluff this morning that we had to fill," Will said. "Someone was digging, I'm guessing."

"A pox upon them," I exclaimed. "This is getting ridiculous." Was it Brady with his metal detector again? I put my hand on Will's shoulder and leaned close. "We're going to meet with everyone tomorrow and get this situation under control. You definitely should be there."

He nodded. "I'll plan on it. Meanwhile, security has been warned to prevent people from wandering away from the official festival area."

I glanced around the crowd. "Far as I know, all our

guests are here—with the exception of Tweedy. I haven't seen him yet." And he was the one we should monitor the most.

Janet and Guy, adorably period correct in their costumes, came across the grass. "Nora," Janet cried. "Join our tug-of-war team. We need you. It's the Villagers versus the Invaders."

I posed as if showing off my arm muscles. "How can I say no? Lead on." As we started off, I waved to Will, who was already moving on to his next post.

The tug-of-war was a hoot. Our team, the Villagers, ended up on the ground in a tangle of arms and legs and cloaks. After, I dusted myself off and continued on my merry way, stopping to sample salmon smoked over birch logs for six days, according to the maker. Yum. Then I stopped by the Lazy Mermaid booth to see Liv and Tom.

Pregnant Liv was seated at the moment while her husband stood ready to wait on people. She fanned herself with a leaflet. "We've been right out straight. This event looks to be a smashing success."

I looked over my shoulder at the milling throng. "It really is. Will is thrilled."

"Why don't you take a break?" Liv said to her husband. "Nora will sit with me." She turned to me. "If you don't mind."

"Of course not." I skirted the edge of the display. "It will give us a chance to chat."

"Be right back," Tom said. "Those kebabs down the way are calling my name. Want anything, Nora?"

"I'm good right now, thanks." He was right, though. The aroma of spicy meat drifting our way was mouthwatering. I wanted to save the remains of my appetite for the ox feast later, though.

"Rolf is fine," Liv said without me having to ask. She

showed me a video on her phone of Rolf romping around with Liv's kids, Lady, and the Beckets' border collie, Sally. "My mother-in-law sent this a few minutes ago."

"Oh, how cute. He's not going to want to come home." I smiled at the memory of the tussle I'd had with him earlier. "It took three Vikings to subdue him after he smelled roasting meat."

Liv laughed. "I know. I saw the video."

I cringed. Was there anyone who hadn't?

A couple approached the ice cream stand and Liv started to rise. "I'll get it," I said quickly. "I know the drill." After popping behind the counter at the ice cream store to help a few times, I knew how to scoop and the right amount of ice cream to include in a serving.

The couple wandered off, feeding each other ice cream, and I returned to my seat. "Finlay wants me to meet his mother." I still felt a mix of elation and fear whenever I thought about it. "She lives in Cornwall."

Liv's mouth rounded. "Oh, that is significant, though I'm not surprised. It's obvious he's head over heels with you. Besides, he already knows your family."

"True. Warts and all. Or should I say, murder and all?" Finlay had been a guest when a local woman was murdered in our garden. He'd had his first local case right here. Not exactly a fond memory or an easy start to his assignment.

"How's it going with your guests this week?" Liv asked.

What to share? Tweedy's midnight trash digging. Georgia's shocking revelation. Ollie's suspected poisoning. The fact that we could actually be sitting above millions of pounds in Viking treasure.

"I have a lot to tell you," I finally said. "Now, unfortunately, is not the time."

She put a hand to her lower back, stretching with a grimace. "Thanks for that. Now I'm dying of curiosity."

"We can talk together tomorrow, after church. When I pick up Rolf." Brady came along the aisle, filming the action. "There's the showrunner now. Wave."

Brady stopped in front of the booth and aimed the camera at us. We put our heads together, hamming it up. Then he moved on.

"The footage from today will make great background shots for the show," I commented. I pictured shots of the Viking games, men grunting and fake swords clashing. A sea of helmets in a crowd. The bonfire, when it was lit. "Especially for the parts about the Red Maiden."

"I don't know much about her," Liv said. "You have a Viking ghost?"

"We do, apparently." I studied the castle, its towers rising above the fringe of trees. "She doesn't appear often. We think she visited the monastery that was here at the time. The castle was built centuries later."

"That is so cool," Liv said. "I wish we had a ghost."

Tom sauntered back into the booth right then, holding two Styrofoam clamshells. Not every detail at the Fest was authentic, I'm afraid. I started to get up.

"It's okay, Nora. I have another chair." He handed Liv and me the clamshells, then unfolded a third chair and placed it next to his wife. He sat and I passed the box over.

"We do have a ghost," Tom said as he flipped the box open to reveal pitas stuffed with meat and fresh vegetables. "A ghost cow."

"What?" Liv and I said in unison. "Hon, are you serious?" Liv asked.

"I am." Tom took a big bite and chewed, then wiped his mouth with a napkin. "She moos during the full moon."

Liv shook her head. "You're pulling my leg." She took a nibble of the pita.

"Honestly, I'm not. Next full moon, hang out in the barn with me."

His wife laughed. "Now there's an invitation." She gave her husband a quick kiss. "You and me, alone in the hay loft? That does sound romantic."

Ghost cows. A new level of haunting unlocked. "We've heard hoofbeats at times," I recalled. "In the courtyard, mostly."

"See?" Tom said triumphantly. "There are animal ghosts."

"Tell us about the Red Maiden," Liv said.

While they ate their meal, I gave them the overview of what we knew. Rusla, the Red Maiden, had been an explorer and pirate from Viking Scandinavia. Her targets had included Ireland and the eastern shore of Britain. "It's said she came to her demise right here in this bay," I said, pointing. "During a skirmish with other ships."

"What a tale," Liv said. "She's appeared to you?"

"Once in a while. Very vaguely. I've never gotten a good look at her." We had heard her speak, though. *Ekki hér—not here.* I refrained from mentioning the encounter because now was not the time to tell my friends about what it might mean.

"I wonder if this event will draw her out," Tom said.

"Yeah, she'll probably say, 'Who are all these fake Vikings?'" I said with a laugh.

"Who are you calling fake?" Tom replied. "I have Viking blood."

I eyed his tall, muscled build, the thatch of reddish-blond hair and pale blue eyes. "Yeah, I can see that. Lucky you, Liv, living with a Viking."

Her smile was smug. "I'll say." She turned to her

husband. "And on that note, love, can you please fetch me a decaf chai tea? I'm dying for a cuppa."

Tom crumpled his napkin, dropped it into the empty clamshell, and closed the lid. "I'd be happy to. Want anything, Nora?"

"I'll take a chai. Regular, please. Thanks."

He set off again. Ice cream seekers arrived and I served them, quite content to stay put at the ice cream tent for a while longer. The main food tent was gearing up for the ox carving and when that started, I'd join the feast.

Liv and I drank our chai and looked up baby things online while Tom waited on customers. I spotted Brady now and then as well as Ollie and Gray. In costume, they blended right into the crowd. I thought I saw Georgia as well. No Tweedy, though. Not that I was looking for him. As for Dad, he was holding court in the tent designated as the throne room. How kind of Will to set that up for him. He was having the time of his life telling tales about Ravensea.

When they lit the bonfire on the bluff, I excused myself. That was the signal for the main meal to begin.

"There you are." Finlay appeared at my elbow while I was waiting in line for food. "Having a good time?"

"I sure am. How about you? I haven't seen you much." I'd spotted him a few times at a distance, keeping watch over the gathering. He did step in when two men had too much to drink and started to punch each other.

"It's interesting," he said, glancing around at the people in the tent. "Some of us are getting a little too much into character."

Just then, a group of raucous revelers lifted tankards and clashed them together with a roar before downing the contents.

"Roadblock in the future?" I asked, only partially jesting.

"Perhaps. Will said the parking attendants will make people use designated drivers, if need be. We'll help with that as well."

We were almost at the serving station so I asked, "Do you have time to sit and eat with me?"

"That was my plan," Finlay said.

We handed over tickets for the first seating and received plates in return. At the serving station, our dishes were loaded with sliced meat, roasted root vegetables, and flatbread. From there, we grabbed two glasses of mead before making our way to spots at a table facing the bonfire.

I was digging into my meal when someone hunkered down next to my chair: Georgia, resplendent in period garb. "Hey," I said. "What's up?"

Her gaze flitted about the tent. "Have you seen Tweedy?"

"I haven't. Not since earlier today, in the castle." Which was strange, actually. Had he come to the Fest at all? Maybe crowded gatherings weren't his thing.

Finlay glanced over. "Hello, Georgia. How are you?" He'd met her during the filming.

"Fine, thanks." She barely spared him a look. "Listen, he sent me a message saying he wanted to meet." She gnawed at her bottom lip. "What do you think I should do?"

I had no idea. "Do you want to meet with him?"

Her face creased up. "No . . . yes, I don't know. He promised me a job on his show. Maybe he changed his mind about me working for him here . . . I desperately need the money. . . ."

I guessed she wasn't banking too heavily on the success of Brady's show or the treasure hunt. "I can't believe you're considering going back after what you told us." That Tweedy was planning to cheat us, I meant. Allegedly. Unless she'd been lying.

She reared back as though I'd slapped her, which I guess I had, verbally. "I'll make it clear that I won't go along with that."

As if she would have that much influence. However, it was moot. Once I had an opportunity to tell Dad, Tweedy would be sent packing, I hoped, agreement or not.

"Okay. Suit yourself." I turned back to my meal, hoping to send a message that we were done here. With a huff of breath, she dashed off. I gave my own sigh and picked up my fork again. "I'll be glad when they're gone."

"I hear you on that," Finlay said. "The situation seems to be pretty unpleasant."

Although it had seemed like a good idea at the time, my decision to talk to Tweedy started weighing on me. Guilt nagged as well. I'd basically taken the ball and run with it in disregard of Finlay's plan to wait.

"I have something to tell you," I blurted out. "I'm really sorry."

He looked up from his plate, startled. "Okay." Although his expression was neutral, I saw concern lurking in his eyes and felt even worse.

"It's not about you and me," I said. "I spoke to Tweedy earlier and I, um, brought up the gloves." Conscious of the people seated around us, I kept my voice low.

He let out a breath. "Nora. I understand the impulse, but you've given away some of our leverage, should it be needed. My plan, once the results come in, was to confront him and mention the gloves as a way to encourage him to tell the truth. If indeed he did use the mushrooms to poison someone."

I felt wretched. "I'm so sorry. I won't interfere again, promise. To be honest, I wanted to spark a response that would put him on notice. We need to get rid of him before he gets his hands on our treasure." I thought of his smug, gloating face if we did discover the hoard. I didn't mind sharing, just not with him.

Finlay put a hand on my shoulder and squeezed gently. "Don't sweat it. If he's guilty, we'll get him."

I hoped he was right. That wasn't a slight against Finlay's skills as a policeman. I knew firsthand how tricky killers could be.

After the meal, Finlay went back on duty and I wandered around the Fest. The main band, Drakkarflame, was performing, the music a compelling blend of driving rock and folklike melodies that evoked a mysterious, long-lost past. The words were in Icelandic, but still, people were making a valiant effort to sing along.

I stood near the bonfire, staring into the roaring, snapping flames, other figures mere silhouettes against its glow. I hadn't seen Georgia again and I wondered if she'd succumbed to Tweedy's invitation for a meeting.

Did he regret firing her? He wasn't going to find readily available clerical help that easily around here. Although that made sense, an uneasy feeling began to grow, nagging at me.

She knew too much about his secrets. If he was indeed planning to double-cross us, he wouldn't want her telling us. Which she had, almost immediately. He didn't have a good grasp on human nature if he'd missed that possibility.

If he had tried to poison Ollie, then he was obviously capable of murder.

Georgia might be in danger and I was the only one who knew that. Besides Finlay. I pulled out my phone and sent him a text. *Going to look for Georgia. Worried.* He'd understand.

I began a methodical circuit around the festival, knowing at the same time that it might well be futile. If she was moving around, I could easily miss her in this crowd. It didn't help that full dark had fallen and it was difficult to see faces clearly outside the circles of light at the tents or by the fire. She could be sitting on the bluff with those other revelers for all I could tell.

A shout went up and arms began to point toward the water. The band finished a song with a great crescendo and then the lead singer said, "Here it is, folks. The journey to Valhalla."

A burning Viking ship nudged around the bluff, on course to drift across our bay. I gasped at the incredible sight, the flames leaping into the air brilliant against the dark sky and water. How had Will pulled that off? Kudos. It was a magnificent, stunning sight.

Barely managing to pull myself away from the spectacle, I went back to searching for Georgia. She wasn't outside, I was almost positive. She must be at the castle with Tweedy.

Moving against the tide of eager spectators pressing toward the cliff's edge, I wound my way toward the castle gardens. Once I located our missing guest, I could go back to enjoying the evening.

Reflections from the bonfire illuminated the castle walls, casting an eerie glow. How often had these walls witnessed fire? In a time when weapons were limited, fire was a potent one. Villages were burned. Ships set on fire. Devastating.

Tonight was merely a play of sorts, I reminded myself. We could enjoy a tingle down our spines without truly being in jeopardy. There was no risk of ravaging hordes kidnapping Tamsyn and me and carrying us away to faraway lands. However, as I trod the familiar path to the dark castle, my foreboding grew.

Something was wrong. I knew it in my bones.

CHAPTER 21

To my dismay, my intuition proved to be accurate.

After hearing a woman scream, Tamsyn and I had huffed and puffed our way up to the northeast tower, holding up our skirts so we wouldn't trip. We burst through the open door, our attention caught and held by the body sprawled at our feet.

Professor Tweedy, friend to none and enemy to many, lay face down, a knife protruding from his back.

"Oh, Nora." Horror etched Tamsyn's face. "Is he dead?"

I took a tentative step forward. "I think he is." Something about the utter stillness of Tweedy's body told me we were too late. "I suppose I'd better check, though."

Not wanting to trample any evidence, I circled wide around his body until I could reach his neck. I crouched on my heels to check for a pulse.

Tamsyn screamed and I fell back, right on my bottom. My helmet tumbled off, hitting the carpet with a thud.

My sister was staring toward the windows, hands to her cheeks. Backing up crab-like, I turned my head to see what had scared her.

The long curtains were moving, even though the windows were closed.

"Who's there?" I called, a distinct quaver in my voice. "Come out now." Ghosts might be mostly invisible but they didn't hide. *The killer.* "Tamsyn, call nine-nine-nine."

She fumbled at her clothing. "I can't find—"

I tossed my mobile phone in her direction and lurched forward to press Tweedy's neck. What if he died while we were faffing about with phones and people playing hide-and-seek?

He was already gone. His skin was cold already.

"He's dead, Tamsyn," I said. "He's been murdered." She put a finger up to indicate she had made the call.

The curtains were ripped aside, the rings jostling, to reveal Georgia. "I didn't do it. I swear I didn't."

I rose to my feet. "Why were you hiding, then? Why didn't you call for help?"

In the flickering light, her eyes were wide and frightened. "I . . . I don't know." She swallowed. "I heard footsteps and I was afraid . . . afraid I'd be next."

"Our footsteps?" I clarified, wanting to be sure someone else hadn't been here.

She grabbed the edge of the curtain and twisted it in her hands. "Yes. Yours. I only came up here a few minutes ago. At the appointed time to meet." She ducked her head. "Sorry, but I decided to go ahead and see what he had to say."

"Don't apologize to me. It wasn't my decision to make."

Tamsyn was pacing by the door. "Yes, we're in the room. No, there isn't any danger."

"Is there?" I asked Georgia. Although the only weapon I saw was already in use. "You're not going to attack us, are you?" Despite her denial that she'd killed Tweedy, she wasn't off the hook. Of course she'd lie.

My gaze inadvertently fell upon the man's body and

I hastily looked away, wishing I could cover him. He had been quite cold already, I thought. I wasn't going to touch him again and confirm it.

Georgia wasn't the only one with a grudge against Tweedy. The three men on the ghost-hunting team despised him for various reasons. We Asquiths did as well. Any of us could have slipped into the castle, which had been locked, and killed Tweedy.

"When was your meeting time?" I asked, to confirm what I thought she'd said. It was just after ten now. The burning ship was the grand finale and the event would soon be over.

"At ten. I can show you the text." Georgia pulled a phone out of her cloak.

She was being quite cooperative, I thought. Maybe she was innocent. Or maybe it was a ruse. *Stop it.* Once rumination began, it was endless and impossible to rein in. We were still in fact-gathering mode, I reminded myself.

Why was I saying *we*? The murder would soon be firmly in Finlay's court. Except . . . unless . . . if we were under suspicion, I would have to get involved. I trusted Finlay, of course, but he wasn't the final word on a case.

Superiors might well override his conclusions. Then another chilling realization dawned: they would probably remove Finlay from the case.

No, make that definitely. He had a major conflict of interest due to our relationship. During our first case, we were only acquaintances.

Who would they send? I prayed the new detective inspector would be reasonable and easy to work with.

"Here it is," Georgia said, waving her phone. Tamsyn and I crowded close to view the message from Tweedy.

Meet me at ten, in my room. A lot to discuss. T.

The time stamp was just before six this evening. Georgia had come to talk to us after that, which lined up.

"You didn't come up here at any time during the evening?" I asked.

She pulled her phone away from under our noses. "No, I did not. What are you saying? That I killed him and then pretended to come to our meeting?"

I hadn't, but that worked. Still, I wasn't going to bluntly say that. "Just working on the timeline." When had Tweedy died, exactly? I hoped the medical examiner could figure it out. It certainly wasn't within the hour. His skin had been far too cold.

"That's a job for the police, surely," she snapped.

Tamsyn put up her hands in a placating gesture. "You're right, it is." She sent me a warning look but then said, "We want whoever is guilty to be caught just as much as the police do. Or anyone else."

Georgia seemed to accept that. "Yeah, it's probably not great to have a guest get murdered, huh?" She looked around with a shudder. "I wouldn't stay any place where that happened."

I guessed she didn't know about the events of last summer and I was certainly not going to bring them up.

"Where is the notebook you mentioned?" Tamsyn asked. "Do you see it anywhere?" According to Georgia, it held Tweedy's notes about the treasure hunt, focused on the sacred spring.

"Yeah, I'd like to take a look at it," I said. "We'll ask the police to give it to us." Why not? Unless there was evidence that pointed to a killer.

Georgia's gaze skittered around the room. "I couldn't find it."

Was she telling the truth? She had just admitted to looking for the notebook rather than call for help, as we had done. If she hadn't killed him, then she'd taken advantage of the opportunity to search. To be honest, I couldn't blame her. The lure of a Viking hoard might overcome many scruples. It had already possibly spurred someone to murder, if that was the motive. The professor seemed to have a habit of making enemies.

Hurried footsteps sounded on the stairs and a moment later, Finlay, with Constable Kumar on his heels, burst into the room. "Nora. We got an emergency call?"

I moved aside so he could better view the scene. "I'm afraid so." The sight of his dear face, creased right now with worry and care, made sudden tears erupt. "Oh, Finlay. Someone killed Tweedy." I threw myself into his arms.

Constable Kumar spoke into the chest microphone hidden under his cloak. "Yes, we are on the scene. We have a male, deceased. We will need the murder bag and the crime scene team."

Finlay wrapped his arms around me and hugged me. After a moment, he said, "Let's get out of the way, okay? The team won't want us in here."

The constable was already ushering Tamsyn and Georgia to the door. "What is the man's name? Professor Norman Tweedy. He was a guest here?" He spoke into the microphone again. "We will need a roadblock at the exits ASAP. Get everyone's name and check their identification."

Finlay groaned under his breath. "I'm almost glad they relieved me of duty. That is going to be a logistical nightmare." His comment meant he'd already gotten the word that he was off the case, as I had suspected would happen.

"The only good news is," I said, "the murderer is almost certainly someone staying here. The castle was locked all day, with only key holders allowed inside."

"Hopefully that will narrow it down," Finlay said.

As we reached the landing, Constable Kumar called after us, "DI, send the team up, will you? As for the witnesses, please assemble downstairs. With everyone else staying here."

"Will do, Constable," Finlay said. "Good work."

"Thank you, sir." The constable looked pleased. "That means a lot coming from you."

We trudged in despondent silence down to the main floor. Another murder at Ravensea. And while I hadn't liked the professor, I certainly hadn't wished him harm. I also felt bad for Will. He'd worked so hard on the Viking Fest and it had been a smashing success. Now I was worried it would be overshadowed by this tragedy, even if a ruined event paled in comparison to an untimely death.

"Why don't we go into the drawing room?" Tamsyn suggested when we reached the Great Hall. "Might as well be comfortable."

"Sounds good to me. I need to sit down." Georgia practically trotted away.

The doorbell rang as we followed her, moving more sedately. The team was here already? I ran to answer, hoping that they would solve this murder quickly. Not only for justice for Tweedy, but to dispel the dark cloud that would now hover over the castle.

I opened the door to reveal two medics and several other officers. "Come in," I said. Finlay and Tamsyn were right behind me.

The team knew Finlay and exchanged friendly greetings with him. "You're off the case, DI?" one officer asked.

"I am. Constable Kumar is securing the scene. Tamsyn, do you mind showing them the way to the tower?"

"The way to the tower," one medic mouthed, a look of amazement on his face. He probably didn't get many calls to castles, I guessed.

"Not at all," Tamsyn said, turning toward the stairs. "Nora, can you put the kettle on? We're going to want hot drinks."

"I'll do that," I said, glad to have a task. "I'll make lashings of hot tea."

"The medical examiner is on his way," the officer told Finlay. "Along with the lead investigator. So keep an eye out for them."

"We will," I promised.

"Just out of curiosity, who did they assign?" Finlay asked.

"DI Hook," she said. "Do you know him?"

"Sure do." Finlay and I watched as the group made their way up the staircase.

"Come with me to the kitchen?" I asked.

He hesitated. "Why don't I go sit with Georgia? Just in a friendly capacity. I'll keep an ear open for the doorbell."

"Good idea all around." He could keep an eye on our suspect. I lowered my voice. "What is DI Hook like? Anything I should know?"

"Roland Hook is a highly skilled officer," Finlay said. "In fact, he has a nickname: 'By the Book' Hook. He can be a bit of a tough nut. Otherwise, he's not a bad bloke. He's a grandfather and a master gardener. Loves his roses."

Very charming about the roses and grandchildren, but I was stuck on Finlay's initial description of his replacement.

By the Book. That meant he probably wasn't going to want my help—or my opinions and insights. Hopefully he wouldn't bungle the investigation, then. Not if we Asquiths were the most obvious suspects.

CHAPTER 22

Cape flying, Dad burst into the drawing room like an avenging warrior, right after I returned with the tea tray. Georgia, Finlay, and Tamsyn were now seated near the fireplace, where a small fire was giving off welcome warmth. I set the tray on a low table near them. The officers and medics were still upstairs, I assumed, and I pictured crime scene tape strung across the doorway.

"What the bloody 'ell is going on?" Dad roared. "The police are stopping everyone and demanding identification. Even from me." He hit his chest with a meaty hand. "The owner of the castle."

I exchanged glances with Tamsyn. Who was going to be the bearer of bad news? She lifted her hand to indicate she would do it. "Dad," she said gently, going to him and taking his arm. I started pouring tea, glad I'd brought extra cups and plenty of sugar. "Please sit down." She guided him, now calm as a lamb, to his favorite chair. I hurried over with a cup holding strong, sweet tea with a dab of milk, the way he liked it.

"Professor Tweedy is dead," she said bluntly. "Someone literally stabbed him in the back. Georgia, Nora, and I came across his body in the tower room a short while ago."

Dad rocked back in his chair, his eyes bulging with shock. After a colorful string of expletives, he said, "I wondered why I hadn't seen him tonight."

I hadn't either, I realized. Not once. Maybe he'd never made it out to the Fest. I returned to the tray to pour tea for everyone else.

My father's gaze went to Finlay. "What are you doing here? Shouldn't you be investigating?"

Finlay's expression was rueful. "I've been told to stand down. My involvement with Nora—and, well, all of you—means I can't take the case."

Dad grumbled, drank tea, and grumbled some more. "That's a shame. You're a dab hand with murder investigations."

"Thank you, sir," Finlay said. "They've assigned another DI. He'll be here shortly."

Georgia was sitting huddled in a corner of a sofa, her fingers fretting at tassels on a pillow. I gently removed the mangled cushion and replaced it with a cup of tea. "Milk, two sugars. Drink it."

Janet and Guy appeared in the doorway. They must have come through the back. Janet's gaze traveled around the room and then she slumped against her husband in relief. "I heard someone was dead. I was so afraid—Just saw Will and he was all right."

Dear Janet. "Someone *is* dead, I'm afraid," I said. "Tweedy." They too were struck by shock. "Come sit. I made tea."

Pouring cups for them used the last of the pot. "I'll go make fresh," I said, picking up the tray. I couldn't sit still right now.

"Has anyone seen Ollie, Gray, or Brady?" Tamsyn asked.

I was thinking the same thing, that one of them had

killed Tweedy, if Georgia hadn't. She could easily have killed him, left, and then pretended to find him. She could even have sent the text to herself from his phone. Which I hadn't seen near his body, I recalled.

Back to the three men. If one of them took off, well, that was probably our killer.

Everyone was looking at Georgia, who shrugged. "I haven't seen them since earlier in the evening," she said. "They were all at the event."

"I saw them, too," I put in. "Brady was filming." The time stamps on the video files might help prove his innocence, after the medical examiner figured out when Tweedy had died.

"I did as well," Janet said. "They sat near us at the ox roast."

Guy made the motion of tipping a drink to his lips. "They were well into their cups by then, the three of them."

If they were drunk, maybe they'd be more likely to confess. We could only hope. A thought struck: What if there was more than one killer? What if it had been a conspiracy among the three of them? Or four?

I rolled my eyes internally at myself. My arms aching from holding the heavy silver tray, I started moving, eager to reach the kitchen and put it down. "I'll be back in a few."

Janet put her cup down. "Right behind you, Nora. I'll put together a plate of sandwiches."

Dad put up a hand. "I'll take one, please. I'm a wee bit peckish." Dad did enjoy a night sandwich, as we called his evening snacks.

I glanced over my shoulder at Tamsyn. "Let us know when the DI arrives, will you?" And keep an eye on everyone and everything, I told her silently.

She gave me a thumbs-up in response. Message received. Finlay sent me a smile. I guessed he understood the subtext and was glad he'd gotten to see our team in action.

As Janet and I went through the Great Hall, the front door opened, revealing the ghost hunters. As Guy had said, they certainly looked the worse for wear. Too drunk to commit murder? Or drunk because one of them had?

"Is this a fair maiden I spy before me?" Brady cried, waving an arm toward me. He closed one eye, swaying. "Make that two fair maidens. I didn't see you there, Mrs. Fagan." The other two laughed and elbowed each other like idiots.

"Go on with you," Janet said, not impressed.

"You'd better sober up fast," I warned. "The police are here." I tilted my chin. "In the tower with Tweedy."

"In the tower with Tweedy?" Gray mocked. "Sounds like that game. What is it? Oh, yeah. *Clue*."

"Which you haven't got," Brady crowed, pointing his forefingers like guns at his friend.

"Boys," Janet rapped out. "Enough. Professor Tweedy is dead."

They froze, their expressions caricatures of shock and surprise. Was Tweedy's death really news or were they acting?

"Dead?" Gray squawked. "How?"

About ready to drop the tray, I set it on a table. It was killing my arms. "Not for us to share," I said. The DI wouldn't thank me for revealing information about the murder to other suspects. "We're waiting in the drawing room for the police. Please go right there. Janet and I are on our way to the kitchen to make sandwiches and tea."

Brady elbowed Ollie. "We're meeting with Inspector

Broom in the drawing room, where it will be announced that the butler did it with the candlestick."

Ollie looked less than amused. "It's not funny, Brady. Guess who will be squirming under the interrogation lights?"

Brady's mouth dropped open in outrage. "Not me. I didn't have anything—"

"Enough," Janet bellowed. "To the drawing room, lads, and step on it."

They scurried away, casting glances over their shoulders at our formidable Janet.

"Wow," I said, picking up the tray again. "I am impressed. You sure set them straight."

Janet sniffed. "Don't get me wrong. I understand the impulse for levity in dark circumstances. In this case, though, they brought trouble to our door, and the least they can do is act like adults about it."

She was right. Tweedy's death must be related to the conflict between the professor and his former students. It certainly had nothing to do with us.

The doorbell rang again. I set the tray down. "Janet, go ahead to the kitchen. I'll be right there."

She picked up the tray and headed off and I opened the door, dread pooling in my stomach. It must be the police. Will would have come in through the back, and he never rang.

A tall, bulky man dressed in an overcoat was standing on the steps. His broad features and deep-set yet piercing blue eyes brought to mind the actor Brian Dennehy. Behind him stood the familiar figure of the medical examiner.

"I'm Detective Inspector Roland Hook," he said. "From the Yorkshire police. You are . . . ?"

"Nora Asquith," I said. "I live here."

His gaze roamed my face and he nodded, as if filing me in his catalogue. He must know that Finlay Cole and I were a couple and he'd been curious about me, I guessed.

I moved back. "Please come in. The team is upstairs in the tower and, well, the rest of us are in the drawing room, waiting." I nodded an acknowledgment to the medical examiner as he entered behind DI Hook.

Hook was still staring at me. "A Tamsyn Asquith made the call, I understand. Did she discover the deceased?"

"That's my sister, and yes, she did. I was there as well, and one of our guests, Georgia Kane." My legs were trembling and I ordered them to stop it.

DI Hook was definitely intimidating, like a mash-up of a strict headmaster big on corporal punishment and a traffic bobby eager to meet his quota.

"I'll want to talk to you three first, then. I'll find you where?"

I gave the directions to the drawing room. "Do you know how to find the team?"

"We have instructions, thank you." With a brusque dip of his head, the DI and the medical examiner began to climb the stairs.

I beat feet for the kitchen, feeling compelled to complete my tasks and hurry back to the drawing room before Hook arrived. I didn't think he'd take kindly to me being absent, no matter the reason. He'd probably think I was destroying evidence or something else nefarious.

Evidence. The thought almost made me trip on the edge of a carpet. What would Hook make of the agreement between Dad and Professor Tweedy? Now that Tweedy was dead, the agreement was null and void. We could claim one hundred percent of the treasure, once it was located.

That was certainly a multimillion-pound motive for murder.

DI Hook appropriated Dad's study for the interrogations. Georgia went first since, as she readily admitted, she was first on the scene. She'd been closeted with Hook and Constable Kumar for ages, and when she'd emerged, she'd immediately run upstairs, crying. Not comforting in the least.

"Nora Asquith?" Kumar inquired, standing in the drawing room doorway. Finlay had already gone home at my insistence, with a promise that I would text updates. The rest of us were slouched around the drawing room in various states of disarray. Gray and Brady were playing cards. Ollie was snoring on a sofa. Janet and Guy were planning a holiday, which they richly deserved. In fact, I was going to ask Dad to pay for it.

As for our patriarch, he had retrieved a pile of books and documents from the study, carefully vetted by Hook, and was deeply engrossed in research. At least he was being productive.

I followed a surprisingly stiff Kumar through the Great Hall. He and I had built a rapport during the last case, and I knew that Finlay valued him. Now he was acting as if I were a stranger. I supposed he had to or else fall afoul of Hook.

A bumping from above drew our attention. The medics were removing Tweedy's body. By unspoken agreement, Kumar and I stopped to watch, as if keeping vigil. It felt wrong to keep going as if he were only a sack of laundry being hauled away.

When I caught sight of the gurney, a sob rose in my throat. Poor Tweedy. This was the first time I'd felt much sympathy for the man, I regretted to admit. He probably had friends and loved ones, people who would miss him. He was human, too. On that basis, I could offer compassion and a modicum of sorrow. In any case, no one had the right to take his life. We needed to find out who had done this heinous act.

"Rest in peace," I whispered as they rolled him to the door. Kumar echoed my benediction.

We moved on as the medics and their sad burden exited, and Kumar opened the study door. "Miss Nora Asquith," he announced.

Hook was ensconced behind the desk, which had been cleared of Dad's belongings. He was going to absolutely hit the roof when he saw this. No one was allowed to touch his things, which were organized according to his own method.

The DI rose to his feet. "Have a seat," he ordered. From his first words, I could tell there was a new sheriff in town, in stark contrast to my incisive yet kind Finlay.

I chose one of the chairs. Kumar took a position on another seat, behind the desk but off to one side where he could view both his superior and the person of interest.

"Ready?" Hook asked Kumar, who replied in the affirmative.

Hook remained standing, looming behind the desk. His first move startled me and I jumped. He tossed an evidence bag holding an antique dagger onto the blotter. "Do you recognize this?"

I studied the knife, which was over a foot long, with a sizable blade and an antler hilt. I recognized the hilt, having seen it recently protruding from Tweedy's back.

"It's the murder weapon."

He gave a small huff. "Besides that . . . occasion, have you seen it before?"

"No, I have not." I was remembering to only answer the questions, not to offer additional information.

Hook lowered himself into the chair, leaving the knife where it lay, an unsettling reminder of why we were here. "To confirm, it doesn't belong to anyone you know? Or to one of the guests? You're certain you've never seen it before tonight?"

To each question he fired at me, the answer was a firm no. Either the killer had brought the dagger with them or it had belonged to Tweedy. I didn't quite dare to voice the latter possibility. It looked like a Viking design and it was possible he had collected artifacts.

The DI now took a step back from questioning me about the murder. He had me give my name and address for the record, then asked, "What is your occupation?"

Unnerved at being treated this coldly, my mind awhirl with questions and theories, I did my best to give him an overview. I told him about Castle Apothecary and the bed-and-breakfast business that we'd launched in June.

"Professor Tweedy was one of your guests? When did he arrive and how long was he staying?"

Now we came to the crux of the matter. Under normal circumstances, I'd give the dates of stay and that would be it. Tweedy's tenancy here was far more complicated.

"He arrived several days ago," I said. "As for how long he was staying, he and my father were, um, working on a project together."

One brow rose as his frigid gaze drilled into me. "What was the project?"

How much should I reveal? How much could I? Surely it was up to Dad to give the details. Plus, to be honest, I wanted to delay. They'd be upon Dad like baying hounds once the treasure hunt agreement was disclosed. I had the strong impulse to throw myself between Dad and those hounds, even if metaphorically.

"Ms. Asquith?"

I decided to rest upon a technicality. "You will need to ask my father for the particulars." I caught movement out of the corner of my eye and glanced over to see that Kumar was looking at me. He'd been working, head down, the entire time. The gleam of what looked like approval in his eyes affirmed my decision.

Thankfully, Hook switched gears. "What about the other guests? We'll need a list of their names, addresses, and stay dates." Since he could ask them that, I guessed he wanted to use it to double-check what they said.

"I can get that for you." I made as though to rise.

"We're not finished, Ms. Asquith," he barked. "Not by a long shot."

With a sigh, I settled in my seat again. "Sorry, I thought—"

Hook made a slicing motion with his hand. "Take me through your movements tonight. Actually, the entire day. I want to get the full picture."

The full picture. That included my visit to the tower room to question Tweedy about his midnight trip to the garbage bin. Lab results on the mushrooms were already in progress. If Hook didn't know about them now, he soon would.

Why had I been so impulsive and reckless? Why hadn't I let the police proceed with the case? I had well and truly put myself in the line of fire.

CHAPTER 23

The silence grew tense. Hook leaned forward across the desk, his gaze never leaving my face. I could feel it, even though I was busy staring at my folded hands.

"Is there something you want to tell me?" he asked quietly. His mild tone was more frightening than a shout.

"Yes," I blurted out. "But I didn't kill him. I . . . we . . . had an encounter with him earlier in the day. In the tower room."

A pause before he said, "Tell us about this encounter."

I scrambled to organize my thoughts. In order for my visit to have context, I needed to give the background. "A couple of days ago, one of our guests, Ollie Agar, suddenly got sick. He was vomiting and weak. Before that, I had spotted a clump of poisonous mushrooms on the property and it looked as if a few had been picked. I have a picture if you want to see them."

Georgia knew they were poisonous, thanks to me. Should I tell Hook that? If it was Finlay questioning me, I definitely would. With this DI, I felt as though I had to think through the implications of everything I said. Which was jarring, because I consider myself a law-abiding person.

"That is quite a leap, Ms. Asquith, to assert that a man was deliberately poisoned."

"I know. You weren't here. There's been a lot of tension . . . Anyway, Georgia came along right after I discovered them. I told her what they were. *Russula emitica*. Which means she, for one, knew they were there. Anyone might have spotted them, actually. They were close to the walking path."

"Why go to the professor, then?"

"I'm getting to that. Finlay and I decided to go through the room garbage to see if anyone had tossed away any mushroom remains. Out of an abundance of caution." I gave the basis for our search, the possibility that one of the guests had made mushroom brew in their room. "Ollie was the only one who got sick. He recovered quickly, which wouldn't necessarily happen if it was flu."

I inhaled deeply. "Finlay found pieces in the trash and those were entered into evidence. Ollie's travel mug was as well. He'd been drinking from it when he was stricken. Lab results are pending. We—I—went to the professor because Janet, our housekeeper, saw Tweedy sneaking inside in the middle of the night. He was wearing disposable gloves."

"Did you tell DI Cole?" Hook asked.

"I did." Now came the uncomfortable confession. "He wanted to wait until the lab results were in." I winced. "I'm afraid I jumped the gun. Although," I was quick to add, "I only mentioned that he'd been seen coming through the back door in the middle of the night. I cited our possible liability if guests wander around in the non-public areas. Which is real."

Hook made a noncommittal grunt. "What was Tweedy's response?"

"He claimed to be looking for a piece of paper he'd thrown away accidentally."

"You said 'we.' Was someone with you?"

"My sister," I mumbled. I'd failed miserably at keeping her out of it. At least she could confirm my version of events.

"Did you mention this incident to anyone else?"

I was on firm footing at last. "You mean the other guests? No. I did tell Finlay this evening, at dinner." I ducked my head. "I know I overstepped, and I regret it."

Hook let me dangle for a long moment. Then he said, "All right. Moving on. What did you do the rest of the day?"

I took him through my movements, aware that he'd probably follow up with Liv and Tom and even Finlay to verify my statement.

"Why did you go into the castle?" Cole asked. "Any particular reason?"

Another tricky situation to explain. A possible ghost sighting, an uneasy feeling, an ominous atmosphere were all I had. Nebulous at best.

"I saw Georgia at dinner. She told me that Tweedy had asked to meet even though he had fired her the day before. She wasn't sure what to do. I told her it was up to her."

I didn't mention my veiled jibe about the cheating claim she'd made. That can of worms could wait until Hook found out about the treasure hunt.

"When I didn't see her later, I got worried. I didn't trust Tweedy and I thought their meeting might have gone badly. I mean, the firing was quite brutal. She was very upset."

I was digging quite a hole for Georgia, I realized with discomfort. "I'm not implying she killed him. I'm just trying to explain why I thought it was odd that he would want to meet with her. So, to be honest, I went to the castle to check on her. Tamsyn and I were inside when we heard a woman scream from the direction of the tower. So up we went."

After a hesitation, I added, "Is it possible that Tweedy didn't send the text to Georgia? Someone might have lured her there, to cast suspicion on her."

DI Hook rocked back in his chair, regarding me with narrowed eyes. "Leave the speculation to us, Ms. Asquith."

Dealing with Hook was proving to be a whole new ball game. Although I understood the reasoning, I wished Finlay was in charge.

The gilded clock on the mantel struck two AM. DI Hook had finally finished interviewing everyone. Georgia and the rest of the ghost-hunting team were in their rooms. Finlay had reluctantly gone home. I was sprawled in the drawing room with Dad, Tamsyn, Will, and the Fagans.

"Who would like a nightcap?" Dad asked, standing at the drinks cabinet. Whiskey poured into a glass with a glugging sound.

"Me." I was both wired and exhausted. Maybe a drink would help me relax enough to calm my mind and allow me to sleep. Doubtful, but worth a shot.

In the end, we all wanted a glass. "Gather round," Dad said, holding his up. "I want to make a toast." We obediently formed a circle, glasses raised. "Tonight we are facing a new challenge at Ravensea, the latest in centuries of war, famine, hard times, and threats to our ownership. I urge you all to take heart. We will overcome. Justice will be served. To Ravensea Castle, long may she stand."

"To Ravensea," we echoed before drinking.

"That was perfect," I said, carrying my glass back to my seat. Dad's toast sparked both hope and determination in me. We would get through this. At the moment, I couldn't see how, but that wasn't anything new. Troubles rarely came with a road map.

Will was slumped next to me, looking absolutely knackered. He'd put his all into the festival and instead of being able to bask in its success, he'd been met with news of a murder. "Did Hook accept your alibi, Dad?"

Dad seated himself in his chair. "He certainly did. There was a constant stream of visitors to my tent, many of them wanting to know more about Ravensea's history."

He must have been in his glory. Usually he was in the position of trying to make people listen.

"I gave him a list of the names I recalled: our parish priest, town council members, a member or two of Parliament, a police commissioner, and a bishop." His smile was satisfied. Then he frowned. "What about everyone else?"

"I'm okay," Will said. "I was busy every minute coordinating the event and I think he understood that."

The rest of us exchanged looks. "None of us really have alibis," I said. "Although I was with people most of the time, every minute isn't accounted for."

"For me, either," Tamsyn said. "They think Tweedy was killed a few hours before we found him, I gathered. Around seven or eight?"

"Dinner was still being served then," Will said. "From six to eight. We had to do three seatings due to the size of the crowd."

"When did you have dinner?" I asked Janet. "The ghosthunters ate at the same time, you said."

"We were at the last seating," Janet said. "Which started around seven-thirty, I think."

"That's right," Will said. "We were running behind."

I logged this information. Any of the three could have killed Tweedy and then joined his companions for dinner.

Still, I didn't envy Roland Hook's job. Unless someone had seen the killer go into the castle at the estimated time, how could he prove who did it? Unless they confessed, unless there was other evidence. I guessed the knife hilt didn't have any fingerprints or an arrest might already have been made.

He'd have to approach the case from another angle while hoping for a confession. We were perfectly placed to keep an eye on the suspects, and that's what I would be doing. Although Dad and Will thankfully seemed to have been cleared, that left the rest of us still under scrutiny. If Hook learned that Tweedy was a huge obstacle standing between us and the treasure with his claim of half or about his plan to cheat us, we'd rise to the top of the list.

"Dad," I asked, needing to know. "Did you tell Hook about the agreement with Tweedy?"

Shifting in his chair, he cleared his throat. "I'm afraid I did, Nora. I didn't want to risk it coming out another way. It would only look worse for us."

I locked eyes with my sister, realizing we had yet another dilemma. We hadn't had a chance to tell Dad that Tweedy planned to cheat us. Again, according to Georgia. If we told Dad, would he also feel compelled by his deep sense of honorable conduct to inform the police?

Probably. And they'd quickly arrive with a warrant to arrest us.

Despite my worries, I slept like the proverbial log until Ruffian insistently nudged me awake. Sunlight was streaming in, a clue that I'd slept well past my usual rising hour. The bedside clock confirmed it was almost ten. Practically noon. No wonder the cat was eager for breakfast.

I threw a robe over my sleep shorts and top, thinking I'd feed the cat and make coffee before showering and getting dressed.

A peek out the window revealed that a cleanup crew was already working on the bluff. The vendors had left last night but there was plenty to do: trash bins to empty, litter to pick up. The stage and tents to dismantle. Five hundred people left a mess no matter how well-trained they were.

Before going down, I checked on my sister. She was still asleep, but when Primrose saw me, she jumped down and padded after us. She was hungry, too.

The rest of the house was silent, the public rooms empty, and the AGA was banked, the burners off. Janet and Guy had slept in, which was rare indeed. Moving about as quietly as possible, I fed the cats and put the kettle on. While waiting for it to boil, I set up three trays: for Janet and Guy, Dad, and Tamsyn. Then I'd start breakfast for our guests.

How many times had Janet brought me coffee in bed? Too many to count. I set two mugs on the tray along with two fat scones, milk, and sugar. Dad's and Tamsyn's trays were similar. Then, feeling highly efficient, I made the cups of tea and a pour-over coffee for me to drink after I delivered the trays.

I went up the winding back stairs to Janet's room. Setting the tray down, I rapped three times before creeping away. As I turned the corner on the staircase, I heard the bedroom door creak open, followed by an exclamation of delight.

"Thank you, Nora," drifted down to my ears.

"I've got breakfast handled," I called back. "Don't even think about coming down for another hour."

Tamsyn's tray was next, which I delivered to her bedside table. The heap of covers grunted when dishes clattered. "Tea and a scone," I told the pillow over her head.

Dad's tray was last and I added my coffee and a scone for me before taking it up. He'd be awake, I was pretty sure, and maybe we could talk.

At the suite of rooms used by every baron in the history of the castle, I knocked and he called, "Enter."

Dad was seated at a table by the windows overlooking the garden, busily writing away in a notebook. He did morning pages every day, writing down the insights and ideas his brain had produced during sleep. Like father, like daughter, except my rumination tended to be about my herbal business and, lately, murder. I always forgot to journal, though, instead carrying my thoughts around like water in a leaky bucket.

"Ah, Nora." Dad set the pen and notebook aside. "Thank you." He shoved aside a stack of books to make room for the tray.

"We're the first ones up." I unloaded the tray before joining him at the table. "It's after ten."

Dad poured milk into his tea. "Our guests are still asleep?" His mouth twisted in a rueful smile. "The sleep of the just?"

"Ha. Doubtful." I picked up a scone and took a bite. "We didn't kill Tweedy, which means they are the top suspects." I chewed. "I'm even reconsidering Tweedy and the poisonous mushrooms." Maybe he hadn't spiked Ollie's coffee. What were the odds of two homicidal maniacs in a group of five people?

Dad's brows drew together in a frown. "What am I missing here?"

I cringed, realizing I hadn't told Dad about the mushrooms or our investigation. Or the claim that Tweedy was going to cheat us. I hadn't deliberately tried to keep my father out of the loop. There just hadn't been time. Or proof, I recalled, letting myself off the hook. The lab results weren't in yet.

"Sit back, Dad," I said. "I have a lot to tell you."

As precisely as possible, I took him through the mushroom saga. Then I touched upon Georgia's accusation. As expected, he grew angrier about that as I went on.

"The glos pautonnier," he growled. "I knew he was not to be trusted. I disliked the smarmy driveler from the moment I set eyes upon him."

"Same," I said. Tweedy was indeed a gluttonous scoundrel. "We were going to tell you about all this, I promise. After the Fest, when you would have a chance to deal with it."

Mug in hand, Dad stared out the window. "I'm glad Tweedy's notebook is missing."

"What? Why?" I hadn't expected him to say that.

He turned to face me, his blue eyes shining with intensity. "Because we need to find the treasure ourselves. If we use clues from a dead man, then the ethics of ownership still come into play."

I put a hand to my head. "Wow, this is complicated. Georgia did tell me that Tweedy was interested in the sacred spring. I already had that thought." I told Dad my reasoning. "Finlay and I intercepted Tweedy coming back from that area one night." I told him about that encounter.

"More proof that he was up to no good," Dad said. "He was supposed to keep me apprised of his movements. We were letting him search our property. He had no intrinsic right to full access."

"Exactly. What are we going to do about the treasure hunt without Tweedy in the picture?" The agreement for the finder's fees hadn't been signed yet. Dad had halted treasure hunting until today because of the festival.

Dad pressed his lips together. "No one will have permission to search until Tweedy's killer is found. We cannot allow the guilty party to benefit from his death."

CHAPTER 24

I left Dad to his pages and returned to the kitchen, planning the breakfast menu as I went. A casserole of eggs, cheese, diced ham, and vegetables would be good and easy to serve. Homemade bread toast and sausages, too.

Janet came down as I was putting two casseroles into the oven. "Did you have a nice lie-in?" I asked, smiling. "You and Guy deserved it."

She stretched with a yawn, blinking. "It was lovely. We both fell back asleep."

My phone lit up. Finlay. *Good morning, love. See you later today? x*

Anytime. Breakfast is on. I need to pick Rolf up at the farm. x

I'll take you. Be right there. x

"I'd better put on a few more sausages," I said. "Finlay is coming over."

Janet fetched the paper-wrapped bundle from the fridge. "I can't believe I'm even hungry after that feast last night."

"I hear you. I'm starving, too." I moved the sizzling sausages over with a long-handled fork and added six more. Breakfast this late was actually brunch and I thought of other dishes to include. A big bowl of yogurt, fruit, sliced meat, and cheese.

Tamsyn wandered down and, still working at a relaxed pace, the three of us got the dining room ready for breakfast. Brady was the first guest to come down, and he sat in front of a laptop at one end of the long table.

"Uploading video from last night," he told us. "I used my phone and the main camera. I got tons of great stuff."

"Did you spot Tweedy anywhere?" I asked as I cut the casserole into squares and slid a server under the first. Maybe he had attended the fest. Brady's footage might hold clues to his death.

"Not yet," Brady said. "I've been looking for him."

Tamsyn carried in the platter of sausages, followed by Janet with stacks of toast.

"We're ready if you want to start," I told Brady. When he made as if to gather his equipment, I said, "Leave it. We have plenty of room." The table could seat twenty people, easy, and we had eight. Janet and Guy preferred to eat in the kitchen.

Shrugging, he left the laptop open and made his way to the buffet table. "This looks amazing. Thank you."

He began serving himself as the other three wandered in. "I could smell those sausages all the way upstairs," Ollie said. Gray and Georgia were ahead of him and he went over to the laptop. "Did you get good footage? The festival was incredible." Ollie bent over the laptop and hit a key.

"Sure did. The burning longboat was out of this world." Brady was still heaping his breakfast plate with two servings of casserole, sausages, and toast.

Ollie gave a squawk. "Seriously? I can't believe it."

"What's wrong?" Georgia was spooning yogurt into a bowl. "Did the camera mess up?"

Serving fork in hand, Brady spun around. "I didn't notice—"

Ollie pointed at Brady. "You've been trolling me. It wasn't Tweedy. It was you."

The fork went up in the air along with Brady's hands. "No, no. You've got it all wrong. I didn't—"

"Yes, you did." Ollie bent to the keyboard and began typing furiously. "In fact, I'm sending myself the proof. I can't believe it," he muttered. "I thought you were my friend."

It took me a moment but I caught on. "You were *prof-skeptic*, Brady? But why?" I distinctly recalled Ollie bringing it up. He had believed the professor was guilty and Brady had gone along with it. Which of course he would.

Brady thankfully returned the sharply pointed fork to the platter before stabbing someone. "Controversy brings eyeballs. I was trying to increase Ollie's follower count to help the show. Brilliant, really. The ghost hunter versus the skeptic. Rather than wait for the criticism, bring it up and demolish it in advance."

"Except it was fake," Georgia put in, her voice dripping with disdain.

"Like your lips and eyelashes," Brady retorted.

"You . . . you jerk." Georgia flung the yogurt spoon at Brady. It hit his chest, leaving a big splotch, and fell to the floor, sending yogurt everywhere.

"Nice," Brady said, regarding his shirt. "Going to throw fruit at me, too?"

Georgia's face reddened. "It would be a waste." Not even trying to clean up, which was annoying, she carried her bowl and mug of coffee to the table.

Gray bent to pick up the spoon and I grabbed a stack

of napkins to wipe up the yogurt. After a futile attempt to clean his shirt, which only rubbed the stain in, Brady picked up his plate and mug and went over to the table. Then, to my amusement, he wavered, obviously caught between the devil and the deep blue sea. Ollie at one end, Georgia at the other. He finally sat right in the middle.

Ollie brushed past Brady, deliberately knocking his shoulder, and went to the buffet line to get his food.

"Thanks," I said to Gray. "Go ahead and eat. I'll finish." I needed to wash the floor with cleaner and a damp rag.

I dashed to the kitchen for these items. Janet and Guy were having breakfast while Tamsyn filled another carafe with coffee. "Food fight in the dining room," I joked before telling them about the argument.

"Good grief," Janet said. "Though I suppose tensions are running high today." She didn't have to elaborate.

"Wait until Dad gets done with them," I said. "He's nixing the treasure hunt until Tweedy's killer is arrested."

"They're not going to like that," Guy said. "It could be months, even years, until an arrest is made."

We all protested. "Please don't say that," I pleaded. "I can't imagine living with an unsolved murder hanging over our heads." All our guests would cancel. The ghost-hunting episode would be axed. Will's festival would be forever marred.

"Ugh," I cried. "What a disaster. Everything is falling apart."

Silence fell over the kitchen. I was usually the one who showed relentless optimism on an uphill road, cold wind in my face and dangerous cliffs on both sides.

Tamsyn came over and hugged me. "Chin up. One step at a time."

Not comforted in the least by her platitudes, though the hug was nice, I cried, "And we have 'By the Book' Hook to deal with. He's probably drawing up the warrants now."

"Eleanor Sibilla Asquith." Janet's voice rang out. "Pull yourself together. There isn't a detective inspector who can match your brain and wits in all of Yorkshire."

"That's a fact I can attest to," a voice said from the kitchen doorway.

I pulled away from Tamsyn's embrace. "Finlay."

"I didn't mean *you*, sir," Janet said, her cheeks flaming.

Finlay brushed that off. "No offense taken. We all know how brilliant our Nora is." Tamsyn stepped aside and he came over to me, gently moving a lock of hair out of my eyes. "I may be off the case but I've got your back, okay? We are going to find Tweedy's killer."

"Okay." I gave him a big hug and a kiss. "Are you hungry? Follow me."

To my relief, the ghost hunters were quiet and focused on their food when we came in. They'd chosen seats far away from each other, which spoke to the conflicts brewing. Before Tweedy's death, they'd often moved as a pack.

I attended to the area of the yogurt spill while Finlay served himself food. The floor would need to be mopped, which we would do later, after the meal.

Georgia picked up her phone. "Does anyone know how to download contacts from the cloud? I'm having trouble."

Ollie looked up from his plate. "I can help you. Why do you need to do that?"

She turned the phone his way. "This is a new, temporary phone. The police took mine."

The police. At this jolting reminder of Tweedy's death, everyone seemed to freeze for a moment.

"They took your phone, G?" Ollie asked. "Why?"

She pouted at him, scowling. "Why do you think? I was supposed to meet Tweedy last night. They wanted to make sure I didn't delete anything, I suppose. Though they can order the records, right?"

"It often takes a few days to get them," Finlay put in.

"Hey," Brady said. "You're a rozzer, aren't you? Here to question us?"

All four regarded Finlay with alarm. He shook his head. "Not I. Not on this case." His gaze slid to me. "Due to personal considerations."

"You're going to wish Finlay was the investigating officer," I blurted out. Why had I said that? I literally bit my tongue to punish myself. It was totally out of bounds for me to discuss DI Hook with the other suspects.

Of course one of them had to ask. "Why do you say that?" Gray asked.

"Um, because I know Finlay is an excellent detective." Which now meant he wouldn't get very far with any covert questioning. I had better stop talking altogether. "Be right back to eat with you, Finlay," I said, gesturing with my rag. I hadn't had breakfast yet and I was getting lightheaded. That must be the reason I was babbling.

I raced to the kitchen, where I put the rag in the laundry and stowed the cleaner under the sink. Then I grabbed the last platter of sausages. "Tamsyn, I need backup." She was seated at the table, chatting with Janet and Guy. "And we'd better feed Dad. I brought him a scone ages ago."

"Be right there," Tamsyn said. "I'm in the middle of a story."

I huffed a breath and hurried out, eager to get back and observe the ghost hunters. Maybe ask them about last night. In an indirect way, of course. All I knew was that they had been quite drunk. Or pretending to be. It was a good cover, a way to pretend you didn't understand or remember.

"More sausages," I announced as I entered the dining room. Dad had come down, I noticed. He was seated beside Finlay, both digging into their breakfast.

I filled a plate and sat across from them. We were in the middle of the table, the other four seated around us, at a distance.

"Delicious," Dad said, forking up the egg dish. "What do you call it?"

"Casserole," I said with a shrug. "No real recipe, use what you have on hand." I'd included green peppers, onions, and mushrooms in this version.

The sausages were fat and juicy, and I devoured two in short order. Tamsyn swanned in and went over to the buffet table. Brady practically leaped out of his chair to talk to her.

"Got some great shots last night," he said. "Perhaps we can review later?"

"Send me the link again," Tamsyn said. "I might share your work with my producer, if you don't mind." She acted in historical television productions, and maybe Brady would be hired to work on one.

He ran a hand through his hair. "I'd love that. I'm perfectly happy to pick up freelance camera projects."

Tamsyn delicately tapped strawberries into her bowl of yogurt. "The answer to your question is yes, we can review together. See what works for the episode."

How clever she was, to imply that the episode would proceed despite Tweedy's death. It worked, too. Brady looked as eager as a donkey being offered a carrot.

"Perfect for the Red Maiden scene, right? Especially the sword fight and the bonfire. And that flaming longboat?" He kissed his fingers. "Chef's kiss."

Tamsyn glanced around, picked up her mug, and carried that along with the bowl to the table, Brady trailing her. She sat next to his setting.

"Are we going to do any more ghost-hunting sessions?" Georgia asked, still playing with her phone. She appeared to have gotten over her earlier spat with Brady.

"I don't know," Brady said, shifting uncomfortably. "We've got the Red Maiden, the friendly ghost, and Sir Percival already."

"What about the monk?" Georgia asked. "Ollie, didn't you say you saw him?"

Ollie nodded solemnly. "I did. The day I got sick." He stared into the distance as if reliving the moment. "What struck me most was the way he glided along. Under his hood, his eyes were dark and piercing, as if he could see right into my soul." He spoke slowly, in a ponderous tone.

Georgia shivered. "Stop. You're creeping me out."

Ollie's delivery had been very effective and even I had shivered a bit. But suspicious me immediately fastened on a possible reason that Georgia had mentioned the monk. He was associated with the sacred spring and that was where Tweedy had been focused. According to Georgia, that is.

"You must be very talented," Dad said. "The monk doesn't usually appear in daylight. I saw him once, after dark. Talk about eerie. I was alone on the path, having visited the chapel to pray for the souls of the departed. The night was moonless and a fog was winding through the trees. A movement caught my eye. His black cloak blended into the night so completely, all I could see was his face, glowing white like bone."

Dad was giving Ollie a run for his money in the scary story department.

"For a long moment, we took each other's measure. Then he lifted his arm and I saw a lantern in his hand. It lit with a spark that quickly became a steady flame. Still holding it high, he turned and glided away as if saying, 'Come, come. Follow me.' And follow him I did, to the edge of the sea." His voice died away, leaving us spellbound.

Tamsyn was the first to speak. "Whoa, Dad. You're amazing."

Dad's smile was sly. "Where do you think the talent came from, my love? Many an Asquith has trod the boards, you know."

Another fascinating aspect of our history, no doubt.

He wasn't finished. "By the way, I've done more digging on Anne Asquith, whom I believe is our friendly ghost. For the stories I'm writing for our guests." He nodded at me. "She was an herbalist and healer." Toward Tamsyn. "And in love with a strolling player."

Tamsyn's mouth dropped open. "Oh, Dad, that's perfect." She turned to Brady. "That's mine, don't use it." She took out her phone and began tapping away. "Not even a hint, okay?"

"This is all preliminary," Dad said, addressing the table at large. "Needs to be confirmed." When my eyes met his, he winked. Pretty much nailed down, I guessed, but he was warning them off.

"Now that I have your attention," Dad said, "I have an announcement concerning the treasure hunt."

If our small audience had been fascinated before, now

they were transfixed. Not that I could blame them. Millions might be at stake.

"I am putting the treasure hunt on hold until an arrest is made in Professor Tweedy's death."

CHAPTER 25

A babble of voices broke out in response to Dad's announcement. He let that go on for precisely thirty seconds before he bellowed, "Quiet!" and thumped his fist on the table.

They complied, settling back like scolded children.

"You may ask questions," Dad said. "I might not answer, but you can ask."

Georgia put up her hand. "How long do you think that will take?" Her voice was timid.

Dad pursed his lips. "If the guilty party confesses, a day. If they continue to evade the police, who knows?" His blue eyes regarded the group with amused cynicism. He was baiting them.

I studied each face closely, looking for signs of guilt. They all merely looked nervous and upset.

"Why are you waiting?" Ollie asked. "Wouldn't it be wise to find it before it becomes common knowledge?"

He did have a point here. News of possible treasure tended to spread with lightning speed. I was actually amazed it hadn't leaked yet.

Dad's brow furrowed. "It would be . . . disrespectful

to search for gold during an investigation of a man's murder, as if that is all we care about. As for the second part of your statement, you have a point. I trust, however, that you all will keep your mouths shut. Anyone who blabs will be disqualified from the team when we do move forward."

Brady pushed his chair back. "Might as well pack up, then. I'll head home to the editing bay, see what I can salvage of this week's work."

His team took a cue from him and began shifting around, as if getting ready to leave.

The front doorbell gave a deep, loud bong. I had a sneaking suspicion who was at the door so I stood and called out, "Hold it, everyone. No one is leaving Ravensea or Monkwell until DI Hook gives the say-so. Am I right, Finlay?"

All eyes turned to Finlay. "Nora is correct. He may want you to stay put for further questioning. It may be today, it may be several days."

They subsided with groans. Gray looked into his mug, then went over to the table for a refill. Brady went over to his laptop.

Tactfully put. I was thinking *until he arrests one of you*. The castle had been locked last night, so whoever killed Tweedy had either been let in by him or someone else, or they were in residence here. My money was on the latter.

DI Hook was indeed at the door, and he put each of us through another round of questioning. He also affirmed Finlay's opinion and told the ghost team that they needed to stay put for "several days."

"Several more days of a pressure cooker," I complained to Finlay as we drove across the causeway late in the afternoon. We were finally on our way to pick Rolf up at Liv's farm. "I'm not looking forward to it at all."

"It is a tough situation," Finlay agreed. "All those suspects cooped up together."

"Maybe the killer will break down and confess," I said without much optimism. "I'm just waiting for them to start sneaking around again looking for the treasure. How can they not? It's too tempting."

"Without your father's permission, the find would be illicit," Finlay pointed out. "They won't be able to claim a finder's fee."

"So they'll steal it all." I folded my arms, barely taking in the village as we passed through. I usually enjoyed studying the quaint, historic buildings and checking out the window displays.

"That is a possibility," Finlay admitted, "when millions of pounds are at stake."

"We need to find it first," I said. "What equipment do I need to explore a cave? It's actually more of a crevice and I have no idea where it goes or how deep it is. It's not easily accessible like the Dragon's Lair."

Located along the shoreline close to the castle, the Dragon's Lair was large and deep enough for boats to enter at certain phases of the tide.

"I can look into it for you," Finlay said. "I have a friend who is a spelunker. He explores underground all the time."

"Maybe he can help us." My stomach tensed at the idea of climbing into a narrow, dark hole. "To be honest, I've always been afraid of being trapped in there."

That was why we hadn't explored the cavern even

as relatively fearless children. The Dragon's Lair, which had tunnels high and wide enough to stand up in, was one thing. Crawling into a crack was another entirely.

Liv and Tom's farm was located out of town a few miles, a classic Yorkshire farm featuring rolling hills edged with stone walls, a stone two-story house, and a number of outbuildings. The largest of these had been refurbished into an ice cream production kitchen, all gleaming stainless steel and modern plumbing.

The cows were grazing on the hillside and they looked up as we went past, their gazes curious. In the farmyard, the younger children, Ava and Thomas, were romping around with Rolf, Lady, and Sally, the border collie. They all, children and dogs, stopped to watch as we pulled and parked. Then they approached in a body, swarming us as we got out.

"Hello," I called over the barking and greetings. "Is your mum home?"

"Mum and Dad are having a cuppa," Ava, age ten, said.

"Will you ask if we can have some biscuits?" Thomas, five, put in eagerly. "She'll probably say yes to you."

I laughed. "I see the ploy. But yes, I'll ask."

They went back to their game and we strolled toward the back entrance to the farmhouse. We entered an enclosed porch crowded with lines of wellies and pegs hung with raincoats, anoraks, and puffers. The kitchen was reached through the opposite doorway.

"You made it." Liv stood to greet me with a kiss on the cheek. "How are you doing, you poor thing?"

They'd heard the news, I guessed. Probably the entire county had by now.

"Hanging in there." I gave Tom a little wave and pulled out a chair.

Tom shook Finlay's hand and gestured to a chair. "Nothing like a busman's holiday," he said.

"You got that right," Finlay said. "Only I'm not on the case. Another colleague caught it." He smiled at me. "Conflict of interest."

"And a lovely one, too," Tom said gallantly, returning to his seat.

Liv opened the lid of the teapot to check the contents, then filled two mugs. "How's that going?" she asked me.

Because she was one of my best friends and I trusted her, I said, "Pretty gruesome. I was surprised DI Hook didn't whip out the interrogation lights and tie me to a chair." I put my hand up, squinting against imaginary spotlights.

She laughed. "It isn't that bad, surely." A nod toward a tin. "Help yourself to biscuits. Lemon curd tarts."

"Almost." I opened the tin and took a tart. "By the way, Thomas would like a snack."

Liv and Tom exchanged looks. "I'll take them some," Tom said. He wrapped four tarts in a napkin.

"Where's Astrid?" I asked. She was fifteen and definitely a teenager.

Liv pointed upward. "In her room, making art on her laptop. She's actually quite good. Plus it keeps the socials in check."

I could imagine. Children of Astrid's age had been born into a time of social media and cell phones, which was a startling thought.

Tom returned. "On a more pleasant topic, the event looked to be a huge success."

"We sold out of ice cream," Liv put in. She reached for her phone. "I got great photos. Look." She opened a gallery and handed me her device.

I smiled at the shots she'd taken of happy customers,

enjoying the juxtaposition of tough, tattooed Vikings—men and women—and ice cream cones. "You need to post these."

"I plan on it," Liv said. "I'm even going to blow up one or two for the shop."

Two figures in the background of one picture caught my eye. I used my fingers to zoom. That looked like Ollie. He was standing with arms folded, frowning, while another man wagged a finger in his face.

Tweedy. Tweedy had come down to the festival. I checked the time stamp on the photo. Six PM.

"Finlay," I said. "Take a look at this."

"What is it?" Liv asked, craning forward.

I turned the phone to face her. "Tweedy and one of our guests. They look like they're having an argument. This was only hours before his death."

Tom came around to look as well. "I remember that. They started yelling at each other. I thought they were drunk and told them to move on."

"That's right," Liv said. "I remember that. I was so busy at the time making cones I barely took it in."

"I'm going to send this to myself, okay?" Then I reconsidered. "Or maybe you should contact DI Hook, Liv? He might think I photoshopped them in."

Liv didn't look thrilled at the idea. "I will, to help you, Nora. Otherwise, I'd rather stay out of it. Officially speaking, I mean."

"Fair enough." I turned to Finlay. "You have his contact info? Or maybe she should send it to Constable Kumar?"

"Oh, Advick," Liv said. "I like him. I'll send this to him right now."

I almost forwarded the picture to myself, then thought better of it. Instead, I snapped a photo of the enlarged image with my own phone. For my records.

"Are you investigating, Nora?" Liv asked under her breath.

I glanced at Finlay, who was chatting with Tom about the cows. I put on a rustic accent. "Do the cows need milking every morning, lass? There's your answer."

She leaned close enough that I could smell her hair, fragrant with the gentle honey and lavender shampoo I made for her. "Keep me in the loop, will you? I'll be anxious until they solve this thing."

"Me too," I said fervently. "You want the details?"

For the next hour or more, we hashed over the events of the previous night with Liv and Tom. It was a different experience having Finlay in the role of peer rather than police officer. He did interject at times, telling us the protocol and chain of evidence needed in a case. In his view, without fingerprints, a witness, or a confession, DI Hook had a tough row to hoe.

Too many suspects, an unobstructed scene in the sense that we were all out of the building during the murder, and a span of hours before Tweedy's body was discovered.

"I have no idea who did it," I mused as we drove back to Ravensea. The dogs were in the back, exhausted, tongues hanging out. Ava and Thomas had worn them out. "Everyone seems equally likely as a suspect."

"There is one thing I haven't shared," Finlay said. "While investigating the mushroom incident, I did a background check on your guests. Brady Benson was questioned during a rash of thefts at the University of York. Student lodgings were broken into and small electronics and the like were stolen."

"Really?" I tried to view Brady through this lens. He

seemed perfectly normal, if somewhat self-serving and pushy. Maybe morally gray, like when he had trolled his friend. But stealing? We didn't need a thief staying at Ravensea, that was for sure.

"He wasn't charged in the end," Finlay noted. "A couple of his buddies were, though. They were expelled and faced charges in court."

"Hmm. I'll take it under advisement." And keep an eye on the lad.

"Lab results from Ollie's coffee should be in tomorrow," Finlay said. "I'm sure Hook will want to see them."

"It might have been attempted murder," I said. "Although fatalities from *russula emitica* are extremely rare, especially in healthy people."

"Would the poisoner know that, though? There is a question of intent."

"True. If they are identified, then their defense will probably be that it was only to make Ollie sick. Not great but better than premeditated murder."

In the case of Tweedy's death, there was no question it was murder. Even if it was an impulse, the professor had died. Ollie had survived, felt better within hours, in fact.

It wasn't up to me to sort it, thankfully. DI Hook could figure out the appropriate charges.

We pulled up in front of the castle. "Do you want to stay for supper?" I asked. I had a sneaking suspicion that he would decline. Not only had we been together all day, tomorrow was a workday for him.

He reached out and touched my cheek. "Rain check? I seriously need to do my laundry tonight."

"Another night." I moved closer and we kissed. "Um, this is definitely the best part of my day." If only we could have spent alone time together, enjoying each other's company, instead of dealing with grim reality.

"Mine too," he said. "We'll plan something fun, I promise. Maybe a weekend away?"

I imagined the two of us on a mini-break, doing whatever we wanted whenever, with no one to interrupt us. No guests. No cases. Only us.

As if reading my mind, which dogs could, Rolf stuck his head through from the back seat and, despite the space limitations, managed to lick my face.

I burst out laughing and pushed his head gently back. "You are not coming on our vacation, Rolf."

"If he did, we'd need two beds," Finlay said. "He weighs as much as I do."

"He's definitely staying home. Even though I love him." I opened the car door, eager to get inside and wash my face. "Talk to you later."

"You bet. Call or text anytime."

I heard the subtext: if another untimely death or disaster occurs. I opened the back car door and finally managed to drag Rolf away from his friend, Lady. Then we went up the steps to the castle entrance, where we stood and watched Finlay drive away.

With a sigh, I opened the door and went in, Rolf barging past me and almost knocking me over. He kept going, right to the kitchen, I knew, to have his dinner. Don't stand between an English mastiff and his food dish.

Voices drifted from the drawing room so I went in that direction, eager to have a glass of wine and relax. The temperatures were getting chilly and I hoped Dad had started a fire. I wanted to sit down and bask and think about absolutely nothing for a while.

Brady, Ollie, and Gray were seated, glasses of wine

in hand, chatting. Tamsyn was over by the drinks table. They all looked over when I walked in.

"Hey," I said, continuing on to the bottles of wine. "Thanks for setting this up," I told my sister. In addition to the wine, she'd put out cheese and crackers with olives and pickles. I could use a snack.

"Where's Georgia?" I asked Tamsyn, half expecting to hear that she'd been hauled down to the station for more questioning. Finding her in the tower room with Tweedy's body definitely put her at the head of the suspect pack.

"I haven't seen her yet," Tamsyn said. "She must be in her room. White or red?"

"Red, please." I filled a small plate with nibbles.

Gray looked over. "She's not," he said. "She went out for a walk."

I pivoted to face him. "How long ago?" She'd done this before, taken off by herself to walk the grounds. "I hope she's okay. It's getting dark."

He shrugged. "An hour ago, maybe? She said she needed to think."

With a sigh, I picked up my wine and my plate and carried them to a chair by the fire. "If she's not back by the time I drink this wine, we're going to go looking for her."

My plan to relax was ruined. How dense could these men be? There was a killer running around Ravensea and they'd let Georgia go off by herself.

I crammed cheese and crackers into my mouth, not even tasting them, then washed them down with gulps of wine.

This was dumb. I gave up and slid out of my chair. "I'm going to go look for her. Anyone want to come with me?"

The trio exchanged glances, then all three reluctantly rose. "I think you're overreacting," Gray said. "Surely she'd call if she was hurt or lost."

Not if she is dead. I pressed my lips together to hold back the retort.

CHAPTER 26

I found a flashlight in the hall and the four of us went out through the terrace doors. Tamsyn stayed behind, charged with contacting me immediately if Georgia came back.

What made sense—staying together or splitting up? The thing was, our extensive property would take ages to search. I didn't feel comfortable letting people search by themselves, though. They might get lost or hurt—or if they had hurt Georgia, try to cover up the evidence.

Even as I was thinking all this, I knew I could be overreacting. She might still be walking or sitting on the bluff, staring at the sea.

I couldn't take the chance, though. Then a solution came to me. Pairs. We'd go in pairs. "Ollie, you're with me. Gray and Brady, you two stick together." I assigned them the bluff and Ollie and I went into the gardens. I knew its secret paths and nooks better than anyone.

This match-up gave me a chance to talk to Ollie. "How are you feeling?" I asked as we strolled through the physic garden, the dried stalks of herbs and flowers rattling in a cold breeze.

"Fine," he said. "Although I drank too much last night."

"No aftereffects from . . . whatever it was?" I didn't want to call it poison until we had the test results.

"Not after I got rid of it all."

I was leading the way, stopping frequently to be sure he was still with me. The path we were on led to a small reflecting pool with a gazebo. This was a nice spot to sit and think and I hoped Georgia would be there.

She wasn't. The gazebo bench was empty.

"Is it true you found Georgia in Tweedy's room?" Ollie asked me. We were standing next to the pool while I debated where to go next.

I almost told him, because I usually answer honestly when people ask me a question. "I'm sorry, I really can't talk about it." I thought of a question for him. "Who told you that?"

His shoulders moved in a shrug. "I'm not sure."

Very helpful. Not. I swung the flashlight around for one last look and the beam caught something on the ground, half under a bush. I went over to take a closer look.

A cell phone. Plain black, so sheer luck I'd noticed it. I bent to pick it up, then thought better of using my bare hand. Ollie was wearing gloves, which had been smart of him. My fingers were freezing.

"Can I use one of your gloves for a minute?" I asked, holding my hand out.

He stripped it off and gave it to me. I slid it on, slightly repulsed by its warmth, and picked up the phone. The screen was not only blank, it was cracked.

"Is this Georgia's phone? The new one, I mean?"

He stared at it. "I have no idea. All those burners look the same, don't they?"

Of course she'd bought a cheap, disposable phone. She was expecting to get her "real" one back from the police.

I slid it into my jacket pocket and zipped it, then gave him back his glove. "Thanks."

"If that is her phone, then she came this way," he said.

The fact that we'd found her phone chilled me. Why had she left it there? Did she not realize that she'd dropped it? Maybe that was it. It had fallen out of her pocket and slid under the bush. If she did know by now, it certainly wouldn't be an easy task looking for a phone in the dark, especially in a garden with a million places to look.

Calling it might be the only way to locate it. Which she could only do back at the castle.

"Hold on," I said, deciding to check in with Tamsyn.

She picked right up. "Did you find her?"

"Not yet. We did find her phone. We think. It looks like it, anyway."

Tamsyn didn't question my assumption. "Where are you?"

I explained our location and told her that we were going to continue in this direction.

"Okay. I'll let you know if there's any news."

"Nothing yet," I said, putting my phone in my other pocket, which I zipped. I didn't want to lose it by accident.

"What's down here?" he asked as we moved on.

"Other garden features. A grotto, a set of stairs leading to an old croquet lawn, a copse of apple trees."

"This place has everything," he said, admiration heavy in his voice. "It's amazing."

"Almost a thousand years in one place will do that," I said. "Every generation added improvements to the property." Even us. We had added upgraded plumbing for the bathrooms, if not all new fixtures. I'd restored the herb garden, too, using the original plans and then expanding upon them.

The faint sound of running water announced the

grotto. This was a stone face set in a wall, the mouth open to allow spring water to trickle out into a basin. This in turn spilled over to water thick beds of ferns, moss, and other shade-loving plants.

Again, I scanned the area for Georgia, although this wasn't really the season to linger here. The grotto's cool moisture was best savored in the burning heat of summer.

Next was the flight of stairs to the croquet lawn. Not that it'd seen a ball or wickets for decades. We kept it mowed, though, and I could easily add croquet as an activity next summer. The guests might enjoy playing such a retro, undemanding game.

"Careful," I warned Ollie as we approached the top of the stairs, remembering one reason we didn't go down here much. The flagstone stairs were steep, mossy, even missing chunks here and there. They'd need to be fixed before guests could use them.

We were partway down when I heard a groan. "Did you hear that?" I asked Ollie.

"I did." We both stopped to look and listen.

The lawn below was swathed in complete darkness. I shone the flashlight in that direction, the beam inadequate to cover the entire expanse.

"Hey," a woman's voice called. "I'm right here."

I moved the beam toward the voice. Georgia, sitting on the grass. She flung a hand up to block the light. Relieved to see her, I started to run down the steps.

Only to slip and almost fall. There wasn't a railing—another improvement we'd need to make—so I teetered until Ollie gripped my arm. Then, with him still helping me, we navigated the rest of the way to the grass.

Once safely on level ground, I ran to her side. "Where are you hurt?"

She had both hands on her ankle. "Here." She tugged

up her pants leg to reveal swelling flesh above her low sock. "I hope it's not broken."

"Me too." Not a medical expert by any stretch, I wasn't going to prod and poke and diagnose. We needed to get her to the emergency room for imaging.

"Can you stand?" Ollie asked. "Nora and I can help you hop along."

"Are you up for that?" I asked. Then I had a better idea. "We'll have someone drive down here on the back lane. Actually, let's do that. It will take hours to hop back."

I stepped aside a few paces and called Tamsyn. After filling her in, she said she'd have Guy drive over in the Land Rover. A pot of soup and homemade rolls would be waiting when we wanted to eat.

"Guy is driving down. We just have to get you to the end of the lawn." I pointed. "That's where the lane comes closest."

With both of us working together, we got her upright and positioned between us. Then we began the slow process of hobbling across the grass, stopping every few steps for Georgia to rest.

"I'm terribly sorry about this," she said between gritted teeth. "For causing so much trouble."

"Don't worry about it," I said. "I'm glad we came out to look for you. Oh, by the way, I found your phone. I mean, I think it's yours."

She panted for breath. "I knew I dropped it somewhere." More panting. "While someone was chasing me."

"Chasing you?" I shouted, right in her ear and Ollie's. "Sorry. Someone was chasing you?" Then I realized we weren't quite to the meeting spot. "Hold on. Let's keep going."

We hobbled a few more yards, to where the single-track

lane wound through the woods. We weren't far from the chapel and the sacred spring. Had Georgia been on her way over there? She hadn't told us what had brought her out here yet.

I warned myself not to come on too strong. I had the feeling she would only clam up. Headlights shone in the treetops and an engine grumbled. A moment later, the vehicle came into view. Once he got closer, I began to wave to attract his attention.

Guy braked and hopped out, then came around. "Got here quick as I could." His gaze swept over Georgia. "Hurt yourself, lass? I'm very sorry to hear that."

"Let's put her in the front seat," I suggested. "It's roomier."

He opened the door and between the three of us, we got her up into the Land Rover. Then Ollie and I climbed in back.

"Where to?" Guy asked once he was behind the wheel.

"Let's drop you and Ollie back at the castle and then I'll take her to the hospital," I said. "That ankle needs an X-ray." The hot soup and rolls I'd been looking forward to would have to wait.

I drove Georgia to the urgent care center attached to the local hospital. It was open until eight and we were barely going to make it. "When we get there, I'm going to grab a wheelchair for you." That would make the transition into the building easier for her.

"Sorry to be such a bother." Georgia was staring out the window, hands clasped between her knees and her shoulders hunched.

"You're not," I said. "Anyone could have fallen down those steps. I almost did. My foot hit a rock."

She turned to look at me. "That's what happened to me. There were a lot of loose rocks and pebbles scattered on the steps."

That was really strange, because there wasn't a source of rocks at the top of the steps. The path was grass in that area. Had they been scattered on the steps deliberately?

I remembered what she had said. "You were being chased?"

She didn't answer immediately. "I think? Now I'm wondering if I was imagining things."

"Well, it is Ravensea," I said, in a probably ill-advised attempt at levity.

"You mean it might have been a ghost?"

"I don't know what I meant. Was someone else in the garden?"

She turned to stare out the window again. "I heard footsteps behind me. I waited, thinking it was one of the guys. Or maybe you or someone in your family. But when I stopped, so did they. I got spooked and started to run. That must be when I lost the phone."

"I found it between the reflecting pool and the grotto."

"Yes, I went by there. At the grotto, I stopped for a moment and heard them coming again. This time they were running. So I ran."

Right down the steps, the only option at that point. Dense bushes lined the path at that point. The person chasing her had funneled her toward the stairs.

CHAPTER 27

An hour and a half later, we were on our way back to Ravensea. Georgia had a broken ankle and it had been quickly and expertly set and put in a cast. A pair of crutches rested on the back seat, which meant we had a dilemma. The stairs to Georgia's room.

"I can't believe I have to wear this cast for a month," Georgia moaned.

Plenty of sympathy here. "Does it hurt?" I asked, hoping the answer was no.

"Not too bad." She folded her arms. "I guess I won't be going on any walks for a while, though."

Which brought up a topic we hadn't discussed: namely, why had she been roaming the grounds in the dark? I'd warned the team about that already.

"Can I ask you a question?" She tensed, darting me a look. "Not about Tweedy." She relaxed a fraction. "Why were you out there in the first place?"

We pulled up in front of the castle entrance. The outside lights illuminated the car's interior well enough that I could see her expression. She was staring, wide-eyed, as though I'd put her on the spot.

"Um." She pressed her lips together, staring out

the windshield. "I was meeting someone. But he didn't show up."

The gardens were a perfect spot for a romantic rendezvous. Or a secret meeting to talk about treasure—or murder. "Who was it?"

"I'd rather not say." She reached for the door handle, then pulled back. "I need my crutches."

"I'll get them for you." I had one more question. "If you were meeting someone, why did you run away?"

Her expression clearly conveyed that I was stupid. "Because it wasn't my . . . my friend. I called out and he or she didn't answer." A trace of spite crept across her face. She'd said "she," which implied that Tamsyn or I might have been chasing her.

I didn't bite. "Got it. Hold on and I'll help you get out."

"Do I still have to sleep upstairs? I don't know if I can make it up there."

"We'll make room downstairs for you." The solar was the best room. The sofa I'd bought for it had a pull-out bed that had never been used.

"I can't wait to go home," she grumbled.

And I couldn't wait for them all to leave, either. Instead, I said, "Let's get you inside."

We got the crutches propped under her shoulders and then I spotted her as she made the short journey into the castle.

"Phew," she said when we reached the hall. "I'm exhausted already."

"They take getting used to. Believe me, I know." I'd been on crutches myself a time or two.

Tamsyn hurried out of the drawing room. "You're back. How are you feeling?"

"Not great," Georgia said. "Nora said I can sleep downstairs."

I explained the plan to Tamsyn. "Do you mind if I pack your things and bring them down?" she asked Georgia.

Georgia's gaze darted from the looming staircase to us to the rooms beyond. "I guess that will be okay. I don't have a choice, do I?"

"We'd rather you didn't climb the stairs," I said crisply. "You might get hurt." I hadn't prevented her first fall. I wasn't going to preside over another. "Are you hungry? Why don't you eat while we get things set up?" I hadn't eaten yet either and my stomach rumbled loudly. After we got Georgia settled, I told it sternly.

I ended up eating in the kitchen, Janet and Tamsyn sitting with me for the updates. Georgia was tucked up in the solar, reading a book, and the other three ghost hunters were off somewhere. Tamsyn had packed Georgia's things, and while she of course hadn't snooped, she hadn't come across Tweedy's notebook in the room. Or a signed confession to his murder.

Between bites of chicken stew, I told them the story of finding Georgia. "She said someone chased her to those stairs. I almost fell down them myself. Ollie saved me."

Tamsyn shook her head. "We might have had two of you on crutches. How would we manage that, Janet?"

"We'd all be hopping," Janet quipped. "Waiting on you both."

I laughed, which was the outcome they were going for, to lighten the mood. "Seriously, though, I'm relieved she wasn't killed. I found stones scattered on the steps, which is why I think she slipped. She said she was meeting someone—wouldn't say who—but whoever it was behind her didn't identify themselves." I didn't mention her gibe that it might have been a woman.

"We need to bell these visitors, like cats," Janet said, shaking her head. "It's the only way we can keep track of them."

Ruffian, who was lurking, hoping for food, stared up at her as though offended. We all laughed again.

"No bell for you, huh, Ruffian?" I crooned, reaching to pat him. Any collar we'd tried on him I ended up finding under a bush or in a flower bed. He managed to get them all off within minutes, if not hours.

I scooped up the last spoonful of stew. "I suppose I'd better report the incident to DI Hook."

"We should," Tamsyn said. "It might have been attempted murder."

I dropped my spoon into my bowl, suddenly unable to finish. If Tamsyn was right, then Tweedy wasn't the only target. We had Ollie's poisoning to add to the list. Maybe it hadn't been a nasty prank. Maybe the person had tried to kill him.

Were they all going to be picked off one by one, like an *And Then There Were None* scenario?

The next alarming twist occurred in the morning. We didn't find out until breakfast had been served. Today's menu was scrambled eggs, kippers, fried mushrooms, bacon, and oatmeal.

"Are those kippers?" Gray asked, peering closely at the platter. "My grandfather used to eat kippers." He used the spatula to scoop up one of the fish filets.

"Mine too," Ollie said. "I love them. Salty goodness."

Georgia had been first out and she was drinking

coffee and looking at her phone. "What's Brady doing? Sleeping in?"

His friends exchanged looks. "I don't know," Gray said. "I haven't seen him yet."

"Not like him, is it?" Ollie asked. "He's usually the first one up."

Uh-oh. Deciding not to alarm them with my worries, I slipped out of the dining room. A simple knock on the door would answer the question about Brady's whereabouts. Hopefully he hadn't gone out with his metal detector again. Strictly forbidden right now. The first time we'd let it slide. Not a chance after Dad's decision to put the hunt on hold.

I didn't allow darker ideas to take root. We hadn't heard screams in the night or any other mysterious sounds. Rolf hadn't barked.

Brady's door was open a crack, I noticed. That was odd. If he was elsewhere, he wouldn't have left it open, I didn't think.

I rapped on the doorframe. "Brady?" Again, louder this time. "Brady? Are you in there?"

No answer. I pushed on the door with my fingertips and it swung inward silently.

The room was empty. The bed unmade. All the luggage was gone.

Brady had left.

I circled the room, searching for Brady. I even looked under the bed to be sure. No, he was gone, all his belongings with him.

The van. He'd been driving when they all arrived. Leaving the door open, I ran downstairs and opened the front door. The rental was still parked in the front courtyard, which meant he hadn't left them stranded. How had he left, then? On foot?

On the way back to the dining room, I tried to collect my thoughts. His disappearance absolutely needed to be reported to the police. Was it a confession of sorts? Had he killed Tweedy? Good way to put a target on his back if not.

"Excuse me," I said loudly as I entered the dining room. Everyone was eating, including Dad and Tamsyn, who had joined the others. Once they were all looking at me, I said, "Brady is gone."

Georgia dropped her fork with a gasp. "He's dead?"

"No, no," I hurried to explain. "He's gone, as in left the building. His luggage, too."

"How about the van?" Ollie asked. "It's in his name."

"That's still here." I studied each face, looking for signs that this wasn't a surprise. They all returned my stare blankly.

Gray was first to look away. Shaking his head, he stabbed at a kipper. "He must have killed Tweedy. Good as a signed confession, right?"

Exactly what I'd thought, but I didn't say anything. Better not to speculate aloud with other suspects. Family, well, that was different. We'd be hashing over this turn of events for sure.

"I'm going to call the police," I said to the room at large before leaving again. DI Hook was going to be furious about Brady's exit, I had no doubt.

I wasn't wrong. DI Hook tried to hide it, but I saw the steely rage lurking in the depths of his small blue eyes. "You didn't see him leave?" he asked me for the third time, as if I were lying.

"I did not," I said. "I sleep on the third floor in the back. We didn't hear anything, either. Not even a vehicle arriving to pick him up." Brady must have called for a ride. I doubted he walked to the train station, which was miles away, or hitchhiked. "You checked local rideshares, right?"

His scowl deepened. "I can't discuss that." He bit off the words. Yes, definitely angry. He switched gears to another topic. "Take me through the incident with Miss Kane again."

I did, doing my best to keep my account short and accurate. Constable Kumar was again taking notes and I was glad to have a friend in the room. Should I reveal what she'd told me about her meeting—and the person chasing her? It was hearsay, really, yet I didn't trust Georgia to tell him anything that put her in a bad light. If I were her, I'd want to play it off as a simple accident.

"Anything else to add?" he asked, which gave me the perfect opening.

"Actually, yes," I said. Trying to recall her exact words, I shared the story she'd told me. Then, to cover myself, I added, "We've told our guests not to wander around in the dark alone on the grounds. It's too dangerous. She's lucky we realized she might be hurt and went after her. Otherwise she could have been out there for hours in the cold."

"She didn't call anyone?" Hook asked.

"She dropped her phone. I found it under a bush." Just more proof that we'd done the right thing to hunt for her.

An uneasy feeling trickled into my mind. Were we making too many assumptions about Brady? Missing baggage pointed to him leaving under his own steam, sure. Had anyone heard from him yet? I had his cell number. The minute DI Hook released me, I would try to call and text him. The police were definitely doing that as well—I had given them the contact information already—but they wouldn't give me an update. I wanted one for myself. To put my mind at ease.

Although, would he answer me if he was on the run? Maybe not. I had to try anyway.

"If you hear from him," DI Hook said, as if reading my mind, "I want to know immediately. Immediately. Do you understand?"

"Yes, I do." I kept my response short. I didn't bother to add how much I hoped and prayed that Brady was all right. That his "disappearance" wasn't a cover-up for murder. I mean, if he could pack and leave without anyone noticing, someone else could have removed all his things and hidden them.

If I didn't hear back from Brady, we were going to search the castle and grounds. Unless the police found him first.

CHAPTER 28

DI Hook and his team had barely left the castle when Finlay arrived in a police car. Official business, then. I saw him pull in through Brady's bedroom window, where I'd been stripping the bed, and rushed downstairs to meet him at the door.

"Good morning," I said, wanting to kiss him but conscious of his role. I peered past him to the parked car. "All alone?"

"Not sure how long I'd be here. Didn't want to tie up another officer." His smile faded. "Nora, we got the lab results back. You were right. The coffee was poisoned."

I gripped the door handle, allowing myself to lean. Although the results were expected, it was still a shock. "Someone targeted Ollie. Tried to make him sick or worse."

"It looks that way, if it's known which cup is his."

"He carried it everywhere. Couldn't miss it with those stickers." I had another question. "It's still your case?"

He shifted the briefcase he was holding. "For the moment. Now that we know for sure, I want to interview the other members of the team."

Belatedly, I realized I was keeping him on the front

stoop. "Sorry. Please come in. They're all still here. Except for Brady." I shut the door behind him.

"What do you mean?" Finlay's eyes lit with alarm.

"He's gone. Missing. Took off in the night. We hope." I pulled my phone out and showed him the texts I'd sent. "He hasn't responded. His phone is going right to voicemail."

"Is DI Hook aware of this situation?" Finlay asked.

"He absolutely is. We called him first thing." I tucked my phone into my pocket. "Georgia is staying in the solar now so I'm not sure where to put you." I'd sent Finlay a text last night about Georgia's accident. I hadn't had a moment to do the same with the Brady news this morning. "Maybe Dad's study?"

"I hate to put Arthur out," he protested.

"He's getting used to it after DI Hook's visits." I rapped on the study door. "It's Nora," I called.

"Come in," Dad shouted. We entered to find him standing behind his desk sorting through papers, books, ledgers, and folders. "Finlay. How are you?"

"Quite well, sir. Yourself?"

Dad grunted. "Be better when the invasion stops." He glanced up. "Not you. You're always welcome."

Seeing my father's annoyance at the state of his office, I thought better of asking if Finlay could use it. "Actually, Dad, Finlay is here about the lab results. Ollie was poisoned."

My father's chin jerked up. "Someone tried to kill him?" His face reddened and he looked ready to explode. "What foul brood of vipers have we cherished in our bosom?"

"A good question, sir," Finlay replied. "That's what I'm here to find out."

"And you have my profound blessing on that endeavor. Did Nora fill you in on the other shenanigans of late?" Dad asked.

"She did. A broken ankle and a missing person. Things aren't trending positive."

Dad snorted. "That's for sure." He glanced around his desk. "You're welcome to use this room—"

"I won't trouble you," Finlay said. "I can set up in the dining room for now."

"Appreciate it, old chap. On another subject, Nora. Have you seen the historic architectural plans? I can't find them anywhere. And before you ask, I've already looked in Tweedy's room. The police are finished with it, they said."

Dad and Tweedy had been studying Ravensea's various maps and plans to come up with possible locations for the treasure. The set he was referencing featured notations regarding the various phases of the castle's construction, starting with the first keep. They would be useful for finding possible locations for the hoard before the castle was built.

I scanned the desk, hoping that, by some miracle, the correct roll of plans would pop out at me. I couldn't see it anywhere. Which probably meant one thing: someone had taken it. I could ask everyone, but I had a feeling they wouldn't be eager to confess taking them. To me this was a sign that someone was still looking for the treasure—without Dad's permission.

Rather than bring up yet another painful subject, I decided to look for the plans while cleaning the guest rooms. If someone had taken them, I'd take them right back.

"I haven't seen the plans but I'll keep an eye out for them," I said. "Right now we'll get out of your way. I'll let you know when lunch is ready." We could eat after Finlay's interviews.

"Hold on," he called after me. I halted in the doorway. "Do you think Georgia would mind helping me with research? She must be awfully bored sitting around."

"I can ask her." I took a step back into the room and lowered my voice. "As long as it has nothing to do with the Viking hoard, okay? I don't trust any of them. Not even Ollie." The fact he was poisoned didn't confer innocence on him.

"Me either," Dad said, his mouth twisting. "I want her to help me research Anne Asquith's life if she's game. Anne was a very interesting woman."

And our friendly ghost. "That's a great idea, Dad. I can't wait to hear what you find out."

Georgia was in the solar, slouched on a sofa staring at her phone, her broken ankle propped on a hassock. A carafe of water, mug of something, and a tin of cookies stood on an end table, within reach. Janet was taking good care of our patient.

"Hey, Nora," Georgia mumbled without looking up when I knocked on the doorframe.

"Can I talk to you for a minute?"

She put the phone down with a sigh. "Sure. You're saving me from another bout of impulse shopping." She picked up the phone and tapped. "There. Shopping cart empty."

I remembered the stack of packages Georgia had delivered here. Did she have a shopping addiction? It was possible—and all too easy to indulge with the internet, even here at remote Ravensea.

"I was talking to Dad," I said, perching on a chair.

"He's got research work if you're interested. Paid, of course."

She struggled to a more upright position, her expression eager. "I'd love to do that. I was quite a research whiz at university, you know. I even helped my friends with their papers."

Friends like the other ghost hunters? Gray had claimed credit for tracing the Red Maiden to Ravensea. Maybe Georgia had contributed to his work and therefore had a stake in the hunt. Beyond the obvious financial rewards.

"I'll let Dad know and he can get you started." I noticed that her cast had several signatures on it, including my family members'. "Can I sign your cast?"

She leaned forward, smiling as she read the signatures. "Sure. It's kind of fun."

I found a felt-tip pen on my desk and knelt by the hassock, looking for a place to write.

Brady had written, *Breaking a leg wasn't supposed to be literal.* The others had only signed their names.

"Have you heard from Brady?" I asked casually, trying to decide what to say.

"Not yet and I'm really worried." She did look concerned, all big eyes and a sad expression. "Do you think he killed Tweedy?"

"I have no idea," I said honestly. "Running away definitely makes him look guilty, though."

She slumped back on the sofa. "Yeah, it sure does. That police officer grilled me about it. Asked me three times if I'd seen Brady in the castle that night. I didn't see anyone."

I stared at a blank spot on the cast, pondering what to write. Unable to think of anything profound or funny, I scrawled, *Get well soon. Nora.* Boring, for sure.

"I'm incredibly disappointed about the show falling

apart," Georgia said. "I was starting to enjoy ghost hunting. I was petrified during that first episode with Sir Percival. Remember?"

"I do." I capped the pen and rose with a creak or two to my feet. "Our ghosts really aren't scary. They're more like departed loved ones still hanging around. In fact, Dad is researching the one we call the friendly ghost, Anne Asquith. He wants to learn more about her life."

"I do, too." Georgia smiled. "I'll never forget how she patted my hair."

"She has a thing about hair, that's for sure. Maybe she liked hairdressing." I put the pen in the desk drawer. "I'll go tell Dad that you're interested."

On the way out of the room, a question about the show footage came to me.

"Did Brady send you video from the show?" The raw files were what I wanted to see, not the carefully edited version. He might have captured something that would give us a clue to the killer's identity.

Georgia shook her head. "He hadn't started editing yet. He was going to do that back in York, in his studio."

Brady was gone, along with his cameras. Had he uploaded the video into the cloud? Tamsyn had mentioned a link and offered to send Brady's work to her producer. Did she still have access?

Eager to track Tamsyn down, I turned to leave and almost barged into Finlay. "Oh, hello. Are you finished with the interviews?" I was hoping we could have lunch together.

"Almost," he said, his gaze warm. "I'm looking for Georgia."

"She's right here," I said, moving aside. How thoughtful of Finlay to come to Georgia, instead of asking her to hobble to the dining room. "Georgia, DI Cole has a few questions for you." He was going to ask her about the mushrooms. Maybe she had been intending to harvest additional pieces when I saw her near the clump, instead of just out for a run.

"What about?" she asked, her expression wary. "I already spoke to the other DI."

Finlay set his briefcase on my desk. "I'm investigating another case. It won't take long."

I shut the door behind me, to give them privacy, then pulled out my phone to text my sister.

Where are you?

In Tweedy's room. Come on up.

You went without me?

A common complaint between me and my sister through the years. The first time in regard to a murder case, however.

I dashed to the study, opened the door and said, "Dad, Georgia wants to work for you. She's with Finlay right now, talking about the mushrooms, so wait before you talk to her, okay?" I caught a glimpse of his startled face before I shut the door and moved on.

Tamsyn was sorting through the mess on the table Tweedy used as a desk. "Help me organize? If the police did this, shame on them. If it was Tweedy, well, he was worse than Dad."

I snickered. Dad was known for his messy desk. I picked up a copy of *Forgotten Vikings* and placed it on the pile of books. "Anything interesting yet?"

"This." She held up a book sitting to one side, called *Sacred Springs of Northern England.*

"More proof that he thought the treasure was in the sacred spring?" I suggested.

I turned over a page lying face down. The text was in a foreign language. "What do you suppose this says?"

Tamsyn took out her phone and pointed it at the page. "It's a Viking curse."

I read over her shoulder. The app she'd used had translated the original text, which was in Old Norse, it reported.

I curse you to be outlawed, to be driven from society, and to find no rest. Your strength shall fail, your luck shall wane, and your life shall end in misery, alone on a desolate rock.

"Wow. That's a death threat." And I'd put my grubby paws all over the page. Tamsyn had touched it, too.

"Sounds like it to me." Tamsyn shook her head. "Kind of cruel to make him translate it first, huh?" She checked the screen. "It's from *Grettir's Saga,* translated into English about a hundred years ago."

I sighed. "I suppose we should show it to DI Hook." I wasn't looking forward to dealing with him again.

"Yes, we should. There's nothing tying it to any particular person, unfortunately." She put the excerpt with the book on sacred springs.

"Why couldn't we find a signed confession?"

"That would be too easy."

We continued to wade through Tweedy's debris. "Tamsyn, do you have access to Brady's video files?"

"Why?" Tamsyn found a stray snack wrapper under a file and tossed it into the trash. We'd found quite a few, as if we were excavating the sedimentary layers of Tweedy's final days.

"Because maybe he filmed a clue. Or caught something on a hot mic. Or . . . I don't know. I think they might be worth looking at."

She picked up her phone again. "Good point. Let me see if I still have access." After a couple of minutes of messing around, she gave a cry of triumph. "I'm in." She scrolled up and down. "Judging by the dates, looks like all the files are still there. New ones, too, from Saturday." The day of the Fest.

"I wonder if the police have seen these files," I said reluctantly. The right thing to do would be to turn them over. They were definitely evidence.

"We can ask." Tamsyn still had her nose in the phone. "I just want to check . . ." She wandered over to a chair and sat.

I kept going, hoping to find something else useful. The castle building plans weren't here, which could mean Tweedy didn't take them. If he had, the person who stole the notebook could have grabbed those as well.

"Nora, come take a look." Tamsyn handed me the phone. "Press play."

A video was already loaded on the screen and I hit the button. Night. In the garden. Jerky camera movements. A whispered male voice: "I'm on my way into the castle. Alone. At night." The viewpoint turned, picking up light and movement, flames shooting into the sky.

"It's the night of the Fest," I said.

Hands in the view, inserting a key and turning the knob.

"He's wearing the camera," I guessed. "Like a headlamp."

"That's what I think, too." Tamsyn touched her forehead. "One of those sports cameras."

Now he walked through the drawing room, the view swinging around to take in various aspects of the room.

"The guests don't have keys to that door," I said. We gave them a front door key, if they went out for the evening.

"He must have stolen the key from Janet," Tamsyn said. "Or you."

We both had full sets for the entire castle. Another worry unlocked. We'd better do an inventory.

Brady entered the Great Hall, the view swooping to take in the high ceiling and the minstrel's gallery. "Such a magnificent building," he whispered. "So much life and death right here. Centuries and centuries. Can you feel the ghosts? I can."

Disappointment struck. "These must be atmosphere shots."

"Keep going," Tamsyn said. "There isn't much more."

He trod stealthily up the main staircase and down the long corridor. When he turned down a side hall, I immediately knew his destination. "He was going to see Tweedy."

CHAPTER 29

The video ended right there and I groaned. Not that I wanted to see him actually kill Tweedy. Seeing Tweedy's face (alive) on camera would have been helpful to establish a timeline.

"Brady—I mean, I assume it was him because this is his account—was in the castle during the Fest. Before Tweedy was killed? Or after?"

Tamsyn took her phone out of my hand. "It's obvious that he killed him, don't you think?" She brought up details about the video. "The time stamp shows he came up here around the time of death, according to the medical examiner."

"And you could be right. I just don't think we should jump to conclusions. What if Brady was a witness and that's why he disappeared? I know the police scoured this place but we need to look for him ourselves. They don't know every nook and cranny the way we do."

The dungeons, for example. They hadn't gone down there. Or the sea caves.

Brady might have left under his own steam, which would be the happiest outcome. I hoped he had. It was possible that he'd been murdered and the killer had removed his belongings. My stomach clenched and I prayed that wasn't the scenario we would discover.

"I wonder if they're pinging his phone," I mused. "Speaking of phones, was Tweedy's ever located?" I hadn't seen it when we found his body. If it was missing, my theory was that the killer had stolen it, either to try to cover up their interactions or to dig into what Tweedy knew about the treasure.

"A question I can't answer." Tamsyn was scrolling through the file thumbnails. "I wish I could go through all these before we tell the police about them." She exhaled. "My conscience won't let me."

She put the phone to her ear and I heard ringing through the speaker. "DI Hook, please. It's Tamsyn Asquith, from Ravensea. Please put me through to him."

Tamsyn tilted her head back and forth, indicating she was waiting for him to pick up. Then her expression changed, a smile breaking out across her face. I knew that trick, to smile while talking made you sound much friendlier.

"DI Hook? We found a couple of things you really need to see." A pause. "Well, one is a threat and the other? Video of a suspect entering the castle before the murder. We think." Another pause. "I'm going by the approximate time of death. It's Brady Benson, filming himself going into the castle. Which is more than we had until now, right? No one witnessed the suspects going inside."

Her expression was smug when she finally disconnected. "He'll be right over, with bells on."

"Thanks for making the call," I said. "I'm trying not to be a lightning rod in this investigation. I'm sure he's heard all about me and the previous case."

"I helped with that, remember?" Once I nodded, she

said, "I don't mind challenging him. He's a bully and bullies wither when you stand up to them."

Or they arrest you and throw you in the clink.

A glance out the tower window revealed that Finlay's car was still here. "Do I have time to go see Finlay? He was interviewing Georgia and that's his last one today."

"Go ahead," Tamsyn said. "Come right back, though. You're my backup witness."

I hurried down the stairs to the main hall and then along to the main staircase. A twirling of dust particles in a certain corner caught my eye. Sir Percival. We hadn't seen hide nor hair of the ghost since we'd filmed his episode.

"Sir Percival? Is that you?" He usually had a reason to show up, I'd learned.

The particles danced more frantically and then an image of his head faded in and out, like poor reception on a television.

"What is it?" I wished I had the EVP recorder, which allowed us to hear ghost voices.

His entire body flickered into view, including his head, which hovered above where his neck should be. Then his head flew up and rolled along through the air, toward me like a bowling ball.

With a yelp, I ran for the main staircase. No words needed to interpret that performance. He was warning me about murder. Too bad Brady hadn't been here to capture it on his equipment.

At the top of the stairs, I turned and called, "Why didn't you warn us before?"

Another interpretation chilled me. He was warning me of a future event. Georgia. Was she in danger? Or Brady? Was someone going to kill him?

"Nora? Are you okay?" Finlay was at the bottom of the stairs.

I started down. "I was just coming to find you. How'd it go?"

He shrugged. "Didn't glean much." He moved toward the front door. "I've got to get back to the station."

"I'll walk you out," I said, buttoning my cardigan against the chill.

Once we were in the courtyard, I said, "Tamsyn and I made a couple of interesting discoveries in Tweedy's room."

Finlay opened the cruiser's passenger door and placed his bag on the seat.

DI Hook hadn't said not to share, so I told Finlay about the Viking curse and the video. "Hook is on his way. We'll see where he takes those clues." He shut the passenger door and started around the car. "Sir Percival made an appearance right before I came downstairs. I'm worried, Finlay. He showed me his head rolling."

"Heads are going to roll?" Finlay guessed.

I couldn't help but laugh. "That's not the meaning I got. Maybe the bad things aren't over. We had a murder, a poisoning, and an 'accident' so far. Now Brady is gone."

Stepping closer, he gathered me into a hug. "This is one benefit of being off the case." He smoothed my hair with one large hand.

My nose was buried against his shoulder and I inhaled his alluring yet comforting aroma of clean cotton and aftershave. "I like it."

Conscious of Hook's impending arrival, I pulled back. "The police looked for Brady earlier. I'm going to search again. They didn't go into the dungeons, for one thing."

I shivered to think about Brady being down there in that cold, dank space. If all his luggage hadn't been gone,

I would have looked for him, thinking maybe he was trapped as we had been. An explorer wouldn't take every pair of clean underwear along.

Now the options were: he'd been killed and the murderer made it look like he'd left; or he actually had taken off.

"I can come back later and help," he offered. "If that's not too late."

"Would you? We can wait. Have dinner with us tonight." I took a breath, then brought up the final topic. "No new clues about who poisoned Ollie?"

He sighed. "Ollie didn't even have any idea, although he thought maybe Tweedy—"

"That's what I thought. He poked through the trash. Sorry. Didn't mean to interrupt."

Finlay smiled to show he wasn't offended. "Anyway, I asked him what Tweedy's motive would have been. He says it was seeing the monk. Tweedy was very interested in that sighting and kept asking him about it."

The monk, who hung out near the spring. Where we thought the treasure might be. Why weren't we mounting a search for it right now? Oh yeah, because we were dealing with injuries and death. And a missing guest.

"Tweedy was interested in the spring. In fact, he thought that was a prime location for the hoard, according to Georgia. He never said that to me directly."

Finlay shrugged. "If Tweedy poisoned Ollie, then that case is closed. Without definite proof, I'm going to leave it open for now." He put his hand on the door handle. "I'd better push off."

"Hold on." I gave him a big kiss. "Thank you. And see you later. Text me and let me know what time."

I stayed outside to watch him drive over the causeway.

He was barely out of view on the other side when another police car approached, this one a large SUV.

Police visit, round three today.

The dungeons hadn't improved since our last visit. In fact, they were danker, darker, and colder than ever. Or maybe that was me. A definite sense of gloom had settled over me this afternoon, not helped by the rainy, foggy weather that had crept in.

"We should break into pairs," Will said. "It will go faster."

Will had made the mistake of stopping by and we'd drafted him to join me, Tamsyn, and Finlay. We couldn't ask Ollie or Gray to help. They were suspects. Georgia was as well, but with her cast, helping us wasn't even a consideration.

"I agree." I was already shivering despite my thick sweater and jeans. It wasn't only the creepy ambiance and discomfort, I admitted. I was worried we would find Brady down here, dead. He would be far from the first person to expire in these dungeons, although the last prisoner had been hundreds of years ago.

After discussion, we decided how to split the task. As Will and Tamsyn set off together, she called, "Make sure you leave the gates open. We don't want you getting stuck."

"Like the last time?" I called back. "Believe me, I remember."

"That's right. You were trapped down here," Finlay said. "Refresh me on the details?" We were both holding flashlights and he was beaming his around. I held mine steadily, being already familiar.

"Ollie and Brady were down here one day. They managed to capture the Red Maiden on video." The heavy stone around us muffled instead of magnifying my voice. A shout for help wouldn't travel far. "The gate between sections got shut and locked somehow and we were trapped. Tamsyn finally came looking for us. There's no signal down here."

"That must have been scary." Finlay shone his light into a small room to one side. "Is that a cell?"

"It is. See the manacles on the wall?" I touched them with my light. "This place has a very dark history."

Finlay shivered. "Might sound odd, but I can sense it."

"Not odd at all." I was dragging my feet, I noticed. "I really hope we don't find Brady. Down here, I mean."

He put his arm around me. "Me either. Let's hope he's somewhere safe and warm. Aboveground."

That made me laugh. "Yeah. In the sunshine. Sipping a drink with an umbrella." That sounded so good right now.

We trudged along, headed toward the place where the ghost hunters had made contact with the Red Maiden.

"I wonder if she's still lurking down here," I said. "Probably not. Last time she told us no—in her language, of course. I thought she meant that the treasure wasn't down here."

"Or she didn't want them bothering her," Finlay suggested.

"That too. She's not as, um, receptive to approach as our other ghosts." I recalled Ollie making another attempt. "She's also been seen on the battlements. Ollie went up there by himself, the idiot. I had to tell him to come back in before he fell to his death."

"Contacting her about the treasure?" Finlay asked.

"Probably. You know, I get it. The hoard could be

worth millions of pounds. That would tempt almost anyone."

"It'd be hard for them to get away with stealing it," Finlay said. "The Arts and Antiquities Unit has alerts set up with Interpol for black market antiquities. It's not a matter of selling things through an online auction site."

"They probably aren't thinking that far ahead," I guessed. I wouldn't have the vaguest idea how to sell anything under the table. Hopefully any would-be thieves would realize the difficulties and be deterred.

We passed through the gate that had trapped us and I stopped to make sure it was still chained to the wall, the way Guy had left it.

"It feels really weird down here," Finlay said when we started walking again. "Am I imagining it?"

"It does." The air was heavy and dense, as if it were pressing down on us and making it difficult to move forward. Our beams of light only illuminated a certain distance and beyond that, the tunnel gaped like an open black mouth. These dungeons were the stuff of nightmares.

I stopped moving. "I have an idea." Handing Finlay my flashlight, I cupped my mouth and yelled, "Brady? Are you down here?" My voice didn't even echo. "Brady," I called again.

"Nora," Finlay said, his expression pained. "That won't help if . . ."

"If he's dead? Maybe we should bring a police dog down to track him." I wouldn't put Rolf through that, though he had a good nose. "I really don't want to do this." The air seemed even more oppressive, making it hard to breathe. Was I panicking? Or was *something* here? I had to struggle to take in enough air.

I grabbed Finlay's arm. "You feel it too, right? It's not

just me." The likelihood that we'd both have panic attacks was pretty small.

"I do, Nora." He rolled his shoulders as if shrugging off a burden. "It's oppressive."

A shape moved in the dark and I jumped with a shriek. "Did you see that?"

He narrowed his eyes, staring into the darkness. "Uh-huh."

I huddled close to Finlay, nestled in the shelter of his wide shoulder. He still had both flashlights and I took mine back. Another movement. This time I bit my tongue to stop myself from screaming.

"Who are you?" I called, my voice wavering. "Show yourself."

The voice was faint as a whisper. "Fylgdu mér."

"What? What does that mean?" Was it the Red Maiden again?

Finlay touched me. "Listen."

This time, she spoke in English. "Follow me."

A rush of shock made my scalp prickle. "Follow her? Should we?"

"I can't see that it can hurt," Finlay said. "She hasn't been known to attack people, has she?"

I snorted. "None of our ghosts go after people. The friendly ghost is the only touchy-feely one and she's gentle." Of course, Anne Asquith wasn't a hardened warrior known for killing enemies and pirating ships.

Every part of my body felt heavy as lead as Finlay and I continued along the tunnel. If he hadn't been here, I would already have fled back to the comfort of the upstairs rooms. There was being brave and then there was being daft. Following a ghostly voice into a dark tunnel had to be a bad idea.

As we proceeded, I tried to keep track of where we

were on a mental map, especially when she led us down a side passage. Her presence was vague, a smudge, a slight movement in the deep gloom beyond our beams.

With every step, I expected to come across Brady. Or his body, rather. Unless she wanted to show us something else. Like the treasure? I didn't even care about that at this point.

"Where does this go?" Finlay whispered.

"No idea." I had never explored this passage, which was more of a tunnel. There weren't any rooms here, just ceiling, walls, and floor hewn from stone.

And another wall straight ahead. We had reached a dead end.

CHAPTER 30

Our wonderful Janet had baked a delicious selection of hot appetizers for the social hour, which went a long way toward easing my bad mood.

"Yum," I mumbled, stuffing warm Brie on a cracker into my mouth. This was followed by a bite-sized sausage roll. "I'm starving." And upset. And confused.

The four of us in the search party had carried loaded plates and two bottles of mead to a corner of the drawing room. Otherwise, it wasn't much of a gathering. Georgia was in the solar and Ollie and Gray had come down, foraged, and disappeared again. Rolf and Lady were sprawled in front of the fire, soaking up heat.

I didn't blame our remaining guests for distancing themselves. I didn't trust them and they obviously didn't trust each other.

"I can't believe the Red Maiden led us to a blank wall," Finlay said for about the fourth time, putting a hand in front of his face to demonstrate. "I don't get it."

"Me either," Tamsyn said. She was curled up in a big chair, a glass of mead in her hand. "You think she'd do something useful."

"Careful," Will warned. "You don't want to get on her bad side."

I rolled my eyes. "Seriously? Are we worried about that?" I was totally disgruntled by the whole situation and not in the mood to look on the bright side.

Maybe it was the weather. The cold rain of autumn was pounding down outside, ripping the leaves off the trees and swamping what was left of my herb beds. Next there would be a frost, followed by long months before spring returned. Ugh.

"Well, at least we didn't find his body," I said, surprising myself with this cheerful remark. "That would have been just too gruesome." Studying my plate, I tried to decide what to eat next—a prawn wrapped in bacon, or cheese puff? The prawn won.

Tamsyn was looking at her phone. "They've put out a bulletin for Brady," she said. "'May be armed and dangerous,' it says."

"Really? With what? Another Viking knife?" I found my own phone and looked for the notice. It was all over the news sites. "'Last seen in Monkwell, Yorkshire.' Good. They didn't mention Ravensea." I turned to Will. "Will Tweedy's murder affect the Fest's reputation, do you think?" I was worried no one would come if he held it again next year.

He took a gulp of mead. "Not sure yet. The attendees I've talked to were rather thrilled to go through a roadblock. Go figure."

"How about the vendors?" Finlay asked. "Have you heard from them?"

Will's smile was wry. "They all cleaned up. A few said it was the best event they'd been to in a while."

"It really was spectacular," I said, still browsing. "That flaming longboat, wow."

My brother grinned. "Now that was a stroke of genius, I have to admit. We built it ourselves, basically a shell stuffed with hay and other flammables. One of the guys went out to the mooring in his fishing boat, lit it, and set it adrift."

I set my phone aside. Brady probably had taken off and hopefully the police would find him. If he did kill Tweedy, then everything would be wrapped up nice and neat. Done and dusted. The books closed.

Why was I convinced that wouldn't happen, though? Mainly because nothing was ever simple, it seemed. Our effort to promote Ravensea with a ghost-hunting show had blown up in our faces, big time.

Janet bustled into the drawing room and, seeing us, came over. "How is everything?" she asked. "It's such a dreary day, I thought I'd make a little extra effort."

"Fabulous as always," Finlay said. "Thank you."

She beamed at him. "You're quite welcome, sir."

Finlay's brows went up and his mouth opened. I guessed what was coming. A futile attempt to stop her from addressing him this way. I elbowed him gently and shook my head.

"I wanted to tell you," Janet said. "I'm making steak frites for dinner. I hope that meets with your approval."

Will straightened in his seat. "I'll say. Is there anything I can do?" This offer was genuine, not just good manners. Will liked to cook.

"How about you toss the salad for me, young sir?" Janet said. "We've got"—she counted on her fingers—"ten of us tonight. I could use a hand with this and that."

Normally the guests would be on their own for dinner, but with Georgia's broken ankle and the murder investigation hanging over our heads, no one had the heart to send them to the village to eat.

Janet and Will went off to the kitchen, Will carrying a tray holding empty glasses, bottles, and platters.

"We need to figure out where that wall is relative to the castle floor plan," Tamsyn said in a change of subject. "Maybe the Red Maiden was giving you a message."

"I'll ask Dad for—" I slumped back. "I forgot. He can't find the big set of building plans that would tell us."

"I remember that, from earlier," Finlay said. Understanding slowly dawned on his face. "What if they're stolen, not missing?"

We asked Dad about the tunnel at dinner, which was just us in the kitchen. The guests were eating in the dining room. Seven of us around the table, cozy and snug. My hope was that, even without the plans, he would be able to help. He didn't disappoint.

"That tunnel used to be an exit," Dad said, cutting a juicy slab of steak. "It came out in the gardens. Then we got a coal furnace and they turned part of the tunnel into a coal bin. When we put in gas, we stopped using coal. Haven't been in there for years."

A coal bin. I could picture it, a dusty, filthy room.

"There's our answer, then," I said. "Not sure why Rusla the Red Maiden led us there."

"That's a real puzzler," Guy said. "Where approximately would it be located?"

Dad pointed with his knife. "Below the old buttery and stillroom." The rooms I used for my herbal products business. "There used to be a door and stairs that led to the old boiler room. Keeping that beast stoked with coal was hard work."

"Is there any way to get inside?" I asked. "Obviously not through the brick wall we ended up at."

"The coal chute is latched shut," Dad said. "The door

from the boiler room is blocked by shelves. No one has been in there for years."

Or had they? It didn't seem like a spot anyone would randomly come across. Unless they had a map. Putting a pin in that thought, I let it go for now and focused on my delicious dinner. Tender steak and thick yet crispy frites were one of my favorite combinations, especially on a cold fall night.

After dinner, we helped clear while Janet suggested dessert options. "I've got part of an apple pie, Will," she said, foraging in the fridge. "Guy, did you eat it?"

"I did not, my love," Guy said.

Muttering to herself, Janet kept looking, pulling items out and setting them on the counter.

"Want to go to my workroom?" I asked Finlay. I was way too full to even think about sweets. "I've got some of that soap you wanted." I made a citrus vetiver that he liked.

We slipped out of the kitchen and down the short corridor to the buttery, where I stored my inventory. The shelves that had once held household goods were perfect for my needs. Plenty of room and the open shelves let me see what I had at a glance. I kept a certain amount of each item on hand, making more when I got low.

"You've been busy," Finlay said, studying the soaps, bottles, jars, and boxes filling the shelves.

"Stocking up for the holidays," I said, scanning the dozen or so soap scents for the right one. I wrapped my cured bars in wax paper secured with a label. "Here we are." I plucked two from the row and popped them into a small brown paper bag.

The half-open door flew back and Rolf barged in. "Rolf," I scolded. "You're not allowed in here." All I needed was dog or cat hair in my products. Or clinging to the package. I grabbed his collar and tried to nudge him back out.

He wouldn't budge. All two hundred pounds stayed put, legs braced, and he woofed. Loudly, like a blast to the eardrums in the small room.

"Good grief," I said. "What's up with you?"

His answer was to paw at the flagstone floor. He jerked his head down, ripping my hand off his collar, and began to snuffle along.

"Is there a scent he likes?" Finlay asked, amused.

"Doubt it." Any time he or Ruffian smelled my soap or lotions, they sneezed.

He sniffed around for another minute before bolting back out.

"Strange." I picked up the bag of soap. "Is there anything else you want? A relaxing herbal tea, perhaps?"

"Anything that helps you deal with a frustrating colleague?" He winked. "You know who I mean." He was referring to "By the Book" Hook, I guessed.

"'Fraid not, although I'm sure that would be huge." I put my hand on the light switch. "All set, then?"

We went back through to the kitchen. On the way, I noticed that Rolf was now standing at the back door.

"Do you want to go out?" I asked him. Rolf was allowed by himself outside. He'd do his business and come back in a few minutes. "It's raining, you know."

He looked up at me and gave another of those deafening barks.

"Okay, then." I opened the door to let him out.

Rolf ran out as though escaping from prison and once in the back courtyard, began barking again. Now I was starting to think something was wrong.

I set the soap bag down and pulled a slicker off the

peg. "I'll be right back. Something is obviously bothering him."

"I'm going with you," Finlay said, reaching for another slicker. He didn't have to state something else that was obvious. He wasn't going to let me stumble around in the dark with a killer on the loose.

Hoods up, we hunched our shoulders against the lashing rain and headed into the back courtyard, which was bordered by the old stables. Rolf was nowhere in sight. We had a choice: try to find him or go back in and assume that he was up to business as usual.

Then I heard that beckoning bark again. "He's over here," I said, pivoting to walk right instead of left toward the kitchen garden and my gardens beyond.

This area was a no-man's-land of sorts, marked by bushes growing in straggly clumps near the castle wall. I recognized the high window in the buttery—and the arched metal door below. The old coal chute.

Which was open, the door swung against the wall.

"Did he go inside?" Finlay asked with a groan. "He's going to be filthy."

"I bet he did." I marched to the open door, wishing I had thought to bring a flashlight. I had my phone so I switched on the light.

Rolf was staring up at me, his tongue hanging out.

"Get out of there," I called. "What are you doing?"

He whined, pawing at the chute itself. Was he stuck? That would mean going around and entering the coal room through the boiler room to get him out. I wasn't climbing down there and pushing his huge body upward. We'd need ropes and pulleys, poor thing.

"Why is the door open, Nora?" Finlay asked. "Was Brady down there?"

A better question: was he still?

CHAPTER 31

Everyone was still gathered in the kitchen around the table, chatting and laughing.

"We have an emergency," I announced. "Rolf is stuck in the old coal cellar." My mouth quivered and I had trouble saying the next words. "I think Brady might be down there."

Gasps and exclamations of shock flew around the room.

"How bloody awful," Dad said. "Did he get stuck?"

"Hold on," I said. "We didn't see him. And he didn't answer when we called. Right, Finlay? I'm only guessing because of what Rolf just did. He came to the buttery, sniffed around, and indicated he wanted to go out. Then he ran over to the coal chute and went inside. We need to get him out." My voice rose. "Poor Rolf. He's trapped." With a dead man? The horror was unimaginable.

"Who opened the chute door?" Guy asked. "We always keep it locked." No one had an answer.

"We need to get in there another way," Finlay said. "We can't get that dog up the chute."

The men pushed back their chairs with scrapes and stood. Dad began to throw out orders. Tamsyn came over to me. "Do you think he's . . . down there?"

I put my hands over my face. “I sure hope not.” What a terrible place to leave a body. Except for Rolf, it might have been decades before the bones were discovered. “Who could have done such a thing?”

“We’ll find out,” Tamsyn promised. “First things first, though. He might not be down there. Maybe someone was snooping around and thought there was something behind that door.” Her smile was grim. “Nothing but black dust.”

The men and I trooped down to the cellar, which was reached through a door in the kitchen. This was where the castle mechanicals were housed. The gas boiler. The water system. The sewage pipes leading out.

“They got the old coal boiler out by cutting it up in pieces,” Dad said. He pointed to a wall lined with shelves holding glass jars and other junk. “The chute is behind there.”

Working as a team. we moved the shelves—and what seemed like millions of jars of unidentified food—out from in front of the access door.

“I’ll get rid of this stuff,” Guy promised. “It’s been on my to-do list for years.”

“Plenty of other priorities,” Dad said. “Who cares about ancient canned peaches?”

Especially when we might be about to discover a body. I hung back, not wanting to see. At the same time, I didn’t want to leave. Rolf had come to me.

The door hadn’t been bricked up, and we were able to quickly pry the wood boards off. Rolf was right there, waiting to get out, covered in coal dust.

“Grab him,” Dad cried. “He needs a bath.”

Will got his collar before he could jump on us and ruin our clothing.

Finlay was standing by the doorway, shining a light inside. As a police officer, he'd gotten the short straw, apparently. "He's not here. But it looks like he has been."

The room was cleaner than I had expected, although Rolf was plenty dirty after sliding down the chute. A pile of bedding sat in a corner, along with bottles, plates, and Janet's pie dish. A bucket stood in the opposite corner, for use as a latrine, I guessed.

When I started to step inside, Finlay put out his arm. "Not yet. Those items might need to go through forensics."

"I don't need forensics to figure it out," Dad said. "Brady must have been hiding down here. Making us think he had left. Or was dead."

"When did he do all this?" I meant stocking the place. "Oh, I know. I bet it was the night someone was watching me while I was in the garage. Remember, Finlay?"

Brady must have clipped the padlock and gone in through the chute, then made the space into his lair.

"Strange behavior," Will said. "What do you suppose he was up to?"

I raised my hand. "He's looking for the treasure. Pretending to leave allowed him to do it without us knowing."

It all seemed obvious now. Brady had crept away in the night, leaving us to wonder where he was. The obvious conclusion was that he'd run away from the murder investigation, which was stupid of him. But if he found the treasure, he'd have enough money to disappear for good, probably to a country without an extradition agreement.

Leaving the coal room untouched, we trooped

upstairs. "Should we call Hook and tell him to call off the manhunt?" I asked Finlay as we trudged up the narrow stairs. "He's probably still on the property."

"Why don't we wait until we have a chance to look for him ourselves?" Finlay suggested. "After I question his friends."

Good point. Maybe they were in on it, too. They'd agreed to let Brady have the freedom to explore without us knowing. I hoped Brady hadn't found the hoard and absconded.

"No body," Dad announced when we entered the kitchen again. "Someone has been sleeping down there, though. Most likely Brady."

"Sleeping down there?" Tamsyn's lip curled. "Gross."

"Phew." Janet fanned her face. "I was worried about what we'd find."

"Me too," I said. "Now I'm just angry. He fooled us."

Will scooted Rolf right outside for a hosing down. Guy followed, to put a new padlock on the outside coal chute door. If Brady came back, he'd get an unpleasant surprise. Where was his equipment? It hadn't been down there. He must have stashed it away from the coal dust. I would have.

"Want tea?" Tamsyn switched the gas on. "Or something more fortifying?"

"Both," I said. "What's next, Finlay?"

"The friends," he said. "We talk to them."

"I'm really glad you're here to lead that charge." Finlay had a way of getting the truth out of people while remaining a perfect gentleman. He played *good cop* to a *T*, I supposed.

Finlay pulled out a chair. "After we chill for a few minutes. We must be strategic."

Case in point why we needed him. With my impulsive

nature and the head of steam I'd built up, I'd barge in like Rolf and bark at Georgia, Gray, and Ollie. *Did you know Brady was still here? Are you working with him? Where did he go? Did you find the treasure?*

I sat beside him, then reached for the tin of molasses cookies. I could use something sweet now. I took two and pushed the tin toward Finlay, who reached in.

Tamsyn poured hot water into mugs holding tea bags. "The Red Maiden was right. She led you to Brady." She pulled out a bottle of brandy and added generous slugs to each mug.

After hastily swallowing a bite, I croaked out, "Yes, she did. She can go through walls, right? She knew where he was." I put my head back. "Tell us where your hoard is. Please?" I said to the ceiling.

"She might not know," Janet said. "She gave it to the monks. Isn't that the theory?"

"Don't ghosts talk to each other?" I asked rhetorically. "Maybe she and the monk ghost hang out."

The sacred spring. Once again, that location nudged at my mind. Even before we'd learned about Tweedy's interest in the spring, I'd had the inkling that the treasure might be there. It made sense.

Tea first. Then we would question Brady's friends.

"I don't know where they are." Georgia cowered back against the sofa, as if we were scaring her. "I haven't seen them since they came down for wine and nibbles."

Her over-the-top fear must be an act, calculated to make us back off and stop asking questions. Finlay's tone and demeanor had been perfectly neutral when he asked about Gray and Ollie.

"Weren't they at dinner?" Finlay asked.

She pointed to a tray holding a dirty plate and utensils. "Janet brought mine in here."

We'd already checked the dining room. They had devoured the steak, frites, and salad down to a puddle of brown sauce and a stray lettuce leaf.

"They were," Finlay said. "They're not upstairs. We thought they might be in here with you."

She ducked her head, fingers fidgeting with her phone, then glanced up at us from under her lashes. "Why do you need to talk to them? Has there been a new development?"

Was this a fishing expedition? Was Georgia aware that her colleague had been hiding in the coal room all along?

I looked to Finlay for a clue as how to handle her question. He stood casually, hip cocked, arms folded, as if he were perfectly at ease.

That's probably why his statement hit her hard.

"Brady was in the coal room, in the cellar."

"What?" She flinched, sitting upright and throwing her arms back. The phone dropped to the sofa cushion. "Is he dead?" Her voice rose to a shriek and she began to gasp and cry and rock. "*Ohnoohnoohno—*"

She was either a stellar actress or she hadn't known about Brady's sneaky plan.

"Georgia," I said, stepping closer. I had to get right in her face. "*Georgia.*"

She mercifully stopped moaning and looked up at me, eyes streaming with tears. "What?" She wiped under her eyes with the back of one hand.

"He's not dead." I amended that. "That we know of. He was hiding." I glanced at Finlay to make sure this was all right to say. He nodded.

"That you know of?" She frowned. "He might be?"

"Listen, forget Brady for now. We need to find Gray and Ollie."

They'd been told not to roam the grounds and, with the rain still streaming down, they couldn't use the excuse of an after-dinner stroll. They were up to something.

"I can't help you with that," she said sourly. "I'm stuck here, remember? I don't know anything." She grabbed a tissue and blew her nose.

"If you see or hear from them, please send me a text," I said. "We're going to try to track them down."

"To ask about Brady?" Another dip of the fishing pole.

"Yes." *And a whole lot more.*

We were leaving the room when she called after us. "Tracing the Red Maiden was my idea, you know." We stopped and turned. Her eyes, dry now, were glittering with anger. "I found her story mentioned in an obscure saga I translated. Gray scoffed. Tweedy scoffed. They all scoffed. None of them believed that a woman could explore and fight and conquer like a man." She paused. "Rusla was one of the fiercest Viking leaders, bar none."

Georgia's revelation gave me greater understanding of the woman and her motives. If she felt Gray and Tweedy had scooped her, then it was understandable that she might try to take back control.

By working for Tweedy so she could spy on him? And stealing his notebook, maybe?

The notebook. Where could it be? If it was among Georgia's personal belongings, I wasn't going to search through them. That was a breach of ethics and privacy.

What if it had never left Tweedy's room?

"Detour," I told Finlay. "It won't take more than a few minutes, promise."

"Lead on," he said.

After stopping for keys, which I combo-locked in my desk now, we went up to Tweedy's tower room. A scrap of crime scene tape still fluttered on the casing and I ripped it down and tucked it into my pocket before unlocking the door. I never wanted to see that ominous yellow-and-black tape anywhere at Ravensea again.

The room appeared untouched, as it should be: Tweedy's books and papers on the table, the bed still needing to be changed. I hadn't had the heart to get up here and clean the room yet. We weren't going to rent it for a while, I didn't think.

Finlay hovered behind me. "Is there any particular reason we're here? The police cleared the room, right?"

"They did. I wouldn't come in here otherwise." I studied the three sets of double windows draped with long velvet curtains. Which set had Georgia been hiding behind? I couldn't remember. Probably not the windows facing the bluff. With the event going on, they would have immediately drawn the eye.

I checked anyway, sweeping the first set of curtains back as far as they could go.

No notebook on the wide stone sill, which was deep enough to sit—or stand—upon. Only a cobweb and a couple of dead flies. Time to hoover.

The second set of windows was also a bust. One more.

And pay dirt. A brown leather notebook was standing upright against the window. A quick glance inside revealed Tweedy's name scrawled on the first page.

We'd found the famous missing notebook. The evidence of Tweedy's betrayal.

CHAPTER 32

Georgia must have tucked the notebook here, hoping to come back and retrieve it. Then the police sealed off the room and I'd made sure it was kept locked.

"Tweedy's notebook," I explained, holding it up. "He was going to double-cross us, pretend not to find the treasure, and then grab it for himself. That's what Georgia said, anyway."

We left the room and I locked the door again. As we walked down the stairs, I began to leaf through. "She told us he was focused on the sacred spring and it sure looks like it." I showed him a hand-drawn map of the spring and chapel area.

Plodding down the steps, I continued to scan. "His theory was that the holy men and women hid in the spring cave during raids. He says, *See local legends warning of the nixie or grindylow.* Evil water spirits. They have those in Viking lore, too."

"I guess the monks weren't above using myths and legends for their own purposes," Finlay said with a laugh.

"Well, the Vikings weren't Christian at that time. Threatening them with God's wrath wouldn't work." I closed the notebook. "We need to go to the spring."

* * *

Will and Tamsyn went with us, all of us wearing slickers and wellies and holding flashlights. The rain had died down, which was a relief, leaving the trees dripping and the footing slippery.

Janet, Dad, and Guy were on standby, ready to act if need be. I had 999 on speed dial. Rolf, we left home. He was too much of an early warning system. I was hoping we could sneak up on the ghost hunters and find out what they were doing before they knew we were there.

We headed across the bluff, where it was easier to see, planning to cut into the woods farther on. I remembered the night Finlay and I were out here and we saw Tweedy. I'd thought he'd been at the spring and the notebook had only confirmed that.

The question was, had he found the crevice that led into the hillside? At a glance, it didn't look wide enough to allow a grown person to slip through.

It could be done. If you held your breath and prayed not to get stuck.

Fog started to roll in off the water, as if coming in with the tide. A thick, smothering fog that soon surrounded us in every direction. Bad enough in the daylight, dangerous at night.

"I'm glad you all know the way," Finlay said. "I'd probably end up falling over the cliff."

"Definitely a danger," Will said. "This fog is no joke. We need to stick together, people."

We moved on, our beams feeble against the murk, providing only enough illumination for us to see the ground and our feet. It was like moving in a bubble. I could see Finlay and my siblings but beyond that, hardly anything.

Only our familiarity with the grounds allowed us to find the path to the chapel. As we moved deeper into the woods, a dense silence shrouded us. Nothing moved and even our footsteps were muffled.

"When we get close to the chapel, we need to turn off our lights," Finlay said. "We don't want to warn them that we're coming. Once we get a read on the situation, we can reveal ourselves."

"Maybe you can arrest them," Tamsyn said.

"I will if they're stealing," was his reply. "I'm obligated to."

"What a relief to have you here, on our side," I told Finlay. If not for the wet and slippery raincoats we were wearing, I would have hugged him.

We continued on, my heart thumping as we drew closer. What would we find? Who would we find? What were they doing?

I wanted Tweedy's murder resolved and for everything to go back to normal. Well, as normal as Ravensea ever was. Clogged toilets and burned toast as the biggest problems of the day sounded wonderful right now.

"Lights off here," Will said, halting. He'd been in the lead.

We did as he said before starting to move forward again, around one last bend in the path to the clearing where the chapel stood.

There were lights in the chapel. And voices. Two male voices.

"I need to hear what they're saying," I whispered. "I'm going to sneak over there."

"Not by yourself," Will said, taking a step.

"Let me," Finlay put in. "I have the authority to intervene if need be."

Will grunted in disappointment and Tamsyn quickly

said, "You and I can keep watch. There's one more person unaccounted for."

She was right. Three ghost hunters, two voices.

Finlay and I crept over to the chapel, making sure to avoid passing by the open door. We went around to the side to one of the windows. After crouching next to the wall, we slowly rose up high enough to peek over the windowsill.

Gray and Ollie were standing near the altar. The candles were lit, which irritated me. They weren't there to worship or remember the dead, I was pretty sure.

"Move over a little," Finlay whispered, nudging me.

We ducked down again to move and as I did, I knocked against a heavy, soft object. My heart jumped and I almost screamed. Was it a body?

No, a knapsack, I realized when I dared to feel all over it. A big one like mountaineers used. What was that doing here? Moving fast, I unclipped the buckle and flipped back the top flap. Using my sense of touch, I groped around and pulled out the first object. A headlamp. Hmm. I dropped it on the ground and felt around inside again. My fingers clasped a length of rope. Lots of it. A big coil. The type climbers used, I guessed by its smooth yet textured surface.

Finlay tugged on my arm. "What are you doing?"

"Found a backpack," I whispered into his ear. "Odd place for it."

"It's not working," Ollie said inside the chapel. "It's not like I can snap my fingers and they show up."

Gray paced back and forth in front of the altar. "I thought you and the monk, um, were best buds."

Ollie barked a laugh. "I saw him, yes. I can't command him to appear."

Gray tipped his head back, closing his eyes and shaking

his head, fists clenched in at his sides. "Why did you drag me out here, then? I thought we—"

"Because of this." With a lightning-fast movement, Ollie picked up a heavy flashlight and beaned Gray on the noggin. Gray collapsed to the floor in a heap.

Finlay's muscles tensed, about to launch into action.

Then Brady ran into the chapel. "Ollie. What did you do that for?"

Ollie was bending over Gray, studying him as if making sure he was out. Or dead?

"What are you doing here?" Ollie's eyes were darting around as if expecting yet another person to appear.

"I escaped from that filthy hole," Brady said in a triumphant tone. "You left the padlock off, you idiot." He started toward Gray, then halted, pointing at the flashlight Ollie still held. "Drop it. Drop it now. I need to check on Gray."

Finlay took off. I was torn between watching the scene and following him. I decided to watch a little longer. If he needed help, I would go. Otherwise I might get in the way.

"You heard the man." Finlay's commanding voice rang out as he charged into the chapel. "Drop the flashlight now." With a swift movement, he pulled out his wallet and displayed his warrant card. "Yorkshire police. You are under arrest for grievous assault."

Ollie dropped the flashlight, which hit the stone floor with a clunk, and raised his hands. "I didn't do anything."

"I saw you," Finlay said. He began to read Ollie his rights.

Thinking of a way I could help, I backed over to Will and Tamsyn. "Call nine-nine-nine. We need the police and an ambulance."

"On it," Will said, the phone to his ear. "Dialed soon as I saw Finlay go in."

"Who's hurt?" Tamsyn asked.

"Gray." I ran a hand over my face. "I'm still in shock. Ollie suddenly picked up a flashlight and hit Gray on the head."

"Ollie?" Tamsyn's mouth rounded in shock.

"I didn't really suspect him either, not after he was poisoned." Then a possible explanation hit me. "Oh. Maybe he did it to himself." If you were going to mess around with a mushroom to fake poisoning, *russula emetica* was a fairly safe choice.

"Call an ambulance," Finlay called from the chapel.

"It's on the way," Will said. He'd been talking with dispatch on his phone.

I ran back to the doorway. "He's alive?"

"Yes, fortunately." Finlay sent a stern look toward Ollie, who was standing with his hands on his head. "For him."

"Ollie kidnapped me," Brady said, anger and resentment heavy in his voice. "He tricked me into going down into that coal cellar, then locked me in there."

Ollie didn't deny it.

"Is that your backpack out there, beside the building?" I asked, pointing. His ducked head was all I needed for an answer. I could use my light now, I realized, so I went outside and around to the pack. I scanned it with my flashlight, up and down, then inside. I was right. That was a climbing rope. And the headlamp? It had a camera attached.

We had assumed the video from the night of the festival was filmed by Brady. What if it had been Ollie? He'd taken a huge risk uploading it. Unless he convinced the police and everyone else to blame Brady.

Ollie had framed Brady for murder. He had faked

being poisoned. Hit Gray and locked Brady up. He'd probably made Georgia fall.

His grand finale? Attempting to grab the treasure out from under all our noses.

Thankfully, he had failed.

CHAPTER 33

Ollie's confession took place in the chapel, a perfect spot for a detailed listing of wrongdoings, one had to admit. He'd been cautioned and arrested for murder (Tweedy), assault (Gray), and kidnapping (Brady). The police were still deciding upon charges regarding Georgia's fall.

DI Hook naturally wanted to follow the rules and interview him at the station, but Ollie insisted on the place—and the people allowed to be there, namely, all of us from the castle and Finlay. "Before you lock me up and throw away the key, I want to tell the truth." He glanced over his shoulder at the shadows near the altar. He shivered. "He wants me to."

Was it his guilty imagination or was the monk present? The air looked thicker in that area, I thought, as if the monk was in the process of materializing.

"I know you think I'm nuts," he told DI Hook, who was regarding him with stoic neutrality. "But I have a gift."

"He does," Brady put in, from behind the camera. He was filming the interview, which was also being recorded by the police. In addition, Constable Kumar was taking notes. They were taking no chances with this case.

Gray had been taken to the hospital. He was expected to recover.

"Tweedy doubted me," Ollie was saying, "when I told him my intuitive gift was helping me study the past. He had a knack for finding a person's weak spot and pressing on it. Later I realized that it was a tactic he used to benefit himself."

I thought of Georgia and Gray, both of whom had claimed to do the research that led to Tweedy's theories about the Red Maiden. He did know how to manipulate his students, it appeared.

"Why don't we stick to the sequence of actual events?" DI Hook said. "You are confessing to the crime of murdering Norman J. Tweedy?"

"I am," Ollie said. "I hadn't planned to kill him. But it happened. And now I'll tell you how." He took a breath. "To give credit where it is due, Gray and Georgia both discovered the Red Maiden and tracked her to Yorkshire. Tweedy stole their work, as we've established."

"Hold on," DI Hook said. "Who has established this?"

"We all have," Brady said. "Gray and Georgia can give you the particulars if you need them."

"Go on," Hook said.

"We've always stayed in touch," Ollie said. "The four of us. Last summer, we got together at the pub where Gray works and came up with a plan. We would come to Ravensea under the pretext of ghost hunting and look for the treasure."

Tamsyn gave a cry of distress, as well she might. Brady had used his relationship with her to get through the castle doors.

"Oh, we were really filming," Ollie said. "But if we found the treasure and scarpered, well, who was going to release the episode? We had plans to leave the country and an offshore account already set up."

Fair point regarding the show. As of right now, I doubted we could use any of it. Or maybe we should. I was pretty sure this story would go viral. We'd have to sort it all out later.

"Gray and Georgia had knowledge," Ollie said. "Brady had film experience, and I had the ability to contact ghosts." Ollie sat up straighter. "The most essential skill, as it turns out."

He took a deep breath, making his chest expand. "After Rusla contacted us, I knew. She wanted me to have the treasure."

DI Hook's face twisted in distaste. Finlay leaned over. "I'll explain later, Roland."

Sending dirty looks in Brady's direction, Ollie went on. "Once she contacted us and we discovered that Tweedy was targeting the spring, everyone started to get greedy. Especially Gray and Georgia. They wanted a bigger share than us, because they'd found the Red Maiden. Brady thought he deserved a bigger share, too, for getting us in here."

Now I saw where it was all going, why Ollie had taken matters into his own hands.

"I decided to cut them out. I went to the roof to try to contact Rusla. Then I realized that the monk might hold the answers. She'd left the treasure with him, I was pretty sure."

Again, he looked at Brady. "You tried to poison me. It was a warning, wasn't it? You didn't like my demands for an equal payout, my threats to go to the family?"

Whoa. So much drama we hadn't known about. Ollie hadn't poisoned himself with the mushrooms. His friends had tried to sideline him.

Brady pulled back from the viewfinder. "I'm not going to answer that. You might want to speak to Georgia."

Georgia, who had a habit of running in the area. Had she been planning to pick more of the noxious mushrooms when I ran into her?

Finlay was making a note. When DI Hook noticed, he said, "Mushroom case is mine. Will keep you in the loop."

Ollie cleared his throat, bringing the attention back to his confession. "After they tried to get me out of the way, I returned the favor once Tweedy was out of the picture and it was just us. I encouraged Georgia to fall. Got Brady out of the way." A pause. "Put Gray out of commission." His face reddened, tears springing to his eyes. "My own mates betrayed me. Surely you can see that wasn't acceptable? I couldn't let them get away with it."

Brady didn't respond but I saw him shuffle his feet. His selfishness had definitely played a role in escalating events.

Ollie sighed. "Anyway, back to Tweedy. I was going to offer him a deal. We would locate the treasure together." He glanced at us. "Sorry, Asquiths. Greed got the best of me. And Tweedy, too."

"All of you," Janet said tartly. "Never seen such an ungrateful lot." We all murmured agreement, our voices rumbling like an unruly mob.

"I understand your feelings," DI Hook said, holding up a hand. "But let the lad continue."

Ollie ducked his head. "This next part is difficult. As you've seen, I filmed myself coming into the castle. Part of my attempt to frame Brady."

Another pause and then he went on. "Tweedy laughed at me. He told me I wasn't needed, that he'd figured it all out. He told me to go find my little ghost friends and get out of his way." He began to sob. "The knife was just sitting there . . . and I"—he swallowed hard—"picked it up and stabbed him."

"And there we have it," DI Hook said. "Take him away."

The next afternoon, we mounted a party and went to the sacred spring. Ollie was in jail, and Brady, Georgia, and Gray had left this morning. Brady promised to be in touch about the show. At the very least, he was going to allow us to use it in our marketing. I expected to see viral posts about the ghost-hunting killer, quite frankly. He'd get more attention from that than an episode on *Britain's Got Ghosts*.

Tweedy left all his effects to the college, and those would be packed up and mailed. As his former students had implied, he didn't have a family, which was sad. While I didn't agree with his methods, obviously, I hoped he would get his due for the work he had done. Thanks to his research and tenacity, the world knew much more about Vikings now. Gray and Georgia should be added as contributors, as they deserved.

Speaking of just deserts, though, academic credit might not be such a concern right now. Gray, Georgia, and Brady were dealing with criminal charges regarding Ollie's poisoning.

Before I sent anything, I planned on making a photocopy of Tweedy's journal, all the pages related to Ravensea. It would be available for public viewing soon enough. We might as well get a sneak preview.

We set off for the sacred spring in a group, an official treasure-hunting party. Dad was wearing his cape, a staff in hand as he stomped along, curly red hair blowing in the breeze. The weather today was clear and cool, with a brisk wind and scudding clouds in a deep blue sky.

Will was next, wearing a big pack with the equipment he was going to use to explore. Then Tamsyn and me and Finlay. And Rolf, of course.

Janet and Guy were driving over later with a portable grill and dinner. However today turned out, we were going to celebrate.

Ravensea had survived another crisis. *We* had survived, battered but unbowed.

And we might be about to find a treasure.

I grabbed Finlay's hand. "I'm so excited, I'm going to explode."

He grinned. "Once-in-a-lifetime adventure, that's for sure."

We stopped to kiss, causing Tamsyn to halt and roll her eyes. "Come on, you two." Still holding hands, we did as she said, sauntering along and bringing up the rear guard.

Inside the spring cavern, Will put on his gear. He donned a helmet with a camera and light strapped on and a climbing harness. Finlay also put on a harness and helmet. He was going to belay Will, even though he wasn't actually climbing. His role was to secure the other end of Will's rope, to prevent him from vanishing underground.

"I hope all this is overkill," Will said, switching on his light. "The monks didn't use any of this equipment."

"Which hopefully means you won't need to go far," Dad said.

Finlay stood with his feet braced. "On belay." A climbing term meaning he was ready to protect Will while he explored.

"Belay on." Will moved toward the crack in the wall beyond the spring, which trickled out of the hillside into a basin. "Climbing." He turned sideways and slipped through. "So far so good," came loud and clear over video. His lamp revealed a rocky passage, bouncing slightly with every step.

The crevice widened and went uphill on a gentle incline. Watching, we all sighed with relief as if enjoying the elbow room ourselves.

Will stopped moving and the video scanned. Up, around, and then down. He was in a cave, about twenty feet across and the same deep.

A heap of small objects lay on the cave floor. He crouched down and picked something up. Rubbed it on his pants leg. A bracelet, shining with the subtle warmth of pure gold.

"I found it," he said. "Guys, I actually found it."

We all cheered and shouted. Rolf barked. Tamsyn and I danced around best we could in the small space. Dad waved his stick. Finlay, hands still on the rope, contented himself with a whoop.

And I tipped my head toward the ceiling and whispered, "Thank you, Rusla. And you too, Brother Monk." I wished I knew his name.

An ancient treasure. Family and friends. And a dog, pushing his nose into my hands and then licking my fingers, as though to say, *Well done.*